Dark Waltz

Elise Morel

Published by Elise Morel, 2024.

This is a work of fiction. Similarities to real people, places, or events are entirely coincidental.

DARK WALTZ

First edition. December 1, 2024.

Copyright © 2024 Elise Morel.

ISBN: 979-8230523420

Written by Elise Morel.

Chapter 1: A Glimpse of Flames

My heart thrums like a war drum, urging me forward as I navigate the chaotic remnants of the city. Each step I take sends jolts of adrenaline coursing through my veins, propelling me toward a confrontation I both dread and crave. The world around me feels surreal, the landscape warped by flickering shadows and the dull glow of distant fires, twisting reality into something almost mythical. This is no ordinary night; it's a tableau of despair and raw power, the air thick with anticipation.

I can see him clearly now, the outline of his form stark against the hellish backdrop. He's more than a figure; he's an enigma, cloaked in the remnants of smoldering ash and illuminated by the erratic glow of embers. Each flicker casts shadows that dance along his chiseled features, accentuating the sharpness of his jawline and the way his dark hair falls across his forehead, wild and untamed like the flames surrounding us. And yet, it's his eyes that ensnare me, twin pools of molten gold that seem to burn with their own internal fire. They hold secrets, old and profound, promising knowledge if only I dare to draw closer.

"Why do you run, Elara?" His voice cuts through the cacophony, deep and smooth like rich velvet, and it sends a shiver down my spine. It's a question laced with challenge, and I can almost hear the smirk that hovers beneath the surface, waiting to be unleashed.

I halt, a mix of defiance and dread coiling in my stomach. "Because you're standing in my way, Kieran. And I don't have time for games." The words come out sharper than I intend, each syllable steeped in frustration. I've dealt with enough men who think they know how to play this game, and I refuse to be another pawn in his scheme.

He steps closer, the heat radiating from him almost tangible, wrapping around me like a shroud. "You think I'm the game?

Sweetheart, you're the one playing with fire." There's a low chuckle that rumbles in his chest, and I can't help but feel my cheeks flush with a mixture of anger and something else entirely—something that sends a thrill spiraling through me.

I push it away. Now is not the time for distractions. "I'm not afraid of you," I declare, though my voice quivers slightly, betraying the truth I'd rather not face. The truth that every instinct screams at me to heed, that Kieran is not just a threat but a spark that ignites something deep within me.

He tilts his head, curiosity sparking in his gaze, and I wonder if he can see the conflicting emotions roiling beneath my skin. "You should be," he replies, a playful lilt in his tone, yet his eyes narrow with an intensity that feels like a storm about to break. "But you're not. That's what makes you interesting."

I take a step back, heart racing, my mind racing even faster. I can't let him draw me in; I can't let his magnetic pull cloud my judgment. "I don't want to be interesting to you, Kieran. I want to survive." The words are an invocation, a reminder of the reality lurking just beyond this strange confrontation. The fires that consume the city, the lives that are already lost—all of it hangs heavy in the air, a reminder that this is no mere dalliance.

Kieran's expression shifts, something darker flickering in those molten eyes. "Survival, huh? A noble cause." He straightens, the momentary mirth evaporating as he scans the horizon, the tension coiling between us shifting like a tide. "But you can't do it alone. There are forces at play here far beyond your understanding."

I shake my head, the stubbornness within me flaring up. "I'm not looking for your help. I can handle this."

A slow grin spreads across his lips, and the sight sends an unwelcome rush of heat through me. "You think so? Then why are you here, in the very heart of it all?"

"Because I'm not running from it," I snap back, steeling myself against the self-doubt that threatens to creep in. "I'm fighting."

His laughter rings out, rich and low, reverberating through the chaos around us. "And yet here you are, face to face with a man who could reduce you to ash."

The moment hangs suspended, the air thick with challenge and unspoken tension. I refuse to back down, clenching my fists at my sides. "Maybe you underestimate me."

"Maybe." He steps forward, invading my space, the world narrowing to just the two of us in the haze of smoke and fire. "Or maybe you're playing a game you can't win."

The heat from him washes over me, a palpable force that stirs something deep within. The warring instincts within me crash together—fear battling with the thrill of challenge. I meet his gaze, defiance burning in my own. "We'll see about that."

As I turn to leave, a sudden explosion echoes behind me, jolting the ground and sending a shockwave of dust into the air. I stumble, catching myself just in time, but when I look back, Kieran is no longer where he stood. Instead, he's now standing beside me, a sudden proximity that leaves me breathless.

"Run," he commands, the gravity of his voice pulling me into his orbit once more. "And don't look back."

With that, we race forward together, the chaos of our world collapsing behind us, and I can't shake the feeling that this is only the beginning of a game far more dangerous than either of us anticipated.

We sprint through the dimly lit streets, the fire's glow flickering behind us like the taunting laughter of a ghost. Kieran's presence is a constant at my side, both a comfort and a curse. Each stride I take is propelled not just by the urgency of escape but also by the magnetic pull of his enigmatic aura. It's as if the chaos around us is a symphony, and we're the only two players in a duet that's both exhilarating and terrifying.

"Where are we even going?" I shout over the cacophony, my lungs burning from exertion. It feels absurd to be running alongside someone who seems to thrive on danger, yet here I am, swept into his orbit.

"Away from here," he replies, glancing sideways at me with that maddeningly charming grin. "Trust me, it's better than sticking around to see what happens next."

"Trust you? That's rich coming from someone who was just standing there like a statue while the world burned." I shoot back, rolling my eyes even as I feel the adrenaline buzz in my veins.

He chuckles, and the sound reverberates through the chaos, a strangely soothing balm. "You have a point, but I'd like to think I'm a more effective statue than most."

"Is that your sales pitch? 'Kieran: the most effective statue in a crisis'?" I can't help but smirk, a part of me relishing the banter even in the midst of our escape.

"Absolutely. If only my resume included a certification in dramatic rescues, I'd be unstoppable." He gives a mock-serious nod, and I can't suppress a laugh, even as the adrenaline sharpens my senses.

Our feet pound the pavement, racing down narrow alleys and past crumbling buildings that seem to loom over us like specters of the past. The city feels alive, its history seeping through the cracks in the walls and whispering secrets of resilience. Each breath draws in the tang of burnt wood and the bitterness of ash, a stark reminder of what we're fleeing. I focus on the rhythm of our movement, pushing aside the weight of fear that lingers like a shadow at the back of my mind.

"What's your real name?" Kieran asks suddenly, the playful tone dropping into something more serious. "I can't keep calling you 'the girl who runs.'"

"Elara," I say, surprised by the simplicity of the truth. It feels strange to let someone in, even just a little. "And you? Are you Kieran the Effective Statue, or is there more to your repertoire?"

He feigns contemplation, his brow furrowing dramatically. "Kieran, the Sometime Hero, Generally Unreliable," he quips. "But I think I prefer 'Kieran the Dashing', don't you?"

"I'll keep it in mind for your superhero application," I reply dryly, but the tension between us shifts slightly, softening the edges of our chaotic flight. There's a flicker of understanding there, a shared moment that sparks like flint against steel.

We round a corner, skidding to a halt as we reach a dead end. The alley is dark and narrow, the shadows curling around us like a shroud. The sudden stop jolts my heart into overdrive. "This is not where I want to die," I mutter, my voice barely above a whisper.

Kieran scans the walls, his brows knitting in concentration. "I'm not planning on dying tonight. Let me think."

"Good plan. Think quickly." I bite my lip, scanning the alley for any sign of escape. The high brick walls loom, forbidding and unyielding, and the distant sounds of chaos echo behind us, a reminder that time is not on our side.

Just as I'm about to voice my panic, Kieran steps forward, glancing up at the fire escape that clings precariously to the side of the building. "Up," he says, determination lacing his voice.

"Up? Seriously?" I can't help the incredulity that creeps into my tone. "You want me to scale a fire escape in the middle of a disaster?"

"Do you have a better idea?" His eyes flicker with challenge, and I feel that familiar push of defiance rising within me.

"No, but I also didn't sign up for parkour training," I reply, eyeing the rickety ladder with suspicion.

"Then just trust me," he urges, the intensity in his voice stripping away the light-hearted banter. "We don't have time to hesitate."

I bite my lip, weighing my options. The chaos behind us is growing louder, the sound of distant shouting mingling with the crackle of flames. With a determined nod, I launch myself toward the fire escape, gripping the cold metal railing as I hoist myself upward. Kieran follows closely behind, his presence a steady reassurance even as my heart races with uncertainty.

As I reach the top, the world opens up beneath me. I pull myself onto the rooftop, gasping for breath as I take in the sprawling city, the smoke curling like fingers around the buildings. The city's skyline, once a proud silhouette against the sky, is now marred by fire and devastation, and an overwhelming sadness washes over me.

"Look," Kieran says, breaking through my thoughts. He points toward a distant rooftop where a flicker of movement catches my eye. "We can cross over there. There's a way down on the other side."

I follow his gaze, my pulse quickening as I realize the enormity of what we're about to do. "Jumping from rooftop to rooftop? You really are crazy," I retort, a mixture of awe and frustration bubbling within me.

"Maybe. But crazy is often the only way out."

"Why does that sound like a motivational poster?" I mutter, shaking my head.

He grins, a flash of mischief lighting up his features. "I could start a series! 'Kieran's Tips for Surviving Apocalyptic Scenarios.'"

"Sure, right next to your career as a statue."

"Exactly! I'll call it 'The Art of Standing Still While Everything Else Burns.'"

His humor is infectious, and for a brief moment, the weight of our situation lifts. But as I look back at the chaos, the laughter fades, replaced by a renewed urgency.

"Let's go before the city decides to implode beneath us," I say, steeling myself.

Kieran nods, and we take a running leap from the rooftop, the rush of air whipping past us as we soar through the night. In that fleeting moment, suspended in the air, there's a strange exhilaration that takes hold. It's not just the fear of falling; it's the thrill of taking control, of embracing the chaos rather than running from it.

As we land safely on the next building, laughter bubbling up between us, it's clear that whatever lies ahead, we'll face it together.

The adrenaline pulses through my veins as we leap from one rooftop to another, the thrill of each landing igniting a spark of defiance in my chest. Kieran's laughter follows me, an infectious sound that momentarily distracts from the destruction below. The city sprawls beneath us, an urban battlefield of crumbling facades and distant sirens, but up here, we are free, unbound by the chaos that seeks to consume us.

"Not bad for a first-time rooftop runner, huh?" he calls, a cocky grin plastered across his face as he deftly maneuvers around a vent jutting out from the wall.

"I'd say you're still trying to convince me that this isn't a terrible idea," I shoot back, my breath coming in quick bursts as I match his pace. "But at least you make it look effortless."

"Years of practice," he quips, his eyes glinting with mischief. "Plus, the occasional reckless decision keeps life interesting."

As we sprint across the rooftops, a sudden wind kicks up, sending a chill racing down my spine. It feels like the city is breathing, an ominous reminder of the turmoil lurking just out of sight. "Where exactly are we headed?" I ask, trying to suppress the rising sense of urgency. "Last I checked, just jumping around wasn't a solid escape plan."

"Relax, Elara. I've got it all figured out," he assures me, though the glimmer in his eyes suggests otherwise. "There's a safe house a few blocks away. A place we can regroup, maybe even catch our breath."

"Catch our breath?" I laugh, incredulous. "I'm not sure you understand what we're doing. Catching our breath is what people do at yoga, not while dodging whatever monster is turning this city into a hellscape."

"Point taken." He slows, suddenly serious as he scans the area. "But let's be real. We need a plan, and if that plan includes a brief moment of not feeling like we're about to be roasted alive, then I'm all for it."

"Fine. I'll humor you," I concede, though a part of me knows I can't let my guard down. It's easy to forget that Kieran is not my ally, not yet. He's an unpredictable variable, a puzzle I'm not sure I want to solve.

As we approach the edge of another building, Kieran pauses, glancing down at the alley below. "Okay, here's the plan. We drop down and head left. There's an entrance to the safe house just around the corner."

"What if it's not safe?" I counter, anxiety curling like smoke in my stomach.

"Then we improvise," he replies, his voice steady, but there's a flicker of uncertainty in his eyes that doesn't escape me.

With a reluctant nod, I follow him to the edge, peering down into the darkness below. The alleyway is littered with debris, a few flickering streetlights casting eerie shadows that dance like ghosts. "Ready?"

"Ready as I'll ever be," I mutter, taking a deep breath before we leap into the unknown. The fall is a whirlwind of adrenaline and gravity, and we land with a muted thud on the damp ground. The impact jolts through my bones, but the moment is brief; we're on the move again, ducking around broken crates and discarded refuse.

As we round the corner, a sudden roar erupts behind us, and I glance back just in time to see flames licking the side of the building we just vacated. "That was close," I gasp, my heart racing. "A little too close."

"Let's just say the city is throwing a welcoming party," Kieran jokes, though there's a tension in his tone that betrays his bravado. We press on, urgency fueling our pace.

The alley narrows, the buildings closing in around us as we rush toward the supposed safe house. The sound of sirens wails in the distance, a chorus of chaos that heightens my anxiety. What if we're too late? What if the safe house is already compromised?

"There it is," Kieran breathes, pointing to a weathered door tucked between two crumbling walls. "It's supposed to be secure. Just stick close to me."

I nod, though my instincts scream at me to hesitate. This could easily be a trap, another layer to the game he's playing. But as he pushes the door open, revealing a dimly lit interior, I can't help but feel a flicker of hope.

"After you, brave knight," I say, forcing a smile to mask my growing apprehension.

"Charming," he replies, stepping aside to let me enter first.

Inside, the air is stale, a musty scent mixing with something metallic and sharp. My senses heighten as I scan the room—shadows linger in the corners, and the faint sound of water dripping echoes through the silence. "What a lovely place," I deadpan, taking in the grim surroundings.

"It has character," Kieran retorts, his voice light, though I can see the tension in his shoulders.

Just as I'm about to respond, a loud crash reverberates through the building, rattling the walls. My heart races as I turn toward the sound, instinctively stepping closer to Kieran. "What was that?"

He frowns, his gaze narrowing as he moves cautiously toward the source of the noise. "I don't know, but we should—"

Before he can finish, the door slams shut with a resounding bang, plunging us into darkness. I spin around, panic rising in my chest. "Kieran!"

"Stay calm!" he urges, the intensity of his voice cutting through the chaos. He reaches for his phone, flicking on the flashlight as he scans the room.

The beam of light dances across the walls, revealing old furniture and dusty crates, but it's the movement in the shadows that grips my heart. A figure emerges from the dark, cloaked in shadow, and I barely have time to react before they step into the light, revealing a familiar face twisted into a menacing grin.

"Thought you could run away from me, did you?" the newcomer sneers, and I freeze, my breath caught in my throat as recognition dawns.

"Lucas," I whisper, dread pooling in my stomach. The last person I ever wanted to see again, standing here in the heart of our fragile sanctuary.

Kieran's stance shifts protectively in front of me, eyes narrowing as he assesses the threat. "You should've stayed away," he growls, the tension crackling in the air like electricity.

I can only stare, caught between the past I thought I'd escaped and the perilous present that threatens to swallow us whole. Lucas takes a step forward, eyes glinting with a predatory gleam. "Oh, but I couldn't resist the party. And now, it's time to play."

As the reality of our situation sinks in, the shadows around us seem to thicken, wrapping around us like a tightening noose. I can feel the walls closing in, the weight of our impending doom pressing down with relentless force. With Kieran by my side and Lucas grinning like a wolf ready to pounce, I realize the game has just begun, and the stakes have never been higher.

Chapter 2: Shadows in the Firelight

The city breathes with secrets, hidden in every shadowed alley and shattered window. As I navigate the crumbling pavement, I can almost hear the whispers of those who came before me, their voices echoing through the damp, heavy air. I find myself in an abandoned corner of town where street lamps flicker like dying stars, casting long, wavering shadows that stretch into the abyss. The faint smell of rain-soaked asphalt mixes with the pungent aroma of something sweet and rotting, creating a sensory tapestry that pulls at my senses. I pull my jacket tighter around me, not from the cold but to shield myself from the weight of the unknown pressing in from all sides.

There he is, leaning against a graffiti-splattered wall, exuding a nonchalance that feels like a challenge. His dark hair is tousled, framing a face that somehow looks both young and old, as if he carries the burdens of a thousand lifetimes in his deep-set eyes. The flickering light catches the sharp angles of his jaw, highlighting a confidence that could easily turn to arrogance if provoked. I approach, my heart thrumming in my chest, a mixture of apprehension and anticipation swirling within me. I know what I want—no, need—to discover. My mission is simple: uncover the truth about his origins. Yet, with each step, I feel the pull of something deeper, a magnetic force that both excites and terrifies me.

"Late night strolls are dangerous around here," he says, his voice smooth, laced with a hint of mockery. The corner of his mouth curls into a smirk that could disarm even the most guarded heart. "What brings you to this charming little haunt?"

I raise an eyebrow, crossing my arms defiantly. "You know exactly why I'm here. Stop playing games."

His laughter is low and rich, echoing through the empty street like the chime of a distant bell. "Ah, but games are the only reason to be out in a place like this, aren't they? Truths are just shadows waiting for the light, and you seem desperate to shine yours on me."

"Is that what you think?" I challenge, forcing my voice to remain steady, even as my insides twist with frustration. "That I'm here for entertainment? I want answers, and you're not going to dodge me this time."

With a slow, deliberate movement, he pushes himself off the wall and steps closer, closing the distance between us. The heat radiating from him sends a thrill racing through me, an electric current that threatens to unravel my carefully constructed resolve. "Answers, huh? What if the truth isn't as pretty as you'd like it to be? What if peeling back the layers only reveals something you'd rather not see?"

"I'd rather take that risk than remain in the dark," I reply, the words spilling out before I can second-guess myself. My determination burns bright, but beneath it simmers a flicker of fear. "You're not some enigma meant to be solved through riddles. You're a person, and every person has a past."

He tilts his head, studying me with an intensity that feels almost predatory. "And every person has a story. But not all stories are meant to be shared, especially not with someone like you." His eyes glint with a mixture of admiration and challenge, as if he's daring me to dig deeper.

"Someone like me?" I scoff, refusing to back down. "What does that mean? You don't know me."

"Perhaps not," he concedes, a flicker of respect sparking in his gaze. "But I know enough to understand that curiosity can be a dangerous game. You might think you're the hunter, but in this dance, you could easily become the prey."

I'm taken aback by the intensity of his words, an uncomfortable truth lacing through his playful tone. I force myself to hold his gaze, refusing to let him see the doubt that simmers just below the surface. "I'm not afraid of danger."

"Is that so?" He leans in, the warmth of his breath brushing against my skin like a whisper. "Then let's make a wager, shall we? You ask your questions, and I'll answer one truthfully. If you can handle the truth, then perhaps I'll reveal more. If not, well, let's just say the shadows might consume you."

The challenge hangs in the air between us, heavy and intoxicating. My heart races, each beat pounding out the rhythm of uncertainty. I know this is a risk, but it's a risk I'm willing to take. "Fine. What's your first question?"

"Tell me," he says, leaning back slightly, a hint of amusement dancing in his eyes. "What is it that you truly seek in the darkness of this city? What truth are you so desperate to uncover?"

His question sends my thoughts spiraling, as I wrestle with my own motivations. This isn't just about him; it's about me, my past, the shadows I carry with me. "I seek... clarity," I finally admit, the word tasting foreign on my tongue. "I want to understand the connections that bind us all, to unearth the secrets that shape our lives. There's a pattern to the chaos, and I want to find it."

He regards me for a long moment, his expression shifting from amusement to something more profound. "Clarity often brings with it a price. Are you prepared to pay it?"

"I've already paid dearly," I reply, my voice firm, though the weight of my past lingers like an unwelcome specter. "I just want to know why."

"Why is always the hardest question to answer," he murmurs, stepping back, an enigmatic smile playing on his lips. "But I admire your tenacity. Very well, let's see how far you're willing to go."

And just like that, the air around us thickens, charged with an unspoken promise and the looming threat of the unknown, as we embark on a journey that promises to unearth truths darker than either of us had anticipated.

The world around us feels suspended in that moment, the air thick with possibilities and unsaid words. His gaze lingers on me, a mix of amusement and challenge, as if he's savoring my resolve. "You're sure you want to play this game?" he asks, tilting his head in a way that makes it seem like he's trying to dissect me, piece by piece.

"Absolutely. Just give me something—anything. I'm tired of this shadow dance we keep doing," I reply, my tone sharper than I intended. The words slip out, revealing a hint of frustration I had tried to keep at bay.

"Shadow dance, huh?" He leans back against the graffiti-laden wall, crossing his arms with an air of casual confidence that both irritates and fascinates me. "What a lovely way to put it. But tell me, when the music stops, and the lights come up, what will you do with what you find?"

I hesitate, taken aback by the unexpected depth of his question. It's as if he's not only probing for answers but also weighing my resolve. "I'll face it," I say, firming my stance. "No matter what it is. I refuse to cower in fear of the truth."

He chuckles, low and dark, the sound wrapping around us like a cloak. "Fear is a natural response, you know. It keeps us alive. But you're not one to shy away from a challenge, are you?"

"Not when it comes to uncovering secrets," I reply, a slight smile creeping onto my lips. "Besides, you make it far too tempting to dig deeper. It's like you're daring me to unearth whatever's lurking beneath your surface."

"Daring you?" He arches an eyebrow, intrigue flaring in his expression. "Is that what you think? I'm simply presenting an opportunity for you to get burned."

"Let me worry about the burns," I shoot back, the heat of our exchange igniting something more than just curiosity. The air around us is electric, charged with an undeniable tension that pulls us closer together, the line between challenge and desire becoming blurred.

"Very well, then. Ask your next question," he says, amusement dancing in his eyes as he leans in slightly, the challenge hanging heavily between us.

"Alright, who are you?" I begin, leaning in myself, desperate to pierce the veil of mystery that surrounds him. "What's your real story?"

He pauses, a flicker of something—vulnerability, perhaps—crossing his face before it's replaced with that familiar enigmatic smile. "My real story is a collection of fragments, like shattered glass scattered across the floor. Each piece reflects a different light, a different truth. But let's just say that the last time I was in a place like this, I wasn't just watching shadows dance. I was one of them."

"Nice metaphor," I say, my voice laced with sarcasm. "But it doesn't answer my question."

He laughs softly, the sound rich and inviting. "You're relentless, aren't you? I admire that."

"Good. Because I'm just getting started."

"Then let's make a deal," he proposes, the gleam in his eyes suggesting he knows exactly how to play this game. "I'll answer your question, but you must share something of your own in return. A fair exchange, don't you think?"

I consider this for a moment, the stakes suddenly feeling higher. "Fine. But let's keep it light, shall we? I'm not ready to dive into the deep end just yet."

"Light, huh? I suppose we can start there." He straightens, the playful demeanor shifting slightly, his expression turning serious. "My name is Asher. It's not the name I was born with, but it's what I've chosen. In this city, names hold power, and I've had to carve my own path."

"Asher," I repeat, tasting the name on my tongue. It suits him somehow, carrying an air of mystery and danger. "So you're not who you say you are. That's a good start."

"Who is, really?" he counters, the corner of his mouth twitching upward. "But I see your point. Now, tell me something about you."

I hesitate, my mind racing. The thrill of the game is intoxicating, but sharing feels daunting. "Fine," I say, bracing myself. "I came to this city to escape my past. I wanted to reinvent myself, but instead, I found myself entangled in its webs of intrigue."

"Interesting. And how's that working out for you?" he asks, leaning closer, an edge of genuine curiosity in his voice.

"Let's just say I'm still figuring it out. But I refuse to be a victim of my circumstances. I'm here to take control, to unearth the truths that haunt me." My voice wavers slightly, but I push through, determined to maintain my composure.

He nods slowly, considering my words. "Control is an illusion, you know. But I respect your tenacity. Most people would have given up by now."

"Maybe they don't have the same fire," I reply, surprised by the intensity of my own emotions. "You'd be amazed at what I'm willing to do to get what I want."

"Then let's see how far that fire can take you." His voice drops to a conspiratorial whisper, a thrill running through me at the implication. "But remember, every flame has the potential to consume."

"Are you trying to scare me?" I challenge, unable to suppress a grin.

"Not at all. I'm merely stating a fact." His tone is teasing, yet there's a seriousness that lingers beneath. "But fear can be a powerful motivator. Use it wisely."

The tension thickens as our gazes lock, an unspoken understanding forming between us. He's right; fear fuels my resolve, igniting a determination I hadn't fully acknowledged until now.

"So what's next?" I ask, shifting slightly, the anticipation building within me. "Do we keep playing this game, or do I finally get to learn more about those shadows you once danced with?"

"Patience," he replies, his eyes glinting with mischief. "The night is still young, and there's much more to explore—both in the city and in each other. Let's see how deep the rabbit hole goes before we make our next move."

"Sounds ominous," I quip, but my heart races at the prospect. "Lead the way, Asher. I'm ready for whatever comes next."

And as he gestures for me to follow, I can't shake the feeling that this is just the beginning of something far more complicated than I ever imagined, a journey fraught with shadows, secrets, and the undeniable pull of the unknown.

Asher leads me deeper into the labyrinthine streets, where the shadows thicken and the city feels almost alive, pulsing with a rhythm all its own. The air hums with a strange energy, each crack in the pavement and rusted lamppost whispering secrets. I follow him through a narrow alley, the walls adorned with faded murals that speak of hope and despair in equal measure. Each step brings us closer to the heart of the city, a place where stories collide and truths hide in plain sight.

"So, what's the plan?" I ask, curiosity bubbling beneath my bravado. "Are we hunting down your dark secrets, or are you leading me to a den of thieves?"

"Why not both?" he replies, glancing over his shoulder with a playful glint in his eyes. "Life is more interesting with a little danger, don't you think?"

"Danger is my middle name," I shoot back, fighting to keep my tone light even as a shiver of excitement runs down my spine. The thrill of the unknown pulls me in, a magnetic force I can't resist. "What's yours? Trouble?"

He laughs, a low rumble that vibrates through the air. "Close, but I prefer to think of myself as a... catalyst. I stir things up, make people question what they think they know."

"Is that what you're doing with me?" I challenge, arching an eyebrow. "Stirring me up like some sort of potion?"

"Precisely." His smirk is maddeningly charming, and I can't help but feel drawn to him, even as I remind myself to tread carefully. "And just like any good potion, you might find that the ingredients can be intoxicating—or lethal."

A flicker of uncertainty gnaws at me, but I push it aside, determined to embrace the chaos. "I've never been one to shy away from a little chaos."

"Then you might just survive this night," he says, leading me to an open courtyard, its cobblestones slick with the remnants of a recent rain. A single, dying streetlamp stands sentinel, casting a weak halo of light that flickers like a heartbeat.

Asher stops, his expression turning serious. "Before we go further, I need you to understand something. The truth can be messy, and it's not always what you expect. Are you ready for that?"

"Ready as I'll ever be," I reply, trying to sound braver than I feel. "But if we're doing this, let's do it right. No more riddles."

He nods, a glimmer of respect in his eyes. "Fair enough. But let's start with a game of trust. You have to promise that whatever I tell you stays between us. There are eyes everywhere in this city, and not all of them are friendly."

"I can keep a secret," I assure him, the weight of his gaze making me feel both vulnerable and empowered. "Just tell me what you need from me."

"Your honesty," he replies, his tone turning grave. "I need you to be open with me, just as I will be with you. We're about to step into a world where shadows can swallow you whole if you're not careful."

"Okay," I say, my voice steadier than I feel. "What do you want to share?"

"I was born in this city, but I didn't choose it; it chose me. My life has been a series of escapes and confrontations, always running from something or toward something. The shadows you see—they're not just in the alleys. They're in me. They're what I'm made of."

"Sounds poetic, but that doesn't tell me much," I reply, my heart racing as the gravity of his words sinks in. "What are you running from?"

"Let's just say I have a past that's more than a little complicated," he says, his voice low, almost pained. "There are people who want me to pay for my mistakes, and they're not the kind to let things go."

"Sounds like you're in deep," I say, my stomach knotting. "But why tell me this? What do I have to do with your mess?"

"Because you're already in it," he replies, his gaze fierce. "Whether you like it or not, you've drawn their attention."

"What do you mean?" Panic bubbles in my chest, but I try to keep my voice steady. "Who's watching?"

He opens his mouth to respond when a distant shout pierces the night, followed by the sound of footsteps echoing against the cobblestones. My heart leaps into my throat as I turn to see dark figures emerging from the shadows, moving with purpose.

"Run!" Asher yells, grabbing my wrist and pulling me along. I stumble after him, adrenaline surging as we dart down another alley, the walls closing in around us. The sound of pursuit grows louder, heavy footsteps echoing behind us, and I can feel the tension tightening like a noose.

"Where are we going?" I shout, trying to keep up as he navigates the labyrinth of darkness.

"To safety," he grits out, glancing back over his shoulder, the fear in his eyes stark against his usually confident demeanor. "But we need to lose them first."

My mind races. "You brought me into this! You said you wanted to share your truth, and now we're being chased?"

"It's complicated!" he shouts, pulling me into a narrow passageway that cuts between two buildings. "But if we don't get out of here, you won't get the chance to hear it."

We sprint into the gloom, the night closing in around us as I struggle to make sense of what's happening. My heart pounds, not just from the physical exertion but from the sheer chaos of this sudden turn. Who are these people? What does he know that I don't?

As we turn another corner, I feel a sharp tug on my arm as he pulls me through a door that leads into a dimly lit room. The sound of the city muffles into a distant thrum, and for a moment, we stand panting, surrounded by peeling wallpaper and forgotten memories.

"What now?" I ask, breathless, my heart racing not just from fear but from the thrill of the chase.

"Now," he says, his eyes narrowing with determination, "we find out just how deep this rabbit hole goes."

Before I can respond, the door bursts open, and the shadows spill into the room, dark figures with eyes that glint like predatory beasts. The air thickens with tension as we stand, cornered, and I realize with a sickening certainty that there's no turning back now.

Chapter 3: Whispers of the Past

Every city has its ghosts, the whispers of history that linger in the shadows, waiting for a curious soul to uncover their secrets. My fingers danced over the brittle pages of the archives, the musty scent of old paper wrapping around me like a shroud. I was knee-deep in the history of our city, a place where brick met ivy, and the cobblestone streets echoed with the footsteps of those long gone. It was here, amid the dust motes glimmering in the sunlight filtering through the tall windows, that I stumbled upon him—a name that sent a shiver down my spine: Larkin Hale.

Larkin's story was woven into the very fabric of our town, a tapestry of intrigue and tragedy that seemed too surreal to be true. His name popped up in the margins of newspaper clippings and in the corner of a weathered photograph, his sharp features unmistakable even in faded black and white. He was a figure caught in the crosshairs of history, linked to events that defied explanation—accidents, disappearances, a fire that had consumed a whole block of buildings without leaving a trace. Each mention of him was like a breadcrumb, leading me deeper into a mystery that I was both thrilled and terrified to unravel.

As I pieced together the fragments of Larkin's past, a knot of tension twisted in my gut. I could feel him watching me, even when he wasn't physically present. It was as if the very walls of the archive whispered his name, urging me forward. And so, with a mix of trepidation and excitement, I decided to confront him. I had gathered enough information to provoke his curiosity—and perhaps unearth some of his secrets.

When I found him, perched on the edge of an old stone bench in the park, the sun setting behind him, he was every bit the enigma I had imagined. The light caught in his tousled hair, painting it in hues of gold, while shadows danced in the hollows of his cheekbones, giving him an air of both allure and danger. My heart raced, an unwelcome but familiar thrill, as I approached.

"Larkin Hale," I said, trying to keep my voice steady, even as the name rolled off my tongue like a forbidden incantation. "We need to talk."

He looked up, his expression shifting from amusement to something darker, a quicksilver change that left me momentarily breathless. "Do we now?" His voice was smooth, rich like dark chocolate, but the underlying edge hinted at mischief. "What could a historian like you possibly want with a ghost?"

"There are stories about you, woven into the very foundation of this city," I replied, my tone firm despite the flutter of nerves. "You're tied to events that defy explanation. I want to know the truth."

He chuckled, a low, dangerous sound that made the hair on the back of my neck stand on end. "Truth is a tricky thing, you know. Sometimes it's better left buried."

My pulse quickened, a mixture of fear and excitement coursing through me. "You're avoiding the question. Why do people say you were involved in those events? Why do you haunt the pages of our history?"

Larkin leaned back, a thoughtful expression crossing his face. "What if I told you I've been waiting for someone like you to find me? Someone brave enough—or foolish enough—to dig into the past."

"And what if I told you I'm not afraid?" I shot back, meeting his gaze with all the defiance I could muster. The tension between us crackled like electricity, each word sparking a potential revelation.

"Ah, but there's a fine line between bravery and recklessness," he countered, a smirk playing at the corners of his lips. "But I suppose you wouldn't be here if you didn't have some sort of reckless streak."

"Maybe I do," I admitted, a grin creeping onto my face despite the gravity of the conversation. "But I'm not leaving until you tell me something—anything—about your past. It feels like a puzzle I need to solve."

His eyes darkened for a brief moment, a flicker of something painful flashing through their depths. "All right," he said slowly, weighing his words as if they were fragile glass. "I'll share a fragment. But be warned, not all stories end happily."

I leaned in closer, eager and desperate for the secrets he held. "I can handle it."

Larkin took a deep breath, as if drawing strength from the air around us. "Years ago, there was a fire—one that changed everything. I was there, a witness to something that shouldn't have happened. A mistake that cost lives." His voice dropped to a whisper, filled with anguish. "And yet, somehow, I emerged unscathed, untouched by the flames."

I felt my heart plummet, the weight of his words pressing down like an anchor. "What do you mean you emerged unscathed? Did you start the fire?"

His laughter was sudden, harsh, and filled with bitterness. "No, I didn't start it. But I might as well have. It's not what you think. The truth is much more complicated."

Before I could press for more, a shadow shifted behind him. My heart raced as I glanced over Larkin's shoulder, dread pooling in my stomach. In that moment, the park, once alive with the soft sounds of evening—children playing, laughter echoing—felt charged with an unseen presence, something lurking just beyond the edge of my vision. I could sense we were not alone, that the secrets we were about to unveil might come with a cost far greater than either of us had anticipated.

The shadow loomed larger, a shroud that clung to the edges of my perception. I instinctively shifted closer to Larkin, my heart pounding a frantic rhythm against my ribs. The park, once a sanctuary of sun-dappled serenity, suddenly felt claustrophobic, as if the air had thickened with an unnameable dread. Larkin turned, his expression darkening, the playful glimmer in his eyes now overshadowed by a flicker of wariness.

"Stay behind me," he instructed, his voice low, laced with an urgency that sent chills skittering down my spine. I obeyed instinctively, drawn not just by the command in his tone but by the magnetism that seemed to pulse between us—a tether that tightened with every heartbeat.

The figure emerging from the shadows was cloaked in an indigo haze, a tall silhouette framed by the dying light of the setting sun. My breath hitched as recognition dawned—Wren, the local historian with a reputation for meddling in things best left untouched. Her intense gaze, often veiled in sarcasm and sharp wit, now bore down on us with a predatory intensity.

"I thought I might find you here," she said, her voice smooth yet edged with malice. "Digging into things that don't concern you, I see."

Larkin's jaw tightened, the muscles in his neck working as he turned to face her fully. "Wren. This isn't your business. Walk away."

"Not likely," she replied, stepping closer, a sly smile curling her lips. "You know how I feel about secrets, especially the ones you think you can keep. They're like weeds in a garden—stubborn and hard to eradicate."

"What do you want?" I interjected, the bravado I had mustered earlier starting to waver. "Can't we have one moment of peace without someone lurking in the background?"

Wren's laughter was a silvery chime, mocking and chilling. "Oh, darling, you should know by now that peace and secrets rarely coexist. Larkin has a way of attracting trouble. Or is it trouble that attracts him? Either way, it's best to tread carefully."

"Thanks for the advice," I shot back, feeling the heat of defiance rise in my cheeks. "But I think we can manage."

Wren raised an eyebrow, clearly amused by my stubbornness. "You're quite bold, aren't you? Or perhaps just naïve. Larkin's allure is a double-edged sword. It cuts deep, and the scars don't fade."

I glanced at Larkin, whose face was a mask of indifference, though I could sense the tension radiating from him. "I'm not afraid of him," I said, trying to sound convincing, even as a sliver of doubt wormed its way into my mind.

"Fear is a healthy instinct," Wren countered, tilting her head slightly. "But it can also be blinding. Remember that."

With that, she pivoted on her heel, the hem of her long coat sweeping dramatically as she disappeared into the encroaching dusk, leaving us with an unsettled silence. I turned back to Larkin, the air crackling with unspoken tension.

"Is she always like that?" I asked, a nervous laugh escaping my lips.

"Pretty much," he replied, rubbing the back of his neck, a gesture that belied his composed exterior. "She's relentless when it comes to her interests, and right now, that interest is me."

"Is there something I should know about you? Something she hinted at?"

Larkin hesitated, his eyes flickering as he weighed his words. "Wren has a knack for weaving tales that blend truth with a hint of fantasy. I've been a part of some strange happenings, but I assure you, I'm not the monster she paints me to be."

"Then who are you?" I pressed, needing to peel back the layers of his carefully crafted facade. "You share just enough to make me curious, yet hold back the things that might help me understand."

He exhaled, a deep, weary sigh that seemed to carry the weight of years. "I'm someone who has seen too much, been caught up in the chaos of fate's design. The stories you uncover—they only scratch the surface. What you find in the archives is my past, a glimpse into a time that should be forgotten."

"But you're not just a ghost, Larkin. You're here, now."

"Exactly," he replied, his tone sharper than before. "And that's why it's dangerous. The more you dig, the more you risk unearthing things better left buried. It's not just my life that could be disrupted."

"Then what are we doing here?" I challenged, my determination pushing against his reluctance. "If there's a chance to understand what happened, to face the truth, shouldn't we at least try?"

His gaze softened, and for a moment, I caught a glimpse of the vulnerability hidden behind his enigmatic exterior. "It's not that simple. Some truths don't come without a price. And it seems you're already entangled in my fate."

The weight of his words hung between us, dense and palpable. Just as I opened my mouth to respond, a chill swept through the park, sending leaves rustling in a sudden gust of wind. I shivered, glancing around as the shadows lengthened ominously.

"I don't think we're alone," I murmured, the hairs on my arms standing on end.

Larkin's expression hardened as he scanned our surroundings. "We should go."

"Go? We can't just run!"

"Trust me, it's better that way." He took a step back, positioning himself protectively in front of me. "Whatever's watching us isn't here for pleasantries."

Before I could protest further, a figure emerged from the encroaching darkness—a man with a striking resemblance to Larkin, yet older, his face lined with the burden of years. Recognition sparked in my mind, a fleeting image from an old photograph I had seen in the archives.

"Larkin," the man called, his voice a rough gravel, full of authority and something deeper, darker. "You need to come with me. It's time to face what you've tried to avoid."

I felt my heart lurch. The air thickened, charged with unspoken tension, a riptide dragging us toward an uncertain fate. Larkin stood frozen, torn between the past that sought to claim him and the precarious present I had unwittingly become a part of. The stakes had just escalated, and as the shadows danced around us, I realized this was only the beginning of a confrontation that would unravel the very fabric of our lives.

The man stepped closer, his expression carved from granite, and I felt the atmosphere thicken, pressing in around us like a heavy fog. "Larkin," he repeated, his voice grave and steady. "We don't have time for games. You know what's at stake."

"Who are you?" I demanded, instinctively moving to Larkin's side, though the urge was equal parts protective and foolish. "What do you want with him?"

The man's gaze swept over me, assessing, calculating. "You're the one digging into things you shouldn't. His past is dangerous, and your curiosity is a liability."

"I think I can handle a little danger," I replied, feigning confidence, though my stomach churned.

Larkin stiffened beside me, his shoulders tense, and I caught a fleeting glimpse of something akin to fear flitting across his features. "Get away from her, Vincent. She has nothing to do with this."

"Everything has to do with this," Vincent snapped, impatience threading his tone. "She's already involved. The moment she started asking questions, she became part of the narrative. And that makes her a target."

"Target for what?" I pressed, desperation creeping into my voice. "What are you two talking about?"

Larkin's gaze softened momentarily, and he turned to me, urgency etched into every line of his face. "You need to leave. Now."

"Not without you!" I protested, unwilling to abandon him to whatever menace Vincent represented. My pulse quickened, the stakes rising as if the ground beneath us was shifting.

"Do you think you can just walk away?" Vincent interjected, his voice a low growl. "They won't let either of you go if they catch you. You don't understand the forces at play here."

I shot a glance at Larkin, who was watching Vincent with a mixture of anger and resignation. "What forces? What's going on?"

"Larkin's past isn't just a series of unfortunate events; it's a chain of mistakes that have consequences reaching far beyond what you see. There are people who want him—want both of us—for what we know, for what we've seen," Vincent explained, his tone shifting from commanding to almost pleading.

"Is that why you're afraid?" I turned to Larkin, my heart racing at the implications. "What have you seen?"

"I can't tell you," he said, frustration tinging his voice. "Not yet. But if we stay here, we won't have a choice."

Vincent sighed, running a hand through his hair in exasperation. "We need to move. Now. You have no idea how close they are."

Before I could respond, a sound shattered the tense silence—a low hum, like the distant drone of an approaching storm. The air crackled with anticipation, and I felt it in my bones: something was coming, and it wasn't friendly.

"Stay close," Larkin instructed, his voice firm as he began to move away from the bench, leading me deeper into the park's shadowed pathways. Vincent followed, his presence a looming specter behind us, and I couldn't shake the feeling that we were being hunted.

As we wove through the trees, the world around us shifted. The once-familiar park morphed into a labyrinth of shadows and whispers, each turn revealing more of the dark secrets hidden within the city's depths. I strained to keep pace, my heart racing not just from fear but from the thrill of the unknown.

"What's the plan?" I asked, trying to keep the panic from my voice as we approached a narrow path that seemed to lead toward the heart of the park.

"Get to the library," Larkin said, glancing back at me. "There's something there—a place we can hide, at least for a little while."

"The library?" I echoed, incredulous. "That's your grand escape plan?"

"Trust me," he insisted, urgency sharpening his features. "The archives have more than just dusty books. They hold answers. Answers that can protect us."

We pressed on, and the hum intensified, vibrating in my chest as if the very earth beneath us pulsed with foreboding energy. "What if we can't find what we need?" I asked, fear creeping into my words. "What if we're too late?"

"We won't be," Larkin replied, determination flaring in his eyes. "I promise you that."

But as we rounded a corner, the path ahead abruptly opened into a clearing, where the moonlight poured down like liquid silver, illuminating a scene that stole my breath away. A group of figures stood waiting, their outlines indistinct yet menacing in the light. They were cloaked in shadows, their faces obscured, but their intent was unmistakably clear—they were waiting for us.

"Larkin," I whispered, panic gripping me like a vice. "What do we do now?"

He stepped in front of me, a wall of defiance against the unknown. "We don't have a choice. We stand our ground."

The figures shifted, their murmurs growing louder, each word an echo of the past entwined with threats for the future. "You can't escape what you are," one of them called out, voice smooth and chilling. "You're tied to us, Larkin. You always have been."

My heart raced as I turned to Larkin, searching his eyes for answers, for hope. But as I looked into the depths of his gaze, I saw the truth—the weight of secrets and the pain of choices made long ago. The realization settled heavily on my shoulders: we were trapped in a web spun by fate and fear, and the strands were tightening with every heartbeat.

"Whatever happens next," he said, his voice steady but low, "remember that you're not alone."

Before I could respond, the group surged forward, shadows elongating as they advanced, closing in around us. I felt the cool brush of the night air against my skin, the sensation both eerie and electrifying. In that moment, a single thought crystallized in my mind: we were standing at the edge of a precipice, teetering on the brink of something unimaginable, and there was no turning back.

With a final surge of determination, I reached for Larkin's hand, intertwining my fingers with his, ready to face whatever darkness awaited us. As the figures loomed ever closer, a whisper of wind carried a promise of upheaval—a storm was coming, and we were at its eye, caught in the tumultuous swirl of fate's cruel game.

Chapter 4: Beneath the Ashes

The dampness clung to my skin as we ventured further into the labyrinth of tunnels. The flickering glow of a lone lantern cast erratic shadows against the jagged stone walls, illuminating patches of charred blackness that told stories I could only guess at. I could almost hear the whispers of the past echoing through the corridor, like distant sighs trapped in time. As he led me deeper, his hand brushed against mine, a fleeting connection that sent a shiver coursing through me, mixing intrigue with unease.

He called this place his home, yet it felt more like a mausoleum—each step reverberating against the heavy silence, each turn steeped in the weight of memories long buried. The air was thick with the scent of soot and something else, something metallic that pricked at my senses. I glanced sideways at him, catching a glimpse of the way his brow furrowed, a hard line of concentration etched across his face. He was a map of contradictions: a fierce protector of his people, yet vulnerable in this underworld of his own making.

"Are you sure it's safe?" I asked, my voice barely a whisper, hesitant to break the fragile atmosphere surrounding us.

"Safe?" He chuckled, a sound low and rough like gravel. "In this city? Safe is an illusion." His eyes glinted with mischief as he added, "But trust me, it's much more exciting down here."

I rolled my eyes, though I couldn't suppress the smirk tugging at my lips. "Exciting isn't the word I'd use for crawling through a subterranean maze with a guy I barely know."

"Yet here you are," he replied, a hint of admiration lacing his words. "Brave enough to follow me into the depths."

"Or foolish," I shot back, unable to suppress a grin.

"Foolishness often breeds bravery," he said, his tone teasing, but beneath it lay a sincerity that caught me off guard.

The winding passageways opened into a larger chamber, and I stepped inside, inhaling sharply at the sight before me. It was a hidden enclave, a sanctuary of sorts, where remnants of a vibrant community lingered. Makeshift tables crafted from reclaimed wood were littered with sketches, each one a vibrant depiction of life above ground, of bustling markets and laughter spilling into the air.

"This is where we gather," he said, gesturing expansively. "When the surface is too dangerous, we create our own world down here."

A warmth blossomed in my chest as I observed the careful touches of life—a row of potted herbs on a window ledge, the flicker of candles casting a golden glow, and the distant sound of laughter echoing through the tunnels like a siren's call. It struck me that despite the shadows and the scars, there was beauty here, a resilience that mirrored the man standing beside me.

"What do you call this place?" I asked, genuinely curious.

"Beneath the Ashes," he replied, his voice dropping to a murmur, as if the very name held power. "It's a reminder that even in destruction, there can be rebirth."

Before I could respond, a figure emerged from the shadows, a young woman with wild curls and a quick smile. She wore a tunic splattered with paint and a belt laden with tools, as though she had just sprung from the depths of creativity itself.

"Who's this?" she asked, her eyes dancing between us, curious and perceptive.

"This is Ava," he said, a protective tone creeping into his voice. "She's...a friend."

"Friend?" The woman raised an eyebrow, a teasing lilt in her voice. "I hope you're not just trying to impress her with your charming underground lair."

"Actually, I'm here to impress her with my wit," he replied with a mock seriousness, crossing his arms over his chest.

"Good luck with that," she shot back, laughter bubbling in her tone.

I felt my cheeks warm as their banter danced around me, an effortless rhythm that drew me in. There was an undeniable camaraderie here, a web of connections that pulled at my heart. I found myself wanting to belong to this world, wanting to be part of their laughter, their resilience.

The tension that had coiled in my stomach began to ease, but just as quickly, I felt it return—a low, simmering unease as I recalled the way he had tensed earlier.

"What's really going on?" I asked, my voice firm but laced with concern. "You said it's not safe."

His expression shifted, seriousness replacing the playful spark in his eyes. "There are factions above ground that want to control what little we have left down here. They don't take kindly to anyone who disrupts their power."

The air grew heavy with unspoken truths, the laughter of the woman echoing hollowly against the weight of his words. I glanced around the chamber, noticing the way the light flickered, shadows lengthening as if they, too, understood the stakes of our conversation.

"And you think they'll come here?" I asked, my pulse quickening.

He nodded, his gaze intense and unyielding. "They won't stop until they've extinguished any light that threatens their reign."

A chill washed over me, an awareness that the laughter, the warmth of the enclave, could be snuffed out like a candle's flame. The thrill of adventure I'd felt earlier began to dissolve into a darker reality, and I realized that I wasn't merely a visitor in this world—I was now a part of its fight for survival.

And as he looked at me, eyes fierce with determination, I understood that my place here was as much about standing by him as it was about discovering my own strength. Beneath the ashes of fear and uncertainty, a spark ignited—a promise of something more profound, something worth fighting for.

The tension in the air was palpable, thick like fog settling over a marsh, and I could feel it wrapping around us, drawing my heart into a tighter knot. He turned to me, his eyes a stormy sea, and for a moment, the world beyond our hidden sanctuary faded into the background. I saw a flicker of something—fear, perhaps, or maybe a deep-rooted worry. It was the kind of vulnerability that beckoned me closer, as if he was inviting me to step into the shadows with him.

"We need to move," he said abruptly, breaking the moment like a glass dropped on stone. The spark in his gaze vanished, replaced by the fierce determination I'd seen before. I wanted to argue, to ask what could possibly be more dangerous than standing still in this place, but the intensity of his expression silenced my protest.

He took my hand, the warmth of his grip grounding me against the uncertainty that swirled in the air. "Stay close," he instructed, leading me through the chamber with purpose. I followed, feeling a strange blend of exhilaration and dread as we navigated through the twisting tunnels.

As we progressed, the walls began to narrow, the air growing colder and the darkness thicker. My heart raced with each echoing footstep, a rhythm of anticipation that matched the tension in my chest. Just as I thought we'd reached the end of the passage, he stopped again, pressing his back against the stone wall.

"Listen," he whispered, his voice low and urgent.

I strained my ears, catching a faint sound echoing from somewhere beyond—a shuffling, the murmur of voices. My pulse quickened as the realization struck: we weren't alone. He turned to me, his expression fierce yet cautious. "If they find us here, it won't end well."

"Who?" I breathed, my mind racing with possibilities.

"People I'd rather not introduce you to," he replied, a hint of bitterness curling his lips. "But we need to get to the escape route before they do."

"Escape route?" I echoed, incredulous. The very notion sent a wave of adrenaline surging through me. "Are you serious?"

He nodded, his grip tightening on my hand as he began to lead us down a side passage. "This way."

The walls seemed to close in around us, the darkness thickening with every step we took. I could barely see anything, relying solely on the occasional flicker of his lantern to illuminate our path. The tension between us was electric, sparking with an intensity that made the air crackle. I felt a rush of warmth at the way he held my hand, like he was anchoring us both in a reality that threatened to unravel.

We turned a corner, and suddenly, the space opened up into a narrow alcove, illuminated by faint daylight filtering through a barred grate above. He pulled me inside, and I pressed against the cool stone, trying to catch my breath.

"What happens if they find us?" I asked, my voice a shaky whisper.

"They'll want to question you," he said, his gaze scanning the shadows, always vigilant. "They think you might know more than you do."

"About what?"

"About me, about us." His voice was steady, but I could see the tension rippling beneath the surface. "They think I'm a traitor, and anyone close to me is a threat."

"Why would they think that?" I pressed, but deep down, I could sense the answer. I could feel the gravity of his situation wrapping around us like a suffocating blanket.

"Because I've chosen to protect my people instead of following their orders," he said, a hint of defiance in his tone. "And in their eyes, that's unforgivable."

A shiver ran through me, the weight of his words sinking in. I had stepped into a world far darker than I had anticipated, and I could no longer deny the reality that surrounded us. But as fear gnawed at my insides, something else surged within me—a fierce determination. I wasn't going to be just a bystander in his fight.

"Then let's fight back," I declared, the conviction in my voice surprising even me.

He turned to me, his expression a mix of surprise and admiration. "You really have no idea what you're asking for, do you?"

"I'm learning," I shot back, a grin breaking through the tension. "And I'm not about to cower in the shadows while you do all the heavy lifting."

His lips twitched in a reluctant smile, the first crack in the armor he wore. "You're either incredibly brave or completely reckless."

"Why not both?" I replied, meeting his gaze head-on.

Before he could respond, the sound of footsteps echoed from the main passage, sharp and purposeful. My heart dropped into my stomach, and I felt a surge of panic.

"Hide," he whispered urgently, pulling me deeper into the alcove.

I pressed against the cold stone, my breath quickening as shadows danced in the flickering light. The footsteps grew closer, and I could see dark figures emerging into the tunnel, their voices low and menacing.

"What if they don't find her?" one of them said, a harsh edge to his tone.

"They will," another replied. "She's connected to him. We can't let that connection put us at risk."

I glanced at him, and the worry etched on his face mirrored my own. The world outside felt surreal, like a twisted dream where danger lurked around every corner, yet here we were, two unlikely allies caught in the eye of a storm.

As they passed, the weight of their presence loomed heavy, and I could feel every heartbeat pounding in my ears. I wanted to scream, to lash out at the injustice of it all, but I stayed silent, relying on him to guide us through this perilous moment.

When the footsteps finally faded, he let out a breath he hadn't realized he was holding, and I could see the tension release from his shoulders. "We have to move, now," he said, urgency threading through his voice.

"Where to?"

"To the old service tunnel," he replied. "It's our best chance."

Without another word, he slipped out of the alcove, pulling me with him. I felt the weight of the world on my shoulders, but with him at my side, I was ready to step into whatever lay ahead. Together, we would navigate this shadowy underworld, finding light in the darkest of places, carving out a path where none existed before.

We slipped through the service tunnel, a narrow passage shrouded in darkness that smelled of damp earth and decay. The walls pressed in around us, each step echoing the thrum of adrenaline in my veins. The lantern's flickering light cast a faint glow, but it did little to chase away the encroaching shadows that felt alive, pulsating with the energy of long-buried secrets. He moved silently beside me, his presence both a comfort and a reminder of the peril that loomed just beyond the veil of darkness.

"Do you ever think about what you'll do if we get out of this?" I asked, trying to keep my voice steady despite the tremor of fear that laced my words.

"Get out?" he repeated, a wry smile creeping onto his face. "Isn't that the goal? You know, to actually survive?"

"Very funny," I replied, rolling my eyes, but the banter was a lifeline, something to cling to as we navigated the uncertainty that surrounded us. "I mean, once we're free, what then? Do you have a plan? A dream?"

He paused, his brow furrowing as he considered my question. "I haven't thought that far ahead," he admitted, his voice turning serious. "Right now, all that matters is getting my people to safety."

"And what about you?" I pressed, my heart swelling with a mix of admiration and concern. "What do you want?"

His gaze locked onto mine, intensity swirling within the depths of his eyes. "I want a world where we can be free, where my people can live without fear. That's the only dream I have right now."

I nodded, the weight of his words settling in the pit of my stomach. It was a noble aspiration, but it also felt impossibly far away. A part of me wanted to weave my own dreams into that vision, to be part of the fight, but another part warned me of the dangers lurking within his world.

We pressed on, the tunnel twisting and turning like a serpent, and I couldn't shake the feeling that we were being watched. My instincts screamed that we weren't alone, that something or someone was trailing us just out of sight.

"Do you hear that?" I whispered, my voice barely breaking the silence.

He nodded, the playful spark in his eyes replaced by the serious focus of a predator. "Stay close," he said, his tone clipped as he pulled me tighter against him.

The sound grew louder, the echo of footsteps mingling with the faint shuffling of what could only be shadows creeping along the walls. My breath quickened, and I felt the heat radiating from him, a stark reminder that we were in this together, tethered by danger and an unspoken bond.

We reached a fork in the tunnel, the right path shrouded in deeper darkness while the left beckoned with a faint glimmer of light. He hesitated for a moment, clearly weighing our options, and I could see the tension in his jaw.

"Which way?" I asked, sensing the urgency in the air.

"Left," he decided, leading us toward the flickering light. But as we moved, the footsteps grew closer, and the shadows began to shift ominously.

"Quick," he urged, pulling me into the narrow passage that opened up before us. I stumbled slightly, my heart racing as I felt the presence behind us growing more tangible, a sensation like icy fingers tracing down my spine.

The light grew brighter, revealing an old maintenance room cluttered with rusted tools and abandoned crates. Dust motes danced in the air, caught in the golden glow spilling from a small window. He stepped inside, his eyes scanning for threats, but as I followed, I could see the relief wash over him momentarily.

"Lock it," he instructed, urgency creeping into his voice as he moved to barricade the door.

"Lock it?" I echoed, looking at the ancient mechanism hanging crookedly on the doorframe. "What if it's not strong enough?"

He glanced at me, a flash of determination igniting in his gaze. "It has to be. We don't have a choice."

I rushed to help him, pushing a heavy crate against the door while he secured the latch, the sound of it clicking into place almost drowned out by the pounding of my heart. We stepped back, breathless and pressed against the cool stone walls, waiting in tense silence for whatever came next.

"Do you think they'll find us?" I whispered, my voice barely above a breath.

"They might," he said, his expression unreadable. "But if we can hold out long enough—"

Before he could finish, the door shuddered violently, splintering against the force of something heavy slamming into it. We exchanged a wide-eyed glance, and panic surged through me.

"What was that?" I demanded, instinctively moving closer to him, seeking the comfort of his strength.

"Stay quiet," he hissed, his eyes wide and alert. He moved toward the door, pressing his ear against the wood, as if he could sense the danger lurking just beyond.

The pounding continued, relentless and chaotic, and I could feel the walls vibrating with each blow. My thoughts spiraled, a frantic dance of dread and adrenaline. I had never imagined I'd be here, locked in a room beneath the city with a man who had already become my protector and my confidant. The uncertainty of it all gripped me tightly, a vise of fear that threatened to crush the resolve I had found.

"What do we do?" I asked, trying to keep my voice steady.

"Just hold on," he replied, his voice a low growl. "If they get through, we'll fight. Together."

The door bucked again, and the crack around the edges widened, dust and debris falling to the floor like a warning. The noise echoed through the cramped space, and I instinctively took a step back, bracing myself for what was to come.

Suddenly, a sharp crack reverberated through the air, and the door burst open, splintering into pieces as dark figures flooded into the room. I stumbled back, my heart racing, and felt his hand grasp mine, the heat of his touch igniting a fire of defiance within me.

"Now!" he shouted, pulling me toward a small window that overlooked the tunnel below.

We had no time to waste. As he hoisted me up, I glanced back at the encroaching shadows, their faces obscured but their intentions clear. They were here to take him, to drag him back into the darkness.

"Go!" he urged, his voice fierce, and I scrambled through the narrow opening, the chill of the air biting at my skin.

I turned, ready to reach for him, but as he made to climb up after me, one of the figures lunged forward, seizing him by the collar.

"Don't you dare!" I screamed, my heart lurching as I watched the chaos unfold.

He fought back, a wild determination sparking in his eyes as he wrestled against his captor. But the odds were stacked against him, and in that instant, I realized that the fragile hope we'd built together hung by a thread, teetering on the brink of destruction.

Just as he was pulled back into the fray, I reached for him, desperate to close the distance. The last thing I saw was the flash of his defiant glare, the promise of a fight still burning brightly in the depths of his eyes, before everything around us erupted into chaos.

"Run!" he shouted, the word echoing through the turmoil as darkness consumed the light.

In that moment, as I fled into the unknown, I couldn't shake the feeling that this was just the beginning, a prelude to a battle that would change everything. And I could only hope that I wasn't running away from him forever.

Chapter 5: A Dance with Darkness

The night unfolded like a silk ribbon, shimmering in the soft glow of chandeliers that dripped like icicles from the ceiling. Each flicker of candlelight painted the room in a warm amber hue, casting shadows that danced playfully against the opulent walls of the grand hall. As I stepped into this lavish world, a swirling sea of silk and sequins, I felt the pulse of the gathering around me, a rhythm filled with anticipation and the promise of secrets waiting to be unveiled.

My costume, a midnight-blue gown that hugged my curves with an almost painful elegance, transformed me. The fabric whispered against my skin, its coolness a stark contrast to the warmth of the bodies moving like a living tapestry on the dance floor. I had chosen a delicate mask that framed my eyes, its silver filigree sparkling like frost under the night sky, shrouding my identity while hinting at the woman beneath. Tonight, I was a ghost in the night, a specter woven from shadows and allure, and I had no intention of being found too easily.

As I surveyed the room, my breath caught in my throat when I spotted him across the crowd. James. His presence commanded attention, even in a sea of finely tailored suits and extravagant gowns. The way he stood there, one hand resting casually in his pocket while the other held a glass of amber liquid, made it seem as if the world had conspired to frame him in a portrait of desire. His dark hair, tousled yet impeccably styled, caught the light just right, illuminating the sharp angles of his face. The mask he wore accentuated the intensity of his gaze, a dark and stormy sea that promised both tempest and calm.

As if drawn by an invisible thread, our eyes locked, and an electric charge shot through the air between us. In that moment, the cacophony of laughter and chatter faded away, leaving only the thrum of our heartbeats. I could feel the weight of the unspoken words hanging between us, the secrets yet to be shared. With a subtle nod, he gestured for me to join him, and the world shifted once more, narrowing to the two of us against the backdrop of lavish splendor.

With each step I took, the air grew thicker, charged with an energy that made my skin prickle. He extended his hand, and I placed mine in his, feeling the warmth radiate through his glove. Our fingers intertwined, a perfect fit, and he pulled me close, guiding me into the flow of bodies moving rhythmically to the music that swelled like a tide around us. It was as if the very universe conspired to push us together, and I lost myself in the dizzying whirl of his presence.

"Didn't expect to see you here," he murmured, his voice low and rich like dark chocolate, melting into the air between us. His breath brushed against my ear, sending shivers cascading down my spine.

"Neither did I," I replied, leaning slightly into him, emboldened by the anonymity of our disguises. "But then again, secrets have a way of drawing us into unexpected places, don't they?"

His lips quirked into a smirk that made my heart race. "Indeed. You look different. I almost didn't recognize you."

"Perhaps that's the point," I said, reveling in the intimacy of the moment. "What good are secrets if they're too easily found?"

The dance floor swirled around us, vibrant and alive, yet it felt as though we existed in a pocket of time, a bubble where nothing else mattered. With each turn, I discovered a new facet of him—how he held me just a little tighter when the music crescendoed, how his eyes sparkled with mischief and intrigue as we spun in perfect harmony.

"Tell me," he whispered, leaning in closer, the warmth of his body igniting the air between us, "what secrets do you carry tonight?"

"Secrets are like shadows," I replied, my voice teasing, "they're only as dark as you allow them to be. But you? You carry a storm in your eyes. What are you hiding, James?"

His expression shifted, the playful glint replaced by a flicker of something deeper, something guarded. Before he could respond, the atmosphere shifted again, and a chill raced through me. The air crackled with tension as another figure approached—a rival who had been a ghost in the corners of my past. Clara, with her sharp smile and sharper tongue, glided into view, her gown a vivid crimson that screamed for attention. She was a firebrand, her presence igniting jealousy and anger, her eyes locking onto us like a predator sizing up its prey.

"Darling James," she cooed, the sweetness in her voice coated with a venomous undertone, "I see you've found yourself a new companion." Her gaze slid over me, dismissive, as if I were an insignificant detail in her grand scheme.

The tension between us thickened, palpable as a taut string ready to snap. I could feel James's grip on my waist tighten instinctively, a protective instinct rising to the surface. The electric connection we shared shifted, evolving into something more profound, more dangerous.

"Clara," he replied coolly, his voice a steely calm that belied the storm brewing behind his eyes. "This is a private conversation. Perhaps you should find another dance partner."

"Oh, but why would I do that?" she purred, her eyes narrowing. "You seem to be enjoying yourself quite a bit, don't you? What a delightful distraction from the real world, wouldn't you agree?"

As she spoke, I felt the ground shift beneath us. The tension swelled, a heavy fog of rivalry and unspoken truths swirling in the air, and I understood in that moment that our connection had been irrevocably altered. I was no longer just an enigmatic stranger to him. I had become a point of contention, a battle line drawn in the shifting sands of power and desire.

Clara's presence shattered the moment like glass, her sharp laughter cutting through the vibrant symphony of the gala, leaving behind a stinging silence. The tension coiled tighter around us, my heart pounding in sync with the thumping music that still pulsed through the hall. I could feel James's body stiffen beside me, a wall of muscle and unyielding resolve. His protective grip on my waist was both a comfort and a challenge, and I sensed the storm brewing beneath his calm facade.

"Don't be such a bore, James," Clara purred, her gaze flicking between us like a lightning bolt seeking its mark. "You know how much I enjoy watching you squirm. And this delightful mystery—" she gestured toward me, her eyes narrowing, "she must have some fascinating tales. Or are we too busy playing dress-up tonight?"

"Leave her out of this, Clara," he said, his voice low but steady, an unspoken promise of protection laced within. "She's not part of your games."

The venom in her smile widened, revealing the kind of pleasure that comes from knowing she held the power to disrupt. "Oh, but she's the most interesting part, isn't she? A new player on an old board. I do hope she knows what she's getting into." With that, she leaned in, her voice dropping to a conspiratorial whisper, "The stakes here are higher than she realizes, James. You of all people should understand that."

A rush of heat surged through me, a mix of anger and the instinct to defend my newfound connection with him. "Perhaps it's you who doesn't understand, Clara," I interjected, forcing my voice to remain steady. "I'm not here to be a pawn in anyone's game. I dance where I please."

Her eyes widened, and for a brief moment, surprise flickered across her features, quickly masked by a practiced poise. "Well, darling, in that case, tread carefully. The dance floor has more than just rhythm; it has its own rules. And trust me, some players don't take kindly to intrusions."

James's jaw clenched, and I could sense the current of tension sparking between him and Clara, a dangerous game of wills playing out in the space we occupied. He turned to me, his expression a mix of admiration and concern. "Let's step away," he suggested softly, as if afraid that any further exchange would ignite a firestorm.

"Ah, running away already?" Clara taunted, her voice honeyed but dripping with malice. "How tragic. I suppose the dark knight needs his damsel in distress."

I bristled at the implication, determined not to be viewed as anything less than my own hero. "I assure you, I'm no damsel," I replied, tilting my chin up defiantly. "And I don't need saving."

A spark ignited in James's eyes, a glimmer of something akin to respect, or perhaps amusement at my boldness. "Let's not give her the satisfaction," he murmured, leading me away from Clara's prying gaze. We weaved through the thrumming crowd, the music swelling once more, each beat resonating with the frantic pace of my heart.

As we distanced ourselves from the tension, I could still feel Clara's eyes on us, a seething heat that seemed to follow our every step. "Who is she?" I asked, my voice low, though I didn't particularly care if Clara heard. "She seems... invested."

James chuckled, a sound both rich and dark, like chocolate melting under the warmth of a flame. "Invested is one way to put it. Clara has a tendency to think of herself as the queen of this little realm, and I suppose I'm the knight she wishes to keep in her court. But I've never been one to play her game."

"Then why not simply say so?" I asked, enjoying the lightness of our banter amidst the heavy undercurrent of the evening. "Why not just remove the mask entirely?"

"Ah, if only it were that simple." He paused, his expression shifting slightly, as if caught between two worlds—the one he inhabited and the one he had just pulled me into. "But here, in this world, masks are worn for protection as much as for concealment. Not every secret is meant to be revealed, and not every truth is safe."

"Then I suppose we're both playing a part tonight," I said, my heart racing with excitement and intrigue. "I'll admit, I wasn't expecting a gala like this. I thought I'd find myself lost among glimmering gowns and idle chatter, not embroiled in a dangerous web of secrets and rivalry."

"Welcome to my world," he replied, a glimmer of mischief in his gaze as he twirled me back onto the dance floor. The space was alive with color and laughter, the air thick with perfume and unspoken promises. "But I can promise you one thing: it's never dull."

As we danced, I surrendered to the rhythm, allowing the world around us to fade away. The whispers of the crowd became a backdrop to our unspoken connection, a magnetic pull that drew us together with each turn and sway. With every twirl, I felt the tendrils of his world wrap around me, tightening like a silken thread woven through the fabric of the night.

But Clara's shadow lingered like a cloud, ever present, and as the song shifted to a slower tempo, I felt the weight of her threat looming over us. "So what happens next?" I asked, my voice barely above a whisper, not wanting to break the spell we had created.

James's gaze bore into mine, his expression serious. "Next, we navigate this world together, as partners. You're in this now, whether you planned to be or not."

"I suppose it's too late to back out," I said, my lips curving into a teasing smile, though the gravity of his words hung heavily in the air. "Especially after making an enemy out of your 'queen.'"

He laughed, a genuine sound that warmed me from the inside. "Consider it a badge of honor. Not many can say they've drawn her ire. You have the makings of a true wild card."

Our laughter melded into the music, and I leaned into him, feeling the warmth radiating off his body, grounding me against the uncertainty of the night. Just as I thought we could breathe easy, a flicker of movement caught my eye. Clara, rejoining the fray with renewed vigor, her expression a storm of determination and fury.

"What now?" I murmured, tension threading through my body once more.

James's grip on me tightened, and I could see the storm brewing in his eyes. "Now, we dance. And we do it well."

In that moment, the world felt suspended, the stakes rising as Clara closed the distance between us, a cat poised to pounce. I steeled myself, determined to meet the challenge head-on, ready to embrace the chaos of the night. As we spun back into the rhythm, I felt the thrill of danger, a potent cocktail of fear and exhilaration that made me feel more alive than ever.

The music swelled, pulling us back into its intoxicating embrace as James and I moved together, our bodies weaving through the throng of masked revelers. Clara hovered nearby, a predator watching its prey, and I felt the sharp edge of her gaze as if it could slice through the air between us. The beat throbbed like a heartbeat, each pulse echoing my growing sense of urgency and thrill.

"Stay close," he murmured, his breath warm against my ear, and I nodded, instinctively inching closer. The kaleidoscope of colors and laughter faded, narrowing my focus to just him, the rhythm of the dance synchronizing our movements into an intimate choreography of defiance. The world around us blurred, yet Clara's looming presence remained an unwelcome shadow at the edge of my mind.

"Do you think she'll give up?" I asked, a hint of nervousness creeping into my voice, my eyes darting toward Clara, who now stood with her arms crossed, her expression an unsettling mix of amusement and ire.

"Not a chance," James replied, a playful grin flickering across his lips. "But that just makes our game more interesting. She thrives on conflict, and right now, we're the main event."

I couldn't help but smile back at him, the thrill of our situation igniting something deep within me. "Then let's give her a show, shall we?"

His laughter was a rich, low rumble that resonated through me, igniting a sense of audacity. We swirled back into the dance, moving fluidly with a shared rhythm that only we could hear. I could feel the eyes of the crowd upon us, whispers weaving a tapestry of speculation and intrigue as we twirled and spun. James was a masterful partner, his movements both confident and graceful, guiding me effortlessly through the sea of dancers.

With each step, the tension between us grew, sparking something that felt dangerously close to recklessness. As we danced, our hands brushed against each other, lingering just a moment longer than necessary, and I could feel the heat radiating from him. I was acutely aware of the way his fingers curled around my waist, the strength in his grip a silent promise of protection against the chaos swirling around us.

Then, as if summoned by the very air we breathed, Clara stepped forward, her voice slicing through the music with a sharp edge. "How charming," she drawled, her words dipped in honey but laced with venom. "The two of you think you can steal the spotlight. But what do you really know about each other? Or are we just pretending tonight?"

James turned, his expression cool yet tense, a warrior poised for battle. "What's your point, Clara? This isn't your stage."

"Oh, but it is, darling. This whole night belongs to me." Her smile was sharp, the kind that could cut glass. "You see, the host has a way of ensuring that the dance floor isn't the only arena where power plays out."

My heart raced, sensing the underlying threat in her words. "What do you mean?" I asked, my voice steadier than I felt.

Clara stepped closer, a cat circling its prey. "You've stepped into a world you don't fully understand. There are factions here, alliances that run deep, and you, my dear, are nothing more than a pawn. A lovely pawn, mind you, but a pawn all the same."

James stiffened beside me, a palpable energy radiating from him. "She's bluffing," he said, his voice low but resolute, though I could see the flicker of uncertainty in his eyes.

"Am I?" Clara tilted her head, a smirk playing at the corners of her mouth. "How naïve, James. You always were the dreamer." She stepped back, a satisfied look on her face. "But let's see how well your little dance partner performs when the lights go out."

Before I could respond, the lights overhead dimmed suddenly, plunging the room into an eerie twilight. Gasps and murmurs rippled through the crowd, a wave of confusion mingling with the underlying current of dread. I could feel the energy shift around us, a collective exhale as panic edged closer.

"What just happened?" I asked, gripping James's arm, the sudden darkness heightening my senses.

"Clara's theatrics, I'd wager," he replied, his voice steady despite the chaos. "Stay close to me."

The music faltered, replaced by the sound of hushed whispers and shuffling feet, the dance floor suddenly chaotic as guests began to scatter. My heart pounded in my chest, adrenaline coursing through my veins. Clara's laughter echoed from the shadows, a haunting melody that sent chills racing down my spine.

"Come now, everyone! Don't be shy! The night is just getting interesting!" she called, her voice rich with delight at the growing confusion.

James tightened his grip on my waist, his breath steadying as he scanned the room, searching for a way out. "We need to find a way to the back," he said, urgency threading his words. "If she has something planned—"

Before he could finish, the lights flickered back on, a dazzling burst of brightness that temporarily blinded me. I shielded my eyes, disoriented, and when I finally blinked them open, the scene had transformed. Guests had taken on a frantic energy, the air electric with fear and anticipation.

And then I saw it—a figure moving through the crowd, cloaked in shadows, their presence commanding attention even in the chaos. It was a man, tall and imposing, with an air of authority that silenced the clamor around him. His eyes gleamed with a feral intensity, locking onto James and me, a predator honing in on its target.

"Who is that?" I whispered, my voice barely escaping my throat.

James's expression turned grave, a flicker of recognition passing over his features. "That's Magnus. He's not someone you want to cross. He controls much of the power in this room, and if he's here, it means things are about to get very dangerous."

Magnus's gaze pinned us in place, and I felt the weight of his stare as though it were a physical force. The air crackled with tension, and I knew in that moment that whatever game Clara was playing had just escalated.

"Run," James urged, his voice low but filled with urgency.

But as we turned to flee, a sharp laugh rang out, cutting through the chaos. Clara, once again, had positioned herself at the center of the unfolding drama. "Oh, don't go just yet! The night is still young, and we have such fun in store for you!"

Before I could process her words, Magnus took a step forward, the crowd parting like waves before him. "You think you can play in my arena without consequences?" he said, his voice deep and resonant, sending a ripple of unease through the gathered guests.

I glanced at James, my heart racing as fear collided with determination. "What do we do now?" I asked, the world around us spinning as the stakes climbed higher.

James's eyes darkened with resolve. "Now we fight back."

And just as the last echoes of his words faded into the air, the lights flickered once more, plunging us into darkness as Clara's laughter danced around us, a sinister reminder of the chaos that lay ahead.

Chapter 6: Chasing Shadows

The city breathed an air of muted desperation, its neon signs flickering like dying stars against the velvet night. As I stepped into the alleyways, the damp concrete crunched beneath my boots, an echo that reverberated in the stillness around me. The scent of rain mingled with the lingering perfume of spilled beer and something else—something darker, almost sulfurous. Shadows clung to the walls like ghosts, and I felt them brush against me, whispering secrets I wasn't ready to hear. Determination hardened in my chest, propelling me forward into the unknown.

I'd promised myself I wouldn't let fear dictate my actions, yet every time I turned a corner, my skin prickled with the sensation of being watched. I cast a furtive glance over my shoulder, half-expecting to see him there, lurking just beyond the reach of the flickering streetlights. Ethan. He had a way of slipping into my thoughts like the chill of the evening air, his presence both unsettling and intoxicating. I had to know why he wouldn't confide in me, why he was so insistent on keeping his distance while simultaneously making it impossible for me to forget him.

The first lead had been a bar, a dive hidden beneath layers of graffiti and neglect, where whispers of the city's underbelly thrived like weeds. The bartender—a wiry man with a face carved by years of hard living—had given me a knowing look when I asked about Ethan's past. His words were sharp, clipped, yet heavy with implication. "Stay out of it, girl. Some things are better left in the dark." I had shrugged off his warning, but it wrapped around me now, tighter than my own fears.

My heart thudded as I recalled our last confrontation. Ethan had pushed me away, frustration etched across his handsome face, a storm brewing behind those stormy eyes. "You don't know what you're asking," he had said, his voice low and grave. I had been too caught up in my need to uncover the truth to see the raw fear that lurked in the depths of his gaze. Now, that fear felt like a thread pulling me deeper into the darkness, and I wasn't sure whether I would emerge unscathed.

My pulse quickened as I rounded another corner, the alley stretching ahead like a yawning chasm. The flickering light above me buzzed ominously, casting erratic shadows that danced along the brick walls. I stepped deeper into the gloom, the air growing heavier, suffused with the scent of damp earth and the metallic tang of uncertainty. Each footfall felt weighted with purpose, but I knew it was also laced with danger.

Suddenly, a movement caught my eye. A figure, barely more than a silhouette, melted into the shadows across the street. My breath caught in my throat as adrenaline surged through my veins. Was this the person I'd been seeking, or merely another shadow in this dark game I had entered? I hesitated, caught between instinct and rational thought. I could turn back, retreat to the safety of the known, but the thought of doing so made my blood boil.

"Why do you always run, Aveline?" The voice was a low murmur, a rasp that sent shivers down my spine. I spun around, and there he stood—Ethan, emerging from the darkness as if summoned by my very thoughts. His eyes glinted like shards of glass in the meager light, and for a moment, the world around us faded away.

"What are you doing here?" I demanded, irritation lacing my tone. "You can't keep shadowing me like this. I deserve to know what's going on!"

He stepped closer, the heat radiating from him like an unspoken promise, and my resolve wavered. "And what would you do with that knowledge? Some truths are weapons, Aveline. They cut deeper than you realize."

"Then tell me how to wield it! I'm not afraid," I insisted, though my heart raced at the thought of what I might uncover. "If you're hiding something, you need to let me in."

A flash of something—fear, perhaps—crossed his features, quickly masked by that impenetrable facade he wore like armor. "You think you're ready for this? The world I inhabit isn't a fairy tale, and you'd be stepping into a nightmare."

I took a step forward, emboldened by a mix of anger and determination. "I've already stepped into this nightmare, Ethan. Don't you see? I want to help you—if you would just let me!"

For a heartbeat, the silence between us crackled with unsaid words and shared tension. The truth hung heavy in the air, suffocating, and I could almost feel it whispering between us. Yet, before I could delve deeper into his soul, the faint sound of a footfall echoed behind me, a disturbance that shattered the fragile moment we'd created.

Ethan's gaze shifted, and I felt a chill sweep over me as I turned. The figure I had seen earlier was back, now emerging from the depths of the alley with deliberate slowness, their presence cloaked in an aura of menace. A flicker of recognition sparked in Ethan's eyes, and for the first time, I saw genuine fear cross his features, twisting them into a mask of tension.

"What have you done?" he hissed, the words barely escaping his lips.

My heart raced as I turned to face the threat, adrenaline coursing through my veins. The world around us had shifted once more, plunging us back into shadows that seemed to twist and coil, hungry for secrets we weren't ready to confront.

The figure stepped fully into the dim light, a hood obscuring their features but not the air of danger that surrounded them. The street was suddenly too small, the walls too close, pressing in with an urgency that made my breath quicken. I shifted instinctively closer to Ethan, seeking both protection and strength. Whatever this was—whatever secrets lingered in the shadows—I wasn't ready to face it alone.

"Who are you?" I called, my voice steadier than I felt. "What do you want?"

A low chuckle escaped the hooded figure, a sound dripping with contempt. "You really shouldn't poke your nose where it doesn't belong, sweetheart. The city isn't kind to those who dig too deep." Their voice was smooth, like honey poured over a wound, and yet it sent a shiver skittering down my spine.

Ethan's body tensed beside me, and for a fleeting moment, I caught a glimpse of vulnerability in his eyes, an emotion that felt entirely foreign against the backdrop of his usual stoic demeanor. "Stay back, Aveline," he warned, his tone clipped and urgent.

"Or what?" I shot back, adrenaline sharpening my senses. "You think I'll just let you handle this alone? You're not the only one with a stake in this fight."

A flicker of surprise crossed his face, quickly smothered beneath a mask of determination. The figure chuckled again, stepping closer, the shadows shifting around them like a living cloak. "Oh, you're feisty. I like that. But sweet girl, you have no idea what you're dealing with."

With each word, the tension in the air thickened, and I felt the electricity crackle between us, binding us in this precarious moment. I couldn't allow fear to take hold, not now, not when I had come so far. "I'm not afraid of you," I declared, my voice steady, though I could feel my heart racing. "Whatever game you're playing, I won't be a pawn."

The figure's laughter echoed through the alley, a sound devoid of mirth. "Aren't you adorable?" they sneered. "But I assure you, this isn't a game, and pawns often find themselves sacrificed."

Ethan moved, stepping slightly in front of me, an instinctual protective gesture that ignited a fire in my chest. "You don't belong here," he said, his voice low and filled with an edge I hadn't heard before. "You need to leave."

"Make me," the figure taunted, raising their hands as if inviting a challenge. "You think you can keep her safe from the truth? The city's secrets are darker than you can imagine, and they don't care about your little love story."

A surge of anger flared within me at their dismissive tone. "You don't know anything about us! This isn't just some romantic escapade; this is about survival!"

Ethan's grip on my arm tightened, grounding me, but I could see the conflict raging in his eyes. It was as if he wanted to tell me something, to drag me deeper into the maelstrom of his world, but fear held him back. My heart twisted at the thought of his turmoil, and I realized that we were not merely in a confrontation with an unknown enemy; we were at the brink of something much larger, a battle of wills that threatened to consume us both.

"Enough of this," the figure snapped, irritation flashing across their face. "I'm not here to play games. I'm offering you a chance to walk away unscathed. You don't want to know what happens when you refuse."

Ethan moved closer, and I felt the warmth radiating from him, a protective barrier against the chilling threat that loomed before us. "You think I'm afraid of you?" he spat, his bravado thinly veiling the dread creeping into his voice. "You don't intimidate me."

"Ah, brave words, but ultimately meaningless. You both have a choice: leave now, or be dragged into the abyss." With that, the figure turned slightly, revealing just enough of their face for my heart to drop—sharp features, cruel lips curled into a smirk. It was someone I recognized from the whispered rumors of the city, a ghost of a past I had never wanted to confront.

"Jules," I breathed, realization hitting me like a slap. The underworld's enforcer, known for a reputation as cold as the steel glinting in their eyes. "You're the one pulling the strings, aren't you?"

"Clever girl," Jules replied, a hint of amusement dancing in their voice. "But knowing the truth doesn't make it any less dangerous. What you want is a fantasy. This world doesn't deal in dreams."

"No," I countered, finding my footing in this precarious exchange. "This world is filled with choices, and I choose to fight for the people I care about."

Ethan's hand gripped mine tightly, and I felt a surge of warmth coursing through me, a reminder of the bond we shared. Whatever lay ahead, I wouldn't face it alone. "You may have the power here, Jules," he said, his voice low and fierce, "but we won't back down. If you think you can intimidate us into submission, you're sorely mistaken."

The smile on Jules' face faded, replaced by an intensity that made the air around us crackle. "So be it. But know this: the shadows aren't merely a backdrop. They can swallow you whole, and you'll find that light isn't as comforting as it seems."

As the words hung in the air, I realized that the stakes had risen significantly. This was no longer just about Ethan's secret; it was about a deeper conspiracy, one that threatened to entangle us both. The city was alive with danger, and I was determined to uncover every hidden truth, even if it meant stepping into the very shadows that sought to consume me.

Jules backed away, melting into the darkness, leaving us trembling in the aftermath of their threat. "What did they mean?" I turned to Ethan, desperation creeping into my voice. "What secrets are we really dealing with?"

But as he met my gaze, I saw that the battle was far from over, and the real fight lay just ahead, shrouded in the complexities of loyalty, love, and the haunting truths that we were yet to uncover.

The air hung thick with tension as I faced Ethan, uncertainty swirling around us like a mist. The remnants of Jules' threat echoed in my mind, intertwining with the fear and anger roiling within me. "What is going on, Ethan?" I pressed, my voice trembling with urgency. "You need to tell me the truth—now."

His eyes darkened, a storm brewing within them as if I had unleashed a tempest. "It's not that simple," he replied, his voice low and strained. "You don't understand what's at stake here. The shadows—"

"Enough with the shadows!" I cut in, frustration boiling over. "I'm tired of vague warnings and half-truths. If we're going to face whatever is coming, we need to do it together. No more secrets."

The muscles in his jaw tightened, and for a moment, I thought he might turn away, retreating into that impenetrable fortress he had built around himself. But then he exhaled, a sound laced with resignation. "Fine. But you have to promise me you'll stay close. I can't protect you if you keep running off into danger."

"Deal," I said, my heart racing at the thought of the truth finally coming to light. I stepped closer, ready to bridge the chasm that had formed between us. "What are the shadows hiding?"

Ethan hesitated, his eyes flickering as if weighing his words. "It's not just about us, Aveline. There are factions within the city, power struggles that run deeper than you realize. Jules is a player in a dangerous game, and they're not the only one. The people in the shadows—they want control, and they will stop at nothing to get it."

"Control of what?" I pressed, desperate for clarity. "What's the prize?"

"The prize is everything," he replied, his voice heavy with the weight of unspoken fears. "The city, its secrets, its people. It's a network, an underbelly that thrives on chaos and fear. They've manipulated events from the shadows for too long, and they won't take kindly to anyone trying to disrupt their plans."

"So what are we supposed to do?" I asked, my mind racing as I processed the enormity of his words. "Just sit back and let them have their way?"

"No," he said firmly, a glint of resolve igniting in his eyes. "We're going to expose them. We'll take back control. But it has to be done carefully. There are lines we can't cross if we want to stay alive."

A chill swept through me as I contemplated the magnitude of what lay ahead. "Carefully," I echoed, feeling the weight of those implications. "You mean we might have to play by their rules to survive?"

"Exactly. We need to learn their moves, understand their motives. Only then can we counteract their strategies." Ethan stepped closer, the air crackling between us. "But I need you to promise me you'll be cautious. One misstep, and we could find ourselves on their radar."

"I can do cautious," I assured him, though the words felt fragile in my mouth. "But I won't stand by while others decide our fate."

He nodded, appreciation flickering in his gaze. "Good. Then let's start by finding out what Jules knows. They might not be the only player, but they're certainly an important one."

Just as I was about to respond, the sound of footsteps echoed from the mouth of the alley, growing closer, steady and deliberate. My pulse quickened as I strained to see through the thick veil of darkness. Ethan's body shifted, instinctively placing himself between me and the approaching noise, a protective barrier that felt both comforting and infuriating.

"Stay behind me," he murmured, his eyes scanning the shadows with predatory alertness.

"Right, because that's worked out so well for us so far," I shot back, a mixture of anxiety and resolve coursing through me. I took a step to the side, determined to stand my ground.

The figure that emerged from the shadows was familiar yet unexpected, a face I had hoped to avoid. "Well, well, if it isn't the brave duo playing detective," said Lena, her voice smooth and dripping with sarcasm. She leaned against the wall, arms crossed, a smirk dancing on her lips. "You really think you're equipped to handle what's out there?"

"Lena," Ethan said with a mix of irritation and surprise. "What are you doing here?"

"Charming to see you too," she replied, unfazed. "I could ask the same. Last I checked, you were busy playing the reluctant hero, and she—" she gestured toward me with an exaggerated flourish, "—was running around in circles. What gives?"

I bristled at her condescending tone, unwilling to let her undermine our mission. "We're not here for your commentary," I retorted. "If you have something useful to say, now would be the time."

"Oh, I do, but you might not like it," she said, her voice dropping to a conspiratorial whisper. "Jules isn't just a shadow. They're the puppet master, and they have eyes everywhere. You two have already made waves, and the current is about to pull you under."

A chill crawled up my spine, the weight of her words settling like a stone in my gut. "What do you mean?" I asked, trying to suppress the trepidation that seeped into my voice.

"They're coming for you," Lena replied, her expression turning serious. "And they won't stop until you're either silenced or... well, you can imagine the alternative."

Ethan's jaw tightened, and I felt the panic rise within me, a tidal wave of fear threatening to consume my thoughts. "What do we do?" I asked, desperation bleeding into my tone.

"First, we need to lay low," Lena advised, her voice cool and measured. "They'll be watching, waiting for any sign of weakness. If we make one wrong move, it's over."

"Great," I muttered, the frustration bubbling to the surface. "And how exactly do we lay low while simultaneously exposing a powerful enemy?"

Lena's gaze shifted, her expression thoughtful. "You don't just go charging in. You need intel, allies—people who can help you navigate the murky waters. But beware, trust is a luxury in our world."

"I'm not interested in luxury," I snapped, my heart racing with defiance. "I just want to protect those I care about."

"Then we'll need a plan," Ethan interjected, cutting through the rising tension. "Lena, if you have contacts—"

"More than you know," she interrupted, a sly smile creeping across her lips. "But be prepared. The deeper you go, the harder it is to find your way back. You'll be hunted, and you'll need to be ready to fight."

A sudden rush of adrenaline surged through me, mingling with the dread pooling in my stomach. "I'm ready," I declared, meeting Ethan's gaze. "Whatever it takes, I won't back down."

"Then let's make our move," Lena said, a glimmer of excitement igniting her eyes. "But remember, in this game, the rules are not yours to define. The shadows will take more than they give, and we'll be lucky if we come out alive."

As her words hung in the air, an unsettling sense of urgency clawed at my insides. I felt the heaviness of impending danger press down on us, and the weight of our next steps loomed like a storm cloud ready to unleash its fury. We turned to leave the alley, but as we did, a sharp noise shattered the night—a sound unmistakably familiar.

Gunfire.

A shot rang out, piercing the darkness with lethal precision, and instinctively, I ducked, my heart pounding in my chest. But before I could process what was happening, I heard Ethan's voice, strained and urgent, call my name. I turned, desperation clawing at my throat, just in time to see him stagger, a look of shock etched across his face as blood blossomed across his shirt.

"No!" I screamed, rushing forward, but the shadows seemed to conspire against me, pulling me back into the abyss, the echoes of danger closing in as the world around us darkened into chaos.

Chapter 7: Sparks and Betrayal

It was one of those mornings where the sun spilled across the sky like molten gold, casting a warm glow over the remnants of last night's chaos. The air hung thick with the smell of burnt wood and the distant tang of iron, a reminder of our latest confrontation. I leaned against the crumbling wall of the abandoned warehouse we'd claimed as our base, the uneven bricks cool beneath my palm. My heart pounded in rhythm with the flutter of memories, fragments of laughter and camaraderie now overshadowed by suspicion and the unspoken words that lingered like ghosts between us.

In the early light, I caught sight of him, silhouetted against the dawn. Caleb had always been the spark to my flame, igniting every conversation with his quick wit and dark, teasing humor. But now, he stood apart, a shadow of the man I had once known. His back was turned to me, shoulders rigid, as if he were bracing against some invisible storm. I wanted to bridge the distance, to throw my arms around him and breathe life back into the remnants of our alliance, but something held me back—a knot of anxiety in my gut that told me to tread carefully.

"Caleb," I ventured, testing the waters, my voice soft but edged with a tension I couldn't quite mask. "We need to talk."

He turned slowly, his expression inscrutable. The sunlight caught the lines of his jaw, emphasizing the weariness etched into his features. "Talk about what? How you've managed to charm your way into the hearts of everyone but me?" His voice dripped with sarcasm, but beneath it lay a hurt that made my chest ache.

I took a step closer, the soft crunch of gravel underfoot almost too loud in the charged silence. "It's not about charm. It's about trust, and you're not giving me any. You've been keeping secrets, Caleb. I can feel it."

The wind picked up, swirling around us like a tempest, and I watched as his eyes flickered with something—guilt, perhaps? Or was it fear? "You're imagining things," he snapped, but even as he said it, I could see the fissures in his facade. This wasn't just a spat between friends; it felt like a fracture, threatening to split us apart entirely.

"Am I?" I challenged, crossing my arms over my chest as if that could somehow shield me from the emotional fallout. "Then tell me why you've been so distant. Why you won't let me in. It's like you've built a wall around yourself, and I'm not sure how to break it down."

He shifted, the tension coiling tighter around us, and for a fleeting moment, I thought I saw a flicker of vulnerability in his eyes. "It's complicated, Elara. There are things you don't understand—things I can't share." His voice lowered, almost pleading, but the distance in his gaze remained, a chasm I couldn't seem to cross.

"Try me," I urged, desperation creeping into my tone. "I've faced everything with you, and I won't turn back now. But you have to meet me halfway."

The moment stretched between us, fraught with unspoken words, until finally, he looked away. "I can't put you in danger. Not like this." His voice was a whisper now, heavy with the weight of unshed emotions, and it struck me like a blow. This wasn't just about secrets or betrayal; it was about protection. But what was the point of protecting someone if it meant pushing them away?

Before I could respond, the world around us erupted in chaos. A sharp crack echoed in the air, and I barely had time to register the sound before a bullet ricocheted off the wall beside me. Instinct kicked in; I shoved Caleb down, the two of us tumbling to the ground as another shot rang out. The warehouse was no longer our sanctuary; it had become a battleground, and in that moment, everything shifted.

"Get down!" I yelled, adrenaline flooding my veins, igniting a primal urge to survive. We scrambled to our feet, ducking behind a stack of crates that had been abandoned long before our arrival. Heart racing, I scanned our surroundings, searching for the source of the attack. Shadows flickered in the periphery, dark figures moving with lethal intent.

"What the hell is happening?" Caleb's voice was laced with panic, his earlier bravado stripped away by the reality of our situation.

"I don't know!" I shouted back, my eyes darting between the chaos. "But we need to stick together."

In that instant, the barriers between us dissolved. Our anger, our doubts—everything else fell away as we focused solely on survival. We moved in tandem, a synchronized dance forged by necessity, dodging bullets and navigating the debris of our former haven. I could feel the heat of his body beside mine, the tension of his presence fueling my resolve.

As we navigated the warehouse, the ambush forced us closer, our bodies brushing against each other with every narrow escape. It was like electricity, the kind that made the air crackle with possibility, but there was no time to process it. Every gunshot was a reminder of the fragile thread that held us together, and I found myself reaching for him, fingers curling around his wrist, anchoring us in the storm.

"Now!" I shouted, dragging him behind a stack of wooden pallets just as another shot whizzed past. The sound was deafening, a stark contrast to the thudding of my heart, and for a moment, we were frozen in time. His gaze locked onto mine, and in the heat of the battle, something shifted—a realization that perhaps, amid the chaos, we had both been hiding behind walls of our own making.

"I'm not letting you go," he breathed, the fierce determination in his voice igniting something deep within me. It wasn't just loyalty; it was a promise. Together, we could weather any storm.

With a shared nod, we burst from our cover, running toward the exit, adrenaline coursing through our veins. As we moved, the anger and betrayal melted away, replaced by a fierce loyalty I couldn't ignore. Whatever secrets lay between us, they no longer mattered in the face of survival. It was time to confront the shadows together, and as we emerged from the wreckage, I couldn't shake the feeling that we had crossed an invisible line. The bond we had once shared was transforming, igniting into something deeper, something fierce and unyielding.

The adrenaline coursed through my veins as we stumbled out into the harsh light of day, breathless and alive, a wild surge of energy battling the disarray of emotions swirling within. Caleb's fingers tightened around mine, a grip that felt both reassuring and electrifying, and as we broke free from the confines of the warehouse, I could almost convince myself that we were escaping the clutches of danger together. The sunlight was bright, blinding even, but it held a certain warmth that made everything feel surreal, as if we had stepped into a different world where the chaos couldn't touch us.

But reality had a way of intruding. The world outside was anything but safe. The sound of gunfire had faded, but the echoes of our heartbeats filled the silence as we darted into the narrow alley that ran parallel to the building. I glanced back, half-expecting to see pursuers, but the street lay empty, save for the distant wail of sirens, a haunting reminder that we were still very much in the eye of the storm.

"Where do we go now?" I asked, my voice low and urgent. The adrenaline rush was beginning to ebb, leaving behind a raw, trembling edge to my thoughts. Caleb's eyes narrowed as he surveyed our surroundings, his brow furrowing in concentration.

"There's a safe house not far from here," he replied, his tone clipped, as if he were mentally mapping our route. "But we need to move fast."

"Lead the way," I urged, trying to keep the tremor out of my voice. I was all too aware of the heavy weight of unspoken truths hanging between us, but the urgency of our situation forced me to push those thoughts aside for now. We couldn't afford distractions; survival was paramount.

As we maneuvered through the backstreets, I couldn't shake the feeling of being hunted. Every shadow felt alive, and I had to fight the instinct to glance over my shoulder every few moments. Caleb moved with an easy grace, his athletic frame cutting through the alleyways with purpose. Yet, despite his outward composure, I could sense the turmoil beneath his surface. The tightness of his jaw and the flicker of his gaze told me he was grappling with more than just our immediate danger.

"Are you going to tell me what you're hiding?" I blurted out, unable to hold back any longer. The question hung between us, and I could see his posture stiffen, the way he seemed to close off as if bracing for impact.

"It's not the time for this, Elara," he snapped, his voice sharper than I anticipated. But then his expression softened, just a fraction, revealing the turmoil I felt mirrored in my own heart. "If we survive this, then maybe we can talk. But right now, we have to focus."

"Survival first, then emotional confrontations," I quipped, forcing a lightness into my tone that didn't quite reach my eyes. It was an attempt to break the tension, to pull us back from the precipice of secrets and doubts.

He shot me a sideways glance, the corner of his mouth twitching into a ghost of a smile. "Always so practical, aren't you?"

"Someone has to be," I replied, nudging him with my shoulder as we turned a corner. "Especially when your secretive tendencies are putting us both in danger."

"Touché." His laughter rang out, a brief respite from the gravity of our situation, but it was short-lived. As we reached the end of the alley, the street opened up before us, and my stomach dropped at the sight of two figures loitering by a battered sedan.

"Stay close," Caleb murmured, instinctively tightening his grip around my wrist. We approached cautiously, and I could see the glint of weapons in their hands, a reminder that not everyone was on our side.

"Caleb!" one of the men shouted, stepping forward, a broad grin breaking across his face. "You made it! We thought—"

"Cut the pleasantries, Kyle," Caleb interrupted, his voice low but firm. "We're not safe yet."

I recognized Kyle, one of Caleb's old acquaintances, a guy who had always been too easygoing for my tastes. But now, that easy grin felt like a fragile mask over an uncertain reality.

"Right, right," Kyle said, the laughter fading from his voice as he took a closer look at us. "You look like you've seen a ghost. What happened?"

"It's a long story," I interjected, feeling the need to assert myself even as I tried to regain my composure. "But we need a place to lay low, and fast."

"Gotcha," Kyle replied, his expression shifting to one of seriousness. "Get in the car, we'll talk on the way."

The tension in the air was palpable as we climbed into the back seat, the metal frame creaking under the weight of unspoken words. Caleb's shoulder brushed against mine, a fleeting connection that ignited a flicker of warmth in the chill of uncertainty surrounding us. I could see him steal a glance at me, eyes clouded with thoughts that seemed miles away.

As Kyle drove, the streets blurred into a tapestry of concrete and color, a chaotic backdrop to our tense silence. "You sure you want to be involved in all this?" he asked, glancing at me in the rearview mirror. "I mean, things are getting pretty dicey."

"It's a bit late for second thoughts," I said, trying to inject levity into my tone. "I'm already knee-deep in this mess, thanks to your charming friend here."

Caleb's head snapped in my direction, surprise flashing across his face before he burst into laughter. "Charming? I think I'll take that as a compliment."

"Don't get used to it," I shot back, a smile breaking through my unease. But beneath our banter, the question lingered—was I really prepared for the consequences of my choices?

Kyle took a sharp turn, and the car jolted, the tension thickening again as we pulled into a dimly lit parking lot behind an inconspicuous diner. "This should do," he said, parking the car and turning to us. "But we need to be careful. There are ears everywhere."

We stepped out, the smell of frying grease and old coffee wafting toward us, a comforting scent amidst the chaos. Caleb moved closer, his presence a steadying force as we approached the back entrance. "So, what's the plan?" I whispered, my voice low as we entered the diner, the clatter of plates and chatter of patrons enveloping us.

Kyle led us to a booth at the back, sliding in first before we followed. "We lay low for a bit, regroup," he said, leaning forward, his tone serious. "And you, Caleb, need to explain why you didn't tell me about the ambush."

I watched as Caleb's expression darkened, a flicker of something—regret, maybe—crossing his face. "I had my reasons," he replied, his voice low.

"Which you're going to share, right?" I prodded, leaning forward, my heart pounding. The atmosphere was electric, charged with unspoken words and unanswered questions. "Because I can't do this alone. I need to know what I'm up against."

Caleb met my gaze, the intensity of his eyes pulling me in. "Fine," he said, taking a deep breath as if steeling himself. "But it's not just about the ambush. There's more at stake here than you realize."

And just like that, the world around us faded, the clatter of dishes and the laughter of strangers blurring into a distant hum as he began to unravel the web of secrets that had ensnared us both, pulling me deeper into a reality I had barely begun to comprehend.

The diner buzzed with life, the clinking of silverware and the murmur of voices creating a chaotic symphony that contrasted sharply with the tension at our table. I leaned in closer, trying to cut through the din and focus on Caleb's expression. His face was a mask of determination and trepidation, shadows dancing across his features as he prepared to unveil the secrets that had festered between us.

"I've been tracking a group," he began, his voice barely rising above the clamor, "one that's been causing trouble in the city for a while now. They're ruthless, and I didn't want to drag you into it." The admission hung heavy in the air, and I could feel my heart pounding in my chest.

"Tracking them how?" I pressed, my curiosity piqued despite the knot of anxiety in my stomach. "Are we talking surveillance, or are we in full-on spy mode here?"

Caleb's lips quirked into a half-smile, but the humor didn't quite reach his eyes. "More like a mix of both. I've had a few contacts feeding me information, but it's all been a bit... fragmented. I thought I could piece it together without involving you, but it turns out I was just being stupid."

"Stupid or noble?" I shot back, refusing to let him deflect my concern. "This isn't just about you anymore. I'm in this, whether you like it or not."

"Believe me, I know that now," he said, running a hand through his hair, frustration evident in the motion. "But there's something else—something I didn't want to burden you with."

My heart raced. "What is it?"

He hesitated, eyes flickering around the diner as if expecting someone to overhear. "The group I'm tracking? They're connected to my past in ways I didn't anticipate. There are people involved that I never wanted you to meet."

A chill ran down my spine. "You mean... they know you?"

"More than that," he admitted, lowering his voice to a whisper. "They know us. They know what we've been doing."

The weight of his words settled over me like a heavy blanket, suffocating and disorienting. I took a breath, trying to gather my thoughts, but the implications sent my mind spiraling. "So they could come after us? After me?"

"Exactly," he confirmed, his eyes dark with concern. "And that's why I've been keeping my distance. I thought it would keep you safe. But now..." He trailed off, frustration marring his handsome features as he struggled with the reality of our situation.

"Now we're both in danger because of your silence," I said, unable to keep the edge out of my voice. "What kind of connections are we talking about here? Criminal? Personal?"

"Both." His tone was grim, and I felt a rush of indignation. How could he think that keeping this from me was protecting me? "I can handle this, Elara. I've done it before."

"But I'm not just a bystander in this, Caleb! I'm not going to sit here while you fight your battles alone." I leaned forward, frustration bubbling to the surface. "We're a team, whether you want us to be or not."

He met my gaze, his eyes piercing through the tension between us. "That's what scares me. I can't let you get hurt because of my past mistakes."

Before I could respond, the diner's door swung open, a gust of wind trailing in, carrying a chill that sent shivers down my spine. A figure stepped inside, silhouetted against the bright light, and I couldn't shake the feeling that something had shifted in the atmosphere. The newcomer scanned the room, and I felt Caleb's muscles tense beside me.

"Who is that?" I whispered, the unease creeping back in.

"Stay low," he muttered, his focus fixed on the entrance. The figure took a few steps forward, and my heart raced as recognition dawned. It was a woman, her long dark hair cascading over her shoulders, and her eyes—a striking shade of green—met mine from across the diner.

"Caleb," she called out, her voice smooth but edged with something sharp, like glass beneath silk. "I was wondering when I'd see you again."

My stomach twisted as I glanced at Caleb, who had gone pale. "Do you know her?" I asked, incredulous.

"She's... an associate," he replied, the word almost tasting bitter on his tongue.

"Associate? That's one way to put it." The woman sauntered closer, her confidence radiating through the space. "I'd call us more like old friends."

"What do you want, Fiona?" Caleb's voice was low and guarded, tension crackling in the air.

She laughed lightly, but it was devoid of warmth. "I heard you were back in town, and I couldn't resist a little reunion. After all, it's been ages since we've had a proper chat."

"What do you want?" Caleb repeated, a hint of menace creeping into his tone.

"I want what's best for both of us," she replied, glancing at me with a cool appraisal. "And I'm afraid your little escapade might have caught some unwanted attention."

"Unwanted attention?" I echoed, anger bubbling beneath my skin. "You mean like the kind that nearly got us killed in that ambush?"

She turned her gaze back to Caleb, ignoring my outburst entirely. "I know things, Caleb. Things you might want to hear, things about the group you're after. But we need to discuss this privately."

"I don't trust you," he shot back, but I could see the flicker of uncertainty in his eyes.

"Trust me or not, it doesn't matter," Fiona said, a sly smile curling her lips. "But if you want to keep her safe, you'll listen. The clock is ticking, and I'm afraid you don't have much time before they find you."

Caleb's jaw tightened as he weighed his options. "What do you mean?"

"Let's just say there are forces at play that are far beyond your understanding," she replied, her voice dripping with satisfaction. "And if you don't act quickly, it won't just be your past that catches up with you. It'll be your future as well."

I felt my heart race, fear slicing through the bravado I'd been clinging to. "What future? What are you talking about?"

Fiona's gaze lingered on me, her smile widening. "Oh, darling, you're in deeper than you know. But I can help. All you have to do is meet me."

"Absolutely not," Caleb interjected, his tone fierce.

But the glimmer in Fiona's eyes suggested she relished the drama unfolding before her. "You can't protect her forever, Caleb. The question is, will you let me help, or will you watch it all burn?"

The weight of her words hung heavily in the air, and just as the tension reached its peak, the door of the diner swung open once more, this time with force. A group of men burst inside, their presence radiating danger.

"Caleb!" one of them shouted, and I felt my stomach drop. "We've got to go. Now."

Panic surged through me as I locked eyes with Caleb. "What do we do?"

His response was swift, but the urgency in his voice sent a chill racing down my spine. "We run."

But before we could make a move, the men advanced, their intentions clear, and in that moment, I realized we were far from safe. With the walls closing in, I braced myself for the chaos to come, knowing that the choices we made in the next few seconds could alter the course of our lives forever.

Chapter 8: The Secret Between Us

I stood on the creaking wooden deck, the evening breeze tousling my hair, a bittersweet reminder of the beauty that surrounded us and the turmoil simmering beneath the surface. The sun dipped low on the horizon, casting a golden hue over the ocean, the waves lapping gently against the shore, as if whispering secrets of their own. My heart raced, an unsettling mix of anticipation and dread swirling within me. How could one man inspire such conflicting emotions?

"Will?" I called, my voice barely cutting through the tranquil sounds of the sea. The air felt charged, heavy with unspoken words that had been building between us like the storm clouds gathering in the distance. "We need to talk."

He appeared moments later, his silhouette framed by the dying light, the shadows playing tricks on my mind. In the fading glow, he looked both regal and haunted, the lines of his jaw sharp against the evening sky, his blue eyes—usually so bright—clouded with something deeper. He crossed the deck, his movements fluid yet cautious, as if he was about to step on a fragile surface. "What's on your mind?"

It was a simple question, yet it hung in the air, fraught with implication. I felt the weight of it, the responsibility of the moment pressing down on me. We had danced around the truth long enough. "I need you to stop dodging my questions," I said, striving for a calm I didn't feel. "You can't keep hiding from me. Not anymore."

Will shifted, his hands sliding into the pockets of his jeans, a defensive posture I recognized all too well. "I'm not hiding," he replied, though the flicker of guilt in his eyes betrayed him. "I just—"

"Just what?" I interrupted, my frustration bubbling to the surface. "You just want to keep me in the dark? I thought we were in this together."

He sighed, a deep, weary sound that resonated with the very core of my being. The walls he had so carefully constructed were beginning to crack, and I felt a desperate urge to break them down, to see the truth that lay hidden behind his stoic facade. "You wouldn't understand," he finally muttered, turning his gaze toward the horizon.

"Try me," I urged, stepping closer, my heart pounding in my chest. "Whatever it is, we can face it together. I'm tired of feeling like I'm in a cage of your making, Will. Let me in."

Silence enveloped us, thick and suffocating, punctuated only by the distant call of a gull and the rhythmic crashing of waves. The air was electric with tension, and I could see him wrestling with himself, fighting a battle that had been raging long before I entered his life.

"I didn't always live here," he began, his voice barely above a whisper, and I could see the shadows of his past flitting across his features like ghosts. "Before this, I was... different. I was lost." He paused, swallowing hard, as if the words were stones lodged in his throat. "I lost everything I cared about—family, friends. I was betrayed in ways I can't even begin to describe. It changed me."

The revelation hung in the air, and I felt the ground shift beneath my feet. "Betrayed how?" My voice was softer now, the edge of accusation giving way to a curiosity that bordered on empathy. "What happened, Will?"

He turned to face me fully, and for the first time, I saw the pain etched in his features, the way his brows furrowed as if even the memory was a physical weight he carried. "I was involved in things I shouldn't have been," he admitted, his voice steady but raw. "Things that put my loved ones at risk. I thought I could protect them, but it only brought them harm."

My heart twisted at the vulnerability in his eyes. I stepped closer, the space between us shrinking, and took his hand, desperate to bridge the chasm that had formed between our truths. "You're not that person anymore, Will. You've changed. You've fought to be better."

He shook his head, a hollow laugh escaping his lips. "But the past doesn't just vanish. It lingers, festering in the corners of my mind, whispering reminders of what I've done."

"You think I don't understand loss?" I challenged softly, my own wounds surfacing, raw and unhealed. "I've lost too. I know what it's like to have that darkness cling to you, to wonder if you'll ever escape it." I took a breath, my voice steadying. "But it doesn't define us. It's what we choose to do with that pain that matters."

For a moment, he simply stared at me, the tempest within him waging a fierce war. I could see it in his eyes—the desire to share, to be understood, and the fear of rejection. I squeezed his hand, urging him to trust me, to let go of the past and embrace the possibility of something brighter.

"I don't want to lose you," he confessed, his voice cracking. "You deserve so much more than the shadows I bring."

"Then let me help you fight them," I said, my heart swelling with a fierce determination. "You don't have to carry this alone anymore."

But just as the barriers began to falter, a chilling presence loomed on the edge of our fragile moment. The faint sound of footsteps on the sand, a shadow creeping into our light, sent a shiver down my spine. My heart dropped, the air turning heavy with a new threat.

I turned, the world shifting around me, my instincts flaring. The ocean continued its relentless dance, but suddenly the waves felt more menacing, the wind howling a warning that echoed in my bones. "Will, we're not alone," I whispered, the realization igniting a sense of urgency.

He followed my gaze, his expression shifting from vulnerability to fierce protectiveness, and I knew that whatever darkness had once haunted him, we would face it together. But the storm was brewing, and it wasn't just the weather that would test us—it was a shadow from his past, one that knew every crack in his armor, poised to strike.

The moment hung in the air, crackling with electricity as I turned away from the encroaching shadows, my heart racing. Will's gaze was like a lifeline, anchoring me amidst the swirling uncertainty. The fading light painted us in shades of amber and navy, a stark contrast to the darkness creeping in from the edges of our fragile moment. I couldn't shake the feeling that whatever had drawn near carried with it the weight of Will's past, and I was determined to face it head-on.

"Stay close," he murmured, his voice low and urgent, yet laced with a protectiveness that made my heart swell. It was a simple request, but the command in it sent a thrill of excitement racing through me, making me feel both brave and terrified. We were in this together, whether the storm came from the ocean or from the ghosts that haunted him.

As the shadow grew more defined, I could see the figure striding purposefully toward us. The sun dipped lower, the last rays of daylight dancing on the waves as I squinted, trying to make out who it was. A familiar silhouette emerged, one that sent a chill creeping up my spine. "Jonas," I breathed, recognizing the man who had once been a friend but now felt more like a specter from Will's past.

Will tensed beside me, his body rigid, as Jonas approached, his expression inscrutable. The air thickened with unspoken history, the kind that crackles like static electricity before a storm. "What are you doing here?" Will demanded, his voice a mixture of anger and surprise.

Jonas stopped a few paces away, a sardonic smile curling on his lips, eyes glinting like shards of glass in the dying light. "I came to check on you, old friend. Heard you were playing house," he said, his tone dripping with condescension. "Didn't think you'd trade in your freedom for... what is it? A cozy little life by the sea?"

The tension in the air was palpable, and I could feel Will's muscles tense beside me, the danger simmering beneath his calm demeanor. "This isn't a game, Jonas," Will shot back, his voice low and dangerously quiet. "You need to leave."

"Or what?" Jonas stepped forward, his presence imposing, his body language a mixture of bravado and menace. "You'll threaten me with your newfound morals? Or maybe you'll let her play the martyr and take the fall for you? Seems like that's your thing now."

A flush crept up my neck at his insinuation, but I refused to let him get under my skin. "You don't know anything about us," I countered, stepping slightly in front of Will, a gesture that felt both brave and foolish. "You're just a shadow of who he used to be, and it's time you moved on."

Jonas's laughter echoed, sharp and biting. "Is that so? Tell me, how well do you really know him? The charming facade doesn't last forever, sweetheart." His eyes bore into mine, a dark challenge hidden behind the mask of his smile.

I could feel Will's gaze on me, steadying, encouraging me not to back down. "What do you want, Jonas?" I asked, my voice steadier than I felt. "If you're here to stir up trouble, you might want to rethink your strategy."

"I want what's mine," he said, his eyes narrowing, the playful veneer slipping away to reveal a predatory glint. "You think you can just swoop in and take him? You don't know the lengths I went to for him, the sacrifices. You think you can just—"

"Enough!" Will's voice rang out, sharp and commanding. The authority in his tone was startling, a glimpse of the man I knew he could be when pushed to his limits. "You need to leave. Now."

Jonas regarded him with a mix of amusement and disbelief, as if he were watching a child trying to act tough. "You think you can just cut me off like that? It doesn't work that way. You think you've escaped the past, but it's still in the shadows, waiting for you. And you'll need me before this is over."

"Not if I can help it," Will replied, his voice filled with determination. "You have no power here anymore."

"Power?" Jonas chuckled, a low, rumbling sound that set my teeth on edge. "Power isn't about control. It's about knowing the right buttons to push. You've forgotten that."

The confrontation was electric, a dance of wills that left me breathless. With every word, the tension coiled tighter around us, an impending explosion of emotions waiting to be unleashed. I could sense the darkness rising, threatening to swallow us whole, but I refused to let fear dictate my actions. "Will," I said quietly, my heart hammering. "We need to go. Now."

But Will didn't move, his eyes locked onto Jonas, and I could see the storm brewing within him, a battle between the man he was and the man he used to be. "You don't have any right to come here and threaten her," he said finally, each word laced with a resolve that cut through the tension. "You're not the man I once knew. You're just a ghost, clinging to the past."

Jonas's laughter was low, rumbling, as if he reveled in the chaos he was sowing. "A ghost? Perhaps. But ghosts can be very real, and they haunt the living, Will. You can't escape your past by pretending it doesn't exist."

"Get out," Will said, his voice now a hard-edged whisper. I could feel the raw energy vibrating between them, and the air felt charged with something dark and dangerous. I took a step back, the reality of the situation settling over me like a cold blanket.

For a moment, the world around us faded—the beach, the waves, the distant horizon. It was just us, three people entangled in a web of history, betrayal, and unresolved pain. I glanced at Will, desperate to show him my support, my loyalty, even as uncertainty twisted in my stomach.

Jonas studied us, his expression morphing into one of feigned curiosity. "What's it going to be, Will? You think you can protect her from everything? You think love is enough?" His tone dripped with disdain, and I felt my stomach churn.

Will took a deep breath, his face hardening, and in that moment, I saw a glimpse of the man I had come to admire—a man who had weathered storms and fought demons. "Love is more than enough. It's everything."

Jonas's smirk faltered, if only for an instant, and I could see the fleeting flicker of doubt in his eyes. "You're a fool if you believe that," he spat, but his bravado seemed to wane, a crack appearing in his confident facade.

"Maybe," Will replied, stepping protectively closer to me. "But I'd rather be a fool in love than a coward hiding behind threats. This ends now."

With that, the atmosphere shifted. The tension seemed to ebb slightly, as if a curtain had been pulled back, revealing the truth that lay behind Jonas's bravado. I held my breath, waiting for the final confrontation to unfold, the air thick with anticipation and uncertainty.

Jonas, however, merely shrugged, a hollow laugh escaping him. "Fine. But remember this, Will. I won't be far behind. Your past isn't done with you yet." And with that, he turned on his heel, striding away, leaving a wake of confusion and apprehension in his path.

As his figure receded into the twilight, I turned to Will, my heart pounding. "What did he mean? What else is there?"

Will's face was set, the shadows of his past creeping back into the forefront of his mind. "It's complicated," he said, his voice barely above a whisper. "But I'll protect you. I promise."

"I'm not afraid," I replied, though the tremor in my voice betrayed me. "Not if you're by my side."

But even as I said it, I felt a sense of dread settle over me, the shadows of Will's past looming larger than ever. The battle wasn't over; it was just beginning.

The cool evening air wrapped around us as the remnants of Jonas's presence faded into the distance, leaving an unsettling stillness in its wake. I could feel Will's tension radiating off him in waves, the way the sea rippled just beyond the deck, a reflection of the turmoil brewing inside him. I took a step closer, my hand instinctively finding his, fingers intertwining in a silent pact. We were allies now, bound together by a truth that both terrified and exhilarated us.

"What does he mean by your past?" I asked, my voice barely above a whisper, afraid of breaking the fragile calm that had settled around us.

Will's jaw tightened, the lines of his face drawn and serious. "It's complicated," he said again, the weight of his past hanging heavily between us like a storm cloud ready to burst. "Things I thought I had buried. Things that I never wanted you to know."

"Maybe it's time I knew," I replied, squeezing his hand gently, willing him to see that I was here, ready to stand beside him, no matter what shadows lurked in his history. "I want to understand you, all of you."

He hesitated, uncertainty flickering in his eyes like a candle struggling to stay lit in a gust of wind. "You really don't want to know the whole story, love. It's messy, and it involves people who won't just walk away."

"Jonas?" I ventured, not wanting to push him but feeling the urgency of our situation. "Is he dangerous?"

Will's expression darkened, his fingers tightening around mine. "More than I'd like to admit. He has a way of manipulating people, using their fears against them. I thought I had escaped him, but..."

He trailed off, frustration flickering across his features like a flame ready to ignite.

"But?" I pressed, unwilling to let him retreat back into himself. The last thing I wanted was for him to slip away behind his walls again, not when we were so close to bridging the gap between us.

He inhaled deeply, as if steeling himself against a wave of memories that threatened to pull him under. "But he knows me better than anyone. He knows how to push my buttons, how to get under my skin. And now that he's here, he'll stop at nothing to get what he wants."

"What does he want?" The question hung between us, heavy with implications.

"Control," Will said sharply, his eyes blazing with a fierce determination. "And revenge. He feels betrayed, and he won't rest until he has what he thinks is owed to him."

A shiver danced down my spine. "And what does that mean for us?"

He looked at me, really looked at me, and in that moment, I could see the turmoil swirling in his mind. "It means we need to be careful. He's not just a threat to me; he's a threat to you too. I can't let him hurt you, not again."

"I'm not some fragile thing that needs protecting," I shot back, a flash of defiance igniting my resolve. "I've faced my own demons, and I won't back down just because he's decided to show up."

Will's gaze softened, the edges of his mouth twitching into a small smile, but the worry lingered in his eyes. "I know you're strong. But this isn't just about strength. It's about strategy. We need to be smart about this."

"Smart?" I echoed, arching an eyebrow. "So what's the plan? Hide out in your cozy beach house until he decides to move on? That doesn't sound like much of a strategy to me."

"Maybe we could turn the tables," he suggested, a spark of mischief igniting in his expression. "What if we gathered some intel on him? We can't let him be the one pulling the strings."

"Now you're talking," I replied, my pulse quickening at the thought. "But how do we even begin to figure out what he's planning?"

Will released my hand and began to pace the deck, the creaking wood echoing under his weight. "We need to be discreet. We could reach out to some of my contacts—people who know Jonas, who might have seen or heard something that could help us."

I nodded, the wheels in my mind spinning. "And we could work together to piece together the information, stay a step ahead of him."

Will stopped, turning to me with a new fire in his eyes. "Exactly. But we need to be careful. If he catches wind of what we're doing—"

"He'll use it against us," I finished for him, my heart racing. "I get it. But we have to take the risk. I'm not going to let him scare us into hiding."

"Agreed," Will said, his voice low and steady. "But we'll need to be careful about who we trust. Even the people I used to rely on might not be on our side anymore."

A sudden thought struck me, a bolt of insight that felt electric. "What about your sister? What if she knows something? She might have information about Jonas or the people he's been hanging around."

Will's face darkened, the glimmer of hope in my suggestion faltering. "Claire? She's been trying to distance herself from all of this. I don't want to drag her back into it."

"Will," I said firmly, stepping closer to him, determination fueling my words. "If there's a chance she can help, we owe it to ourselves to try. Besides, she's family. You should be looking out for her, too."

He hesitated, weighing my words against his reservations. "You're right. I just don't want to put her in danger."

"Then we'll approach it carefully. We'll keep it low-key, see what she knows without alarming her," I suggested, my mind racing with the possibilities. "It's the best chance we have to get ahead of Jonas."

Will nodded slowly, his resolve hardening. "Okay. Let's do it. We'll go see her tomorrow. But we need to keep our plans close to our chest. No one else can know what we're up to."

As the plan settled between us, a sense of purpose surged through me. Together, we could face this, confront the shadows of his past and unearth the secrets lurking in the dark. I could feel the weight of our shared determination, a force that would shield us from the encroaching storm.

But just as the tension in the air began to shift from anxiety to anticipation, the distant sound of tires crunching on gravel reached my ears, a sound that sent a cold wave of apprehension washing over me. My heart raced as I turned toward the driveway leading to the house, squinting into the darkness. "Will," I whispered, fear creeping into my voice. "We're not alone."

He stepped closer to me, eyes narrowed, scanning the shadows. "It can't be anyone good at this hour," he murmured, every instinct honed, alert.

The headlights of a car cut through the night, illuminating the driveway, and I felt my breath hitch in my throat. "Should we go inside?" I asked, my heart pounding.

"No. Let's see who it is first," Will said, his voice low and controlled. He slipped his phone from his pocket, readying it as a precaution, and I couldn't shake the sense of dread coiling tighter within me.

As the vehicle drew nearer, I recognized the sleek black SUV that rolled into view, the insignia glinting ominously in the light. My stomach dropped, a chilling realization settling over me. "It's them," I breathed, my eyes widening in horror.

Will's grip on my hand tightened, a silent reassurance that we would face whatever came next together. But as the car door swung open, revealing a figure cloaked in shadows, the air grew heavy with the weight of impending confrontation, and the ominous truth lingered like a specter in the night.

"Stay close," Will whispered, his voice steady, but I could hear the tension that lay just beneath the surface. We weren't just fighting against Jonas anymore; this was about to become a battle against the very forces that threatened to unravel everything we had fought for.

The figure stepped forward, and just as I braced myself for what would come next, a chilling laugh echoed through the night, sending a shiver racing down my spine. "Well, well, if it isn't the lovebirds." The voice dripped with mockery, and in that moment, I knew we were standing on the precipice of chaos, ready to plunge into the unknown.

Chapter 9: The Edge of Loyalty

The air crackled with the kind of tension that made the fine hairs on the back of my neck stand at attention. I stood in the half-light of the cavern, shadows flickering like the ghosts of memories I wished to forget. The walls were damp, their surfaces glistening with moisture that mirrored the unease coiling in my stomach. Each breath I took felt heavy, laden with unspoken fears and the weight of a past I was barely beginning to understand. Just a few weeks ago, my life had been a routine of small town dramas and the occasional thrill of a new book release. Now, I was caught in a web spun from old grudges and newfound loyalties, with the man at the center of it all—Ethan—looking like a tempest wrapped in a heartbreaker's charm.

Ethan shifted beside me, his broad shoulders tense as he surveyed the darkness ahead. I could feel the pulse of his anxiety in the air, thick and suffocating, and I hated that it affected me too. A fragment of his past had reemerged, an old rival who seemed to know him better than I ever could. That thought alone was enough to keep me awake at night, haunted by the idea that there were parts of him still buried, still hidden from me. "We need to move," he said, his voice low and steady, but there was an edge to it that suggested he was barely holding it together.

I turned to him, searching his eyes for answers that felt just out of reach. "Are you sure you want to do this?" The question slipped from my lips before I could censor myself. Doubt bubbled up like the darkness surrounding us. "We don't know what we're walking into."

His gaze hardened, a flicker of something unyielding passing through his expression. "I can't let him dictate my life anymore. Not after everything." The passion behind his words ignited something within me, a stubborn flame that refused to be snuffed out by fear.

"What if it's a trap?" I pressed, unable to quell the instinct that urged me to protect him at all costs. "What if he wants you to come out into the open? This could end badly, Ethan."

He stepped closer, the space between us charged with an unspoken understanding. "Then we'll face it together. I'm not losing you to this—whatever it is." His determination wrapped around me like a cloak, and I felt my heart lurch at the prospect of standing beside him, facing whatever shadows lay ahead.

We ventured deeper into the cavern, the flicker of our flashlight revealing the jagged stones that jutted from the ground like the teeth of some slumbering beast. Each step was fraught with uncertainty, my instincts screaming at me to turn back, but I couldn't abandon him—not now. We'd formed an alliance, one rooted in trust but threatened by secrets and the lingering ghost of betrayal. I could see it in the way he clenched his jaw, the way his eyes darted around, searching for something he couldn't quite name.

As we rounded a bend, a low sound echoed through the darkness—a laugh, cruel and mocking. I froze, fear gripping my heart like a vise. Ethan's hand shot out, gripping my arm, his touch both grounding and electric. "Stay behind me," he whispered, his voice barely above a breath, thick with the tension of unspoken fears.

"Who is it?" I asked, trying to keep my voice steady as I leaned closer to him, the warmth of his body anchoring me. The darkness seemed to pulse around us, alive and hungry, and I fought against the urge to flee.

He didn't answer, his focus entirely on the shadows ahead. I could see the muscles in his back tense, the set of his shoulders revealing a man caught between his past and the present. Then, out of the murky gloom, a figure emerged, tall and menacing, with a grin that could curdle milk.

"Ethan," the figure drawled, his voice a silken thread woven with malice. "I wondered when you'd finally show up. You've been avoiding me for far too long."

My breath hitched in my throat. This was the enemy, the specter from Ethan's past. The air shifted, electric with the tension of a confrontation long overdue. I watched as Ethan's expression hardened, the vulnerability I had glimpsed moments before retreating behind a wall of steely resolve. "What do you want, Marcus?" he asked, each word dripping with disdain.

"I think you know exactly what I want," Marcus replied, stepping forward, his confidence palpable. "You've always been too good at hiding, but not good enough. I've come to settle old scores."

I could feel Ethan's body tense beside me, the storm brewing in his eyes a stark reminder of the man who had been shaped by hardship and betrayal. "This isn't just between you and me," Ethan said, his voice firm. "I'm not the only one you'll have to answer to."

Marcus turned his gaze to me, an amused smile playing at the corners of his lips. "Ah, the charming companion. A bold move, Ethan, bringing her into this mess. Doesn't she know the danger she's in?"

I straightened, my own resolve hardening at the challenge in his tone. "I'm not afraid of you," I shot back, my voice steady, even as my heart raced. "You don't scare me."

Marcus laughed, a low rumble that reverberated in the cavern. "Brave words from a pretty face. But bravery doesn't always translate to survival."

In that moment, as the echoes of his laughter faded into the oppressive silence, I felt the weight of our situation settle heavily upon me. The stakes were higher than I had ever anticipated, yet I couldn't back down. Ethan needed me—now more than ever. The bond we shared had become a lifeline in the darkness, and I was determined not to let it slip away.

"Together," I whispered, a vow formed in the depths of my heart. The air between us shimmered with the promise of what was to come, and as I glanced at Ethan, I saw the flicker of hope ignite in his eyes. We were no longer just two people caught in a web of danger; we were allies, partners forged in the heat of uncertainty, standing firm against the shadows that threatened to engulf us.

And for the first time in a long while, I felt the stirrings of something more profound than fear—a fierce loyalty that bound us together, ready to face whatever Marcus had in store.

The silence that followed Marcus's taunt was thick enough to cut through. I felt the moment stretch, like a taut string ready to snap, and the uncertainty swirled around us like fog. Ethan's jaw clenched, his eyes narrowing as he faced his nemesis. The contrast between the two men was striking—Ethan, with his rugged handsomeness and the weight of burdens too heavy for any one person, and Marcus, sleek and predatory, dressed in dark clothing that clung to him like a second skin.

"Your bravado is amusing, but let's not pretend this is a game, shall we?" Marcus drawled, his voice dripping with disdain. He stepped forward, the shadows clinging to him as if drawn by his very essence. "You're out of your depth here, Ethan. This is my territory."

"Territory? You think you own this place?" Ethan's voice held a low, steady rumble, like distant thunder threatening a storm. "This ends tonight. I won't let you drag me back into your hell."

"Such noble intentions," Marcus replied, his grin widening, revealing the glint of teeth that resembled a shark's. "But I'm afraid loyalty only gets you so far, my old friend. Perhaps your lovely companion here would like to take your place instead."

I bristled at his words, feeling a mix of fury and fear. "You don't know anything about loyalty," I spat, my voice stronger than I felt. "It's not just a word to toss around when it suits you."

Marcus chuckled, a sound that reverberated through the cavern like a sinister echo. "Oh, but I do. Loyalty can be a double-edged sword, especially when it's misplaced. Isn't that right, Ethan?" He stepped closer, the air thickening with his malevolence. "You could protect her, but at what cost?"

Before Ethan could respond, a loud crash echoed from deeper within the cavern, reverberating off the walls. The sound startled us, jolting me from my rising dread. "What was that?" I whispered, my heart racing in my chest.

"Just a little welcome gift," Marcus said, his smirk fading as he turned his attention to the darkness beyond. "Seems your arrival hasn't gone unnoticed."

My instincts kicked in, and I grabbed Ethan's arm, pulling him back. "We should move. We can't stay here."

"Right," he agreed, his voice clipped but his focus still on Marcus. "You won't win this, Marcus. You're outnumbered, and you're losing your grip on whatever this is."

"Am I?" Marcus replied, his tone mocking. "It's cute that you think you can make threats in my territory. But I have all the cards. You're the one who's bluffing."

With a sudden movement, he lunged toward us, and I felt a rush of adrenaline. "Ethan!" I shouted, pushing him to the side just as a jagged rock whizzed past us, missing by mere inches.

"Run!" Ethan commanded, his voice fierce as he shoved me ahead. I took off, the rough terrain beneath my feet stumbling me. My heart raced, not just from fear, but from the overwhelming need to keep Ethan safe.

The darkness enveloped us, but I didn't dare look back. I could hear Marcus's footsteps pounding behind us, a menacing sound that drove me to run faster. "This way!" Ethan shouted, grabbing my wrist and pulling me into a narrow passageway that twisted away from the open cavern.

I stumbled after him, the sound of rushing water growing louder, mingling with the sound of our footsteps echoing in the claustrophobic space. The walls felt closer here, damp and uneven, and I could almost taste the fear that hung in the air between us. "Do you know where this leads?" I gasped, my breath coming in ragged bursts.

"Somewhere safer," he replied, glancing over his shoulder. "But we need to keep moving."

Suddenly, the ground beneath us shifted, a sharp crack slicing through the air. I caught my balance just in time, but Ethan stumbled, and I turned, grabbing his arm to steady him. "We can't stop!" I urged, the urgency in my voice propelling us forward.

Just as we rounded a corner, we emerged into a small chamber filled with shafts of moonlight filtering through cracks in the rock. It was a breathtaking sight, the shimmering light dancing on the water pooling in the center of the room. I caught my breath, momentarily mesmerized by the beauty, but Ethan's voice yanked me back to reality.

"Get to the water!" he shouted, urgency lacing his tone. "If we can reach the other side, we can—"

Before he could finish, Marcus appeared in the entrance, his silhouette framed by the darkness. "Did you really think you could escape me?" he taunted, his voice smooth, like silk concealing a knife.

Ethan's eyes flared with determination. "You're not getting her, Marcus," he declared, positioning himself protectively in front of me.

"Oh, Ethan," Marcus drawled, his tone dripping with condescension. "You think this is just about her? You're mistaken. This is about your weakness—your inability to let go of the past."

"Letting go isn't the issue," Ethan shot back, his voice low and fierce. "It's about standing up to monsters like you."

I felt the tension swell between them, a storm brewing in the space of mere heartbeats. "Ethan, we need to go," I urged quietly, my heart pounding with both fear and something else—an unshakeable connection to the man in front of me, one that was growing stronger with every moment we faced together.

But as if reading my thoughts, Marcus moved closer, his smirk returning. "You think you're his savior, don't you?" He stepped forward, his gaze piercing. "You're just a pawn in this game, and he's willing to sacrifice you for a chance at redemption."

"No!" I said, my voice rising with desperation. "You're wrong. He would never—"

"He would never hesitate to protect what's his," Marcus interrupted, his tone triumphant. "You're not as safe as you think, little girl."

In a split second, everything changed. With a fierce cry, Ethan lunged forward, his fist connecting with Marcus's jaw, the sound reverberating like a crack of thunder. It was a move born not just from anger, but from a deep-seated need to protect, to fight back against the shadows that had haunted him for too long.

I stood frozen, the adrenaline coursing through me, shock momentarily paralyzing my thoughts. But then, instinct kicked in. "Ethan, behind you!" I shouted, rushing forward, my heart pounding in rhythm with the chaos around us.

Ethan turned just in time to see Marcus recover, fury flashing in his eyes. I knew we had to get out, but I felt the weight of our situation, the perilous balance of loyalty and danger. We were running out of time, and I couldn't let him sacrifice everything for me.

In that moment, as we braced for the inevitable confrontation, I realized that our fight wasn't just about survival—it was about breaking free from the chains of the past, together.

The cavern erupted in chaos as Marcus reeled from Ethan's blow, but he quickly regained his composure, a dangerous glint igniting in his eyes. "Is that all you've got, Ethan?" he sneered, wiping a trickle of blood from his lip with a casual flick of his wrist. "You'll have to do better than that if you want to protect her."

Ethan's breathing was heavy, the weight of the confrontation pressing down on him like the darkness surrounding us. I could see the rage simmering beneath his skin, a fierce protector rising to the surface. "You won't touch her," he growled, positioning himself between Marcus and me, an unyielding barrier of defiance.

I felt a rush of affection mixed with anxiety. How had we found ourselves here, locked in a battle that felt almost surreal? "Ethan, we can't—" I began, but he shot me a look, fierce and protective, and I knew better than to argue.

Marcus chuckled, the sound devoid of warmth. "You think you can save her? This isn't just about her, you fool. It's about everything you've tried to bury. You're only digging your grave deeper."

"You don't know anything about me," Ethan snapped, every word laced with the kind of anger that burned bright and hot. "You think I'm afraid of my past? You think I care about your twisted games? I've fought demons far worse than you."

With a sudden shift, Marcus lunged, his body a dark blur against the moonlit backdrop. My heart raced, and without thinking, I rushed forward, ready to do anything to protect Ethan. "No!" I shouted, but I was too late. The two men collided with a heavy thud, grappling like wild animals, their movements fierce and desperate.

I felt a surge of panic rising in my chest as I sprinted toward them. "Ethan!" I cried, but the sounds of their struggle drowned me out, each punch thrown echoing in my ears like a death knell.

As I reached them, I caught a glimpse of Marcus's face twisted in rage, and I seized a nearby rock, raising it as a makeshift weapon. "Get off him!" I screamed, adrenaline coursing through my veins. I swung the rock, aiming for Marcus, but he twisted just in time, dodging my attempt. The rock hit the ground with a dull thud, and Marcus turned to me, eyes gleaming with mockery.

"You think you can save him?" he taunted, brushing off the dust from his shirt as if he hadn't just been in a scuffle. "Look at you—just a pawn in a game you can't possibly understand."

In that moment, fury ignited within me. "I might be a pawn, but I'm not without my power. I will fight for him."

"Then let's see how far that will get you," Marcus hissed, lunging again, but this time Ethan was ready. With a swift movement, he sidestepped, using Marcus's own momentum against him. The force of the blow sent Marcus crashing against the rocky wall, a grunt escaping his lips as the wind was knocked out of him.

"Now!" I shouted, urgency pulsing through me. "We need to get out of here!"

Ethan nodded, his focus shifting back to me, the intensity in his gaze softening momentarily. "Go! Find the exit; I'll hold him off."

"No! We can't separate. I'm not leaving you," I insisted, the idea of running without him felt like jumping into a dark abyss.

"Do you trust me?" he asked, and the sincerity in his voice tugged at my heart.

"Of course, I trust you!" I replied, frustration bubbling. "But I won't just abandon you!"

"Then you need to get to safety so I can fight him without worrying about you." His eyes burned with urgency. "Please. I can't lose you."

The gravity of his words anchored me, and I hesitated, my heart torn between loyalty and the primal instinct to flee. But before I could respond, Marcus regained his footing, eyes narrowing as he stalked toward us with renewed ferocity. "Your little moment is over, Ethan. Time to end this."

Ethan's expression shifted from determination to desperation. "Go!" he shouted, urgency lacing his tone. "I'll find you. Just run!"

With my heart pounding in my chest, I turned and dashed toward the cavern's exit, adrenaline propelling me forward as I stumbled through the narrow passage. My mind raced as I navigated the twists and turns, each shadow a reminder of the danger lurking behind me. I could hear their voices—the clash of fists, the grunts of exertion—but I forced myself to keep moving, driven by a mix of fear and the need to protect what we had fought so hard to build.

Finally, I burst into a wider chamber, the moonlight spilling in from an opening high above. The sight took my breath away. This place was an underground oasis, a hidden sanctuary untouched by the turmoil of the world outside. Water glimmered like stars scattered across the floor, and bioluminescent moss clung to the rocks, casting an ethereal glow. But I couldn't linger; I had to keep going.

I moved through the chamber, desperately searching for another way out, my heart thrumming in sync with the echo of my footsteps. "Ethan!" I called, my voice bouncing off the walls, swallowed by the shadows.

The silence that followed felt ominous, and I pressed forward, determined not to let the darkness win. Each step felt heavy with dread, and just as I reached another narrow passage, I heard a roar of rage behind me. The sound was followed by a crash that reverberated through the cavern, shaking the ground beneath my feet.

"Ethan!" I screamed again, panic rising in my throat. My pulse quickened as I pushed through the passage, desperation fueling my legs. I stumbled into a winding tunnel, the path narrowing as I went deeper into the earth, my breath coming in short gasps.

The tunnel twisted and turned, leading me deeper into the darkness. I had no idea where I was going, but the sound of the fight echoed in my ears, a chilling reminder of the stakes. Every fiber of my being urged me to turn back, to find him, but I knew I had to find a way out first.

As I rounded a corner, I caught sight of faint light flickering ahead, a promise of escape. But just as I was about to reach it, a shadow loomed in the entrance. My heart dropped as I skidded to a halt, the realization dawning on me that I wasn't alone.

The figure stepped into the light, and it wasn't Ethan. It was Marcus, his expression a blend of triumph and malice. "Looking for someone?" he purred, blocking my only route to safety.

I froze, my heart pounding furiously against my ribcage. There was no way back now. The only path lay ahead, and I had no choice but to confront the very threat I had tried to escape. "Let him go!" I shouted, my voice steadier than I felt.

Marcus chuckled, a low, menacing sound that sent a shiver down my spine. "Why would I do that? This is so much more entertaining."

In that moment, the gravity of our situation hit me like a freight train. My body tensed, ready to fight, but I was painfully aware that I was outmatched. Yet, deep within me, a flicker of resolve ignited. I wasn't just fighting for survival; I was fighting for Ethan, for the bond we had forged in the fires of adversity.

"Get away from me!" I shouted, and without thinking, I lunged at him, my instincts screaming for me to protect what was mine.

But as I did, the ground shook violently beneath us, and the cave began to tremble, the rock walls groaning ominously. I lost my balance, the world spinning around me as I struggled to regain my footing. And in that split second, as the shadows began to close in and the ground quaked, I saw Marcus's expression shift from amusement to shock.

Then, the world around us shattered, and the ground gave way, plunging me into darkness.

Chapter 10: A Shattered Alliance

The narrow street stretches ahead, littered with shards of broken glass and crumpled newspapers, remnants of a world that was once vibrant and full of life. Now, it feels more like a tomb, each step echoing with the memories of laughter and love that used to fill this place. I can still hear the ghosts of our past conversations, laughter ringing out under the flickering neon signs of the shops that line the alley. A hairpin turn takes us deeper into this urban labyrinth, where the air is thick with the scent of rain-soaked pavement and distant smoke from an unseen fire. The sky is bruised with the hues of twilight, casting long shadows that seem to stretch out and grasp at us, a tangible reminder of the uncertainty that looms.

I take a breath, letting the chill of the evening air wash over me. My heart is still racing, a percussion of adrenaline from the narrow escape we had just made. The memory of the chaos feels like a live wire in my mind, crackling with the danger we barely eluded. I glance sideways at him, the betrayal still fresh, a bitter taste on my tongue. He is handsome, with tousled dark hair that falls just above his striking blue eyes, eyes that used to sparkle with mischief and warmth but now seem cold and guarded. The tension between us is palpable, like an invisible thread pulling tight, ready to snap at any moment.

"Do you ever think we'll find our way back?" I ask, the words escaping before I can stop them. I didn't mean to, but the question hangs in the air, heavy and loaded.

He shifts, his jaw tightening, and I can see the conflict brewing beneath the surface. "Back to what? A life that was built on lies? Or the illusion of trust we once had?" His tone is sharper than I expect, a jagged edge slicing through the fragile atmosphere.

I wince at his words, feeling the truth in them. Our alliance, once so solid, now feels like a fragile web spun from mistrust and deception. I want to argue, to defend the bond we shared, but the memories of his secrets flood my mind, drowning out any response. "It doesn't have to be like this," I murmur, my voice softer, edged with a vulnerability I'm reluctant to reveal. "We can still salvage something from this mess."

His eyes soften for just a moment, a flicker of the man I thought I knew, but it vanishes as quickly as it appeared. "Can we really? How do I know you won't turn around and stab me in the back when it suits you?"

The accusation stings, igniting a fire of indignation within me. "You don't get to throw that at me after everything! I fought for us!" My voice rises, each word fueled by the frustration of a thousand unspoken fears. "I stood by you when no one else would."

His expression hardens, and in that moment, I see a flicker of regret mixed with defiance. "And I lied to you. I kept things from you because I thought it would protect you. I thought I was doing the right thing."

"Protect me?" I scoff, incredulous. "You think betrayal is protection? You put me in danger the moment you decided to keep me in the dark." The echo of my words hangs heavily between us, the truth of our situation bearing down like the oppressive weight of the storm clouds above.

As silence envelops us again, the distant sound of sirens wails through the air, a reminder that we are not yet free from the chaos that seeks to reclaim us. I steal a glance down the alley, shadows darting at the edges of my vision, and a shiver skates down my spine. Fear mingles with anger as I contemplate our next move. We need to decide, and quickly, or risk losing ourselves entirely to the shadows.

"Look," he finally says, his voice a low murmur as he steps closer, bridging the gap just slightly. "I didn't mean for it to go this far. I didn't plan on..." He hesitates, struggling with the words as if they are heavy stones lodged in his throat. "I didn't plan on you getting hurt."

"Then stop pretending this is just about you," I reply, my heart pounding. "I'm in this too, remember? I'm the one who fought to be by your side. You're not the only one who has something to lose."

He nods slowly, and I see a flicker of something—maybe understanding, or perhaps resignation. "I know. But if we're going to get through this, we need to trust each other again. No more secrets. No more lies."

The sincerity in his tone pulls at the edges of my resolve, and I want to believe him. I want to lay down the weapons we've drawn against one another and return to the moments of shared laughter and whispered dreams. But the reality of the betrayal lingers like a bitter aftertaste, making it hard to swallow the idea of reconciliation.

"Trust doesn't just come back like that," I say, my voice tinged with both hope and caution. "It takes time, and right now, I don't know if we have any left."

His gaze holds mine, and in that silence, an unspoken promise hangs in the air, fragile yet potent. I take a step back, the distance between us stretching once more, and I feel the weight of the decision looming ahead. Together or apart, we are teetering on the brink of something monumental, and I can't shake the feeling that whatever happens next will change everything.

The silence stretches like a taut wire between us, each heartbeat a reminder of the decisions we both must make. I can hear the faint hum of the city beyond the alley, a cacophony of life that feels worlds away from the tension simmering in this shadowy corner. As I turn my back to him, an inexplicable heaviness clings to my chest, a paradox of relief and sorrow coiling tightly. With each step away, I steal glances over my shoulder, caught between wanting to flee and longing for him to call me back.

Just as I reach the mouth of the alley, a sudden commotion erupts behind me. The sound of boots pounding against pavement sends a jolt of adrenaline coursing through my veins. Instinctively, I duck behind a dumpster, the cold metal biting into my skin as I peer around its edge. My heart races, and the once-comforting shadows now seem ominous, alive with the potential for danger. I catch a glimpse of him as he slides into cover beside me, eyes wide with a mix of fear and determination.

"What the hell was that?" I hiss, the urgency in my voice slicing through the tension like a knife.

His gaze is fixed on the entrance to the alley, where a group of men in dark clothing approaches, their movements slick and purposeful. "Looks like they're looking for someone," he mutters, his tone low and steady.

I can feel the electricity in the air, the kind that crackles right before a storm. "Do you think they're—"

"Related to what just happened?" He finishes for me, his brow furrowing. "Yeah, I'd say so."

The men step into the light, revealing faces I recognize from the whispered conversations at the edges of my life, shrouded in rumors and veiled threats. My stomach sinks. "We need to get out of here. Now."

He nods, but his expression is indecipherable, a complex web of emotions that makes my heart ache. I can see the shadows of his past swirling in his eyes, the burden of choices that led us to this moment. "You head left, I'll go right. We'll meet at the diner two blocks down."

"No!" I whisper sharply. "We stick together. We can't split up now."

"Splitting up might be the only way we survive," he counters, his voice firm but laced with an edge of desperation. "Trust me."

Trust. The word lingers in the air between us, heavy and loaded. I hesitate, the weight of his past choices bearing down on me. But the urgency of our situation forces a decision. "Fine. But I'm leading."

With that, we inch backward, blending into the shadows like phantoms. My pulse quickens as we navigate the tangled web of alleys, each step filled with a mix of dread and determination. The stench of garbage and the distant echoes of laughter from unsuspecting passersby feel worlds apart from the reality we're entangled in. As we move, I can't shake the feeling that our escape might not be so simple.

The alleyways twist and turn like a labyrinth, but my feet seem to know the path, each corner a reminder of the city I once loved. The familiarity brings me comfort, even as my heart pounds with the knowledge of the danger stalking us. Just as I start to breathe easier, a shout rings out, cutting through the air like glass breaking.

"There they are! Don't let them get away!"

Panic floods my veins, and without thinking, I grab his hand, pulling him deeper into the maze of concrete and shadow. "Run!" I shout, urging him forward, my instincts kicking in. We weave through the alley, the air thick with tension, my mind racing as I try to recall every escape route I've ever memorized.

"Where to?" he gasps, his breath coming in quick bursts as we turn another corner, the echo of footsteps drawing closer.

"The subway!" I respond, heart hammering in my chest. "It's just ahead. We can lose them there."

As we sprint toward the flickering lights of the subway entrance, I feel the heat of their pursuit like a shadow on my back, relentless and hungry. We reach the steps leading down, the cool air of the tunnel a welcome reprieve. I pause at the entrance, glancing over my shoulder to see the figures emerging from the alley, their faces obscured but their intentions clear.

"Go!" I urge him, shoving him forward. He hesitates, searching my face for something—reassurance, perhaps. But what can I offer him that won't crumble under the weight of reality? The decision has to be made in a heartbeat. "We'll be fine. Just—go!"

He nods, and we plunge into the dimly lit subway, the scent of metal and sweat filling my nostrils. The clatter of our footsteps reverberates against the tiled walls, a frantic rhythm that propels us further into the bowels of the city.

We reach the platform just as a train screeches to a halt, its doors sliding open with a rush of air. We hop on, collapsing into the nearest seats, hearts racing in synchrony. As the train pulls away, I look out the window, the city blurring into streaks of light and shadow, a fleeting reminder of everything we're leaving behind.

"Do you think they saw us?" he breathes, glancing around the nearly empty car, his voice laced with tension.

"I don't know," I reply, still catching my breath. "But we can't let our guard down. Not yet."

He leans back, running a hand through his hair, the weight of the world pressing down on his shoulders. "I'm sorry," he says suddenly, the words tumbling out like a confession. "For everything. For the lies, for dragging you into this."

I open my mouth to respond, but the truth is more complicated than any apology could encompass. Instead, I simply nod, the truth of his actions and my feelings swirling in a complicated dance. This moment, raw and unfiltered, is the beginning of a new chapter, one that I can't predict but know will change us both forever. As the train speeds through the dark tunnel, I can't help but wonder what awaits us on the other side.

The train rattles forward, a metal beast devouring the dark, its rhythm a hypnotic lull that masks the chaos just beyond the platform. I lean my head against the cool glass, watching the flickering lights zip by, a montage of yellow and white streaks that seem to mirror my racing thoughts. The noise of the train is a cocoon, muffling the world outside while the shadows swirl, reminiscent of the tangled emotions thrumming through my veins.

Beside me, he shifts, tension coiling around his shoulders. "What's our next move?" he asks, his voice a mixture of urgency and uncertainty. The intensity of his gaze catches me off guard, a mirror reflecting my own unease.

I take a breath, steeling myself for the reality of our situation. "We need to lay low for a bit. I have a friend who runs a small coffee shop near the docks. If we can make it there, we can figure out what to do next."

His eyes narrow slightly, skepticism mingling with curiosity. "Your friend? You trust her?"

"More than I trust anyone right now," I reply, determination lacing my words. "She's been a lifeline in this city long before any of this happened. If anyone can help us, it's her."

A flicker of something passes through his expression—relief or resignation, I can't tell. The weight of shared trust, however fragile, lingers between us, and I can't help but wonder if it's enough to guide us through the murky waters ahead.

As we pull into the next station, the train lurches, and the doors hiss open, revealing a bustling platform filled with commuters, their faces a blur of indifference and routine. I nod toward the exit, and we step into the fray, moving quickly to blend in with the crowd, our hearts racing to a frantic rhythm. The air is charged, a mix of dampness from the rain outside and the musty scent of the underground, an unsettling reminder that we're not free yet.

Navigating through the throng, I try to keep my mind focused, but the unease gnawing at my gut is hard to shake. With every footstep, I half-expect to see the dark figures from the alley reappear, their predatory instincts honed in on us. I'm struck by the absurdity of our situation; two people caught in a whirlwind of danger and secrets, trying to outpace a past that refuses to let us go.

When we finally emerge into the rain-soaked streets, I lead him toward a narrow side road, the dim lights from storefronts casting long shadows that flicker with each passing car. The familiar neighborhood wraps around us, but the comfort I once felt has been stripped away, leaving only a sense of vulnerability in its place.

"There's the shop," I say, gesturing to a small, unassuming building with a faded sign that reads "Bella's Brew." The aroma of freshly brewed coffee wafts through the air, a welcoming scent that stirs memories of lazy afternoons and warm pastries. I push open the door, the little bell above chiming cheerfully, a stark contrast to the turmoil brewing inside me.

Bella, a middle-aged woman with a head of curly hair and a smile that could brighten the gloomiest of days, looks up from behind the counter. Her eyes widen as she takes in my disheveled appearance and the man beside me. "Oh my goodness, what happened?"

"Just a little trouble," I say, forcing a smile that doesn't quite reach my eyes. "Can we talk?"

"Of course, dear. In the back." Bella leads us to a small room filled with mismatched furniture and the faint scent of cinnamon. She closes the door behind us, her expression shifting from concern to determination. "You two look like you've been through a war zone. Sit down."

We take our seats at a rickety table, and I can feel the tension begin to ease slightly, the safety of Bella's presence wrapping around us like a warm blanket. But as Bella pours us each a cup of coffee, I can't shake the nagging feeling that this sanctuary could quickly be compromised.

"What's really going on?" she asks, her gaze flicking between us. "You can't just drop in here looking like you're on the run without some serious backstory."

I exchange a glance with him, and in that moment, the gravity of the truth hangs in the air, almost tangible. "We've been caught up in something dangerous," I begin, hesitant but resolute. "People are after us. We need to find a way to stay safe, to regroup."

Bella's expression hardens, and I can see her weighing the risk of getting involved. "You know I can't just—"

"I know," I interrupt, urgency threading through my voice. "But I wouldn't ask if it wasn't serious. We're running out of time."

Her eyes soften, and she nods, reluctantly accepting the gravity of our plight. "Alright. You can stay here for a bit, but you'll have to keep your heads down. If anyone comes looking for you, I can't—"

"Bella, you're the only one we can trust right now," he interjects, the plea in his voice raw and genuine. "Please."

She pauses, glancing between us as if weighing her options. Finally, she exhales a resigned breath. "Okay. But we have to be careful."

As we settle in, sipping the hot coffee and allowing the warmth to seep into our bones, I can feel the tension between us subtly shift. It's as if the act of sharing our burden has lightened the load, if only just. But the comfort is short-lived; the reality of our situation looms like a storm cloud.

"I need to make a call," Bella says suddenly, standing up with purpose. "Just to check on a few things. Stay put, and don't talk to anyone unless it's me."

As she slips out of the room, I look at him, my heart racing again as uncertainty swirls in my mind. "What if they find us here?"

"We'll figure it out," he says, trying to sound confident, but the tremor in his voice betrays him. "We have to stay ready."

Just then, the sharp sound of the bell jingling interrupts the quiet. My heart lurches as the door swings open, a gust of wind sending a chill through the room. I exchange a frantic look with him just as I hear Bella's voice raised in alarm.

"Get back! You can't come in here!"

The words hang in the air like a death knell. My stomach drops, and I jump to my feet, adrenaline surging through me. The unmistakable sound of heavy footsteps approaches the back room, and my heart pounds as the door handle rattles. I glance at him, fear coursing through me, the realization sinking in that we may not escape this after all.

And then the door bursts open, revealing a figure cloaked in darkness, a face obscured by shadows but unmistakably filled with intent. My breath catches in my throat, and the world around me shrinks to a single, terrifying moment, the confrontation of our past crashing into the present, ready to shatter whatever fragile safety we had left.

Chapter 11: The Enemy's Face

The alley smells like stale beer and old regret, an aroma that clings to the back of my throat as I edge deeper into the shadows. My footsteps echo against the cracked pavement, each sound swallowed by the oppressive darkness that clings to this part of town like a shroud. It's a place that thrives on secrets, where the buildings lean together as if sharing hushed confessions. The dim, flickering neon lights above buzz like angry wasps, casting an unsettling glow that dances across the graffiti-laden walls, a chaotic tapestry of color and despair.

I pause, pressing my back against the rough brick of a building, my heart pounding a steady rhythm of anticipation and fear. Somewhere out there, he lurks—the ghost who has turned this city into a playground of terror. His face haunts me, a phantom lingering just beyond reach. I've never been one to back down from a challenge, but this feels different. The whispers have grown louder, curling around me like smoke, wrapping me in a cocoon of paranoia.

My mind races back to the dossier I had poured over for hours. A name scrawled in frantic handwriting, notes hastily scribbled in the margins. Every detail was a piece of a puzzle, each clue leading me deeper into a labyrinth of deceit. But the most chilling entry was the photograph—a blurry image of a man with dark hair and piercing eyes, his expression obscured yet achingly familiar. I shake my head, trying to dispel the thoughts. I can't afford to get distracted. Not now.

But then, just as I begin to question my resolve, a figure steps from the shadows, and my breath catches in my throat. He is tall, his frame draped in a long coat that billows slightly as he moves, an ethereal presence that sends a shiver racing down my spine. And when he turns, locking eyes with me, the world shrinks to the two of us, suspended in a moment that feels like it could fracture reality itself.

I recognize him instantly. The face is a jagged shard of memory, someone I thought was lost to time—a ghost from my past. His lips twist into a sardonic smile, and I can't decide if it's an invitation or a warning. "Didn't expect to see you here, Detective," he says, his voice smooth like silk, but laced with an edge that cuts deeper than I'd like to admit.

"Neither did I, Adam," I reply, forcing my voice to remain steady, even as my insides twist like a coiled spring. "What are you doing in a place like this?"

"Just enjoying the ambiance." He glances around, his expression a mix of amusement and disdain. "You know how it is—some of us are drawn to the dark."

"Or perhaps you are the darkness," I retort, unable to keep the bite from my words. I take a cautious step back, assessing him, the tension in the air thickening. Every instinct screams at me to retreat, but curiosity anchors me to this spot. I need to understand how he fits into the chaos that has consumed the city.

"I'm here to help," he says, raising his hands in a gesture of surrender. "You've been chasing shadows, and I can lead you to the light."

I scoff, the sound sharp in the silence. "You're not exactly the beacon of trust, Adam. You have your own ghosts to contend with."

"True," he concedes, the glimmer of mischief dancing in his eyes. "But your ghosts might just be my specialty."

In that moment, something shifts in the atmosphere. A creeping sense of danger clings to the air, tightening like a noose around my throat. I glance over my shoulder, instincts honed from years of experience screaming at me that we are not alone. It's a trap—an unsettling revelation that makes my skin crawl. I feel the weight of unseen eyes, a presence lurking just beyond the periphery.

"Listen," I say, my voice dropping to a whisper, "this isn't the time for games. If you know something, now would be the moment to share it."

He steps closer, the grin fading into something more serious, more vulnerable. "They're watching, you know. The enemy isn't just some nameless face; he's calculated, patient. He'll exploit any weakness—"

Before he can finish, the sound of a scuffle erupts from the mouth of the alley, breaking the fragile tension. Shadows shift, and the hairs on my arms stand on end as three figures emerge, their intentions clear in the glint of metal. They are not here for pleasantries.

"Run!" I shout, shoving Adam aside as I pivot, adrenaline surging through me. But even as I turn, I know it's too late. The alley feels like a trap closing in, the walls narrowing, squeezing the air from my lungs. There's no escape now, only the fight against whatever hell has just been unleashed.

As the figures close in, a whirlwind of instinct takes over. I glance back at Adam, our eyes locking in a shared understanding that our fates are entwined, whether we like it or not. With a quick flick of my wrist, I reach for my sidearm, the cold metal a reassuring weight against my palm. "You better be useful, Adam," I hiss, my heart racing with the knowledge that the time for hesitation has passed.

He smirks, a defiant glimmer in his eye as he takes a step forward, his own resolve sparking to life. "Trust me," he says, the confidence in his voice oddly comforting amid the chaos. "This is just the beginning."

The trap snaps shut with a finality that leaves me breathless. I'm standing in the alley, shadows pressing in from all sides, the slick pavement beneath my feet a mirror reflecting the chaotic swirl of my thoughts. The familiar face before me bears the scars of time and experience, a visage marked by betrayal and unspoken words.

"You didn't think I'd let you wander around uninvited, did you?" he says, his voice dripping with a condescension that feels like ice water thrown over my resolve.

I take a step back, heart pounding in my chest, the adrenaline coursing through my veins sharpening my senses. This man, with his knowing smirk, is not just a remnant of the past; he's a piece of a larger puzzle, and I can't afford to lose sight of that. "You're playing a dangerous game," I shoot back, trying to mask my unease with bravado. "You know what happens when you underestimate me."

He chuckles, the sound low and mocking, as if he relishes the tension. "Underestimating you was the best mistake I ever made. But here we are, and you've stepped right into the lion's den." His gaze flicks over my shoulder, and for a brief moment, I sense his confidence wavering. Instincts flaring, I pivot to scan the alley, but I find it empty, a hushed void that only amplifies my sense of vulnerability.

The silence stretches, thickening the air between us. "You've changed," I say, feigning indifference. "Or maybe I just see you for what you are now. A coward hiding behind illusions." My words are sharp, a gambit designed to provoke a reaction, to peel back the layers of this twisted encounter. His expression falters for just a second, a flash of anger sparking in his eyes, but then he regains his composure, a mask slipping back into place.

"You think you know me?" he replies, his tone now laced with a simmering rage. "You haven't seen the real me in years. I've survived in ways you wouldn't even begin to understand." There's an undercurrent of desperation in his voice, a hint that his bravado is paper-thin. I can see it now, the cracks in his carefully constructed facade, and my heart races with the possibility of exploiting them.

"I know exactly who you are," I counter, stepping closer, letting the distance between us shrink. "You're a man who craves power but fears it too. You hide behind shadows because the light reveals your true self—a coward, a manipulator." The intensity of our standoff shifts as I speak, the tension electrifying the air. My words hang between us, a double-edged sword that could either cut deep or shatter entirely.

His expression hardens, and I brace for his retort, but it doesn't come. Instead, he studies me, his eyes narrowing as if he's weighing his options. "Maybe I've underestimated you," he finally admits, his tone less condescending and more contemplative. "But let's not pretend you have the upper hand here. You're out of your depth."

And just like that, the precarious equilibrium tips. My instincts scream at me to flee, but my feet remain rooted, drawn into this psychological duel. "What do you want?" I ask, my voice steadier than I feel. "You think you can toy with me, but you've got it all wrong. I'm not afraid of you."

He leans against the alley wall, a relaxed posture that belies the tension thrumming beneath the surface. "Oh, but you should be. Fear can be a great motivator. It drives people to make mistakes." He smirks again, but this time there's something darker behind it, a glint of malice that sends a shiver down my spine. "And mistakes? They can be fatal."

Just as the air feels as though it might crack open with the weight of our confrontation, a distant siren wails, echoing through the alley. His smirk fades, and the tension shifts yet again. "Looks like our little chat is about to be interrupted," he says, straightening with a sudden urgency. "But don't think this is over. You're not as clever as you think you are."

In that instant, I realize this is my chance. The moment he turns away, I seize it, my legs propelling me forward as I dart past him, the narrow alley offering only fleeting cover. I can hear his footsteps behind me, heavy and deliberate, the sound mingling with the cacophony of the city waking up to the chaos of the night.

Each breath I take is a reminder of my fragility, a stark contrast to the adrenaline that fuels my escape. I weave through the streets, heart racing, the glow of neon lights painting a surreal landscape around me. I can't let him catch me—not now, not when I'm so close to unraveling the truth.

As I round a corner, the cold bite of the night air hits my face, a stark contrast to the warmth of my determination. I slip into a crowd, the bodies moving in a chaotic rhythm, a sea of anonymity that momentarily shields me from his relentless pursuit. I slow my pace, blending in, but my heart pounds like a war drum, each beat echoing my fear and resolve.

"Thought you could outrun me?" His voice cuts through the noise, smooth and mocking, yet laced with a familiar undertone of urgency. He's closer than I'd hoped, the gap between us narrowing with every second. Panic flares, but I refuse to let it consume me. I can't let him define this moment.

With a sudden burst of clarity, I pivot into a narrow side street, the shadows swallowing me whole. I press my back against the cool brick wall, forcing myself to take a deep breath, to listen for the sound of his approach. Each second stretches into eternity, the quiet punctuated only by the distant hum of the city. It's a game of cat and mouse, and I'm determined to emerge not as the hunted, but as the hunter.

The darkness wraps around me like a cloak, heavy and suffocating, as I stand frozen in place. He knows I'm there, lurking in the shadows, and I can feel his gaze piercing through the fog of my uncertainty. The moment stretches, taut and electric, every nerve in my body screaming at me to act. But here I am, tethered by fear and a sense of foreboding that has a weight of its own.

"Quite the reunion, isn't it?" he says, his voice smooth yet laced with an edge that sends shivers down my spine. "I'd say it's been too

DARK WALTZ

long, but I'm not sure you ever really left." The audacity of his words slices through my paralysis, igniting a flicker of anger within me.

"I'm here to finish what we started," I retort, summoning courage from somewhere deep inside. "You think you can just waltz back into my life and dictate the terms? You have no idea who you're dealing with." I take a cautious step forward, the bravado in my tone barely masking the tempest of emotions swirling within me.

His laugh is low, mocking, and it reverberates off the brick walls surrounding us. "Ah, the fire still burns. But tell me, how do you plan to extinguish the blaze I've set? You're not prepared for what lies ahead." There's a glimmer of something dark in his eyes, a hint of the danger he embodies, and my instincts kick into high gear.

"We'll see about that," I reply, willing my voice to remain steady. But doubt creeps in, curling around my resolve like a vine tightening its grip. He shifts slightly, a predator assessing its prey, and I can't shake the feeling that he's waiting for me to make the next move. I glance around, desperate for an escape route, but the alleyway feels like a trap, a cage of my own making.

Just then, the distant sound of sirens pierces the stillness, a siren's song of hope and impending chaos. "You should run," he advises, his tone eerily calm. "They won't find you if you're smart enough to disappear."

I narrow my eyes at him, the defiance within me sparking to life again. "I'm not afraid of you or your games. You may have the upper hand now, but it won't last." Each word is a battle cry, a reminder that I have a strength he has yet to reckon with.

His expression darkens, the humor fading from his face as reality sets in. "You're playing a dangerous game, and the stakes are higher than you think. I hope you're ready to lose everything." The gravity of his words weighs heavily in the air, and I can feel the tension shift, like the calm before a storm.

With a sudden surge of determination, I turn on my heel, sprinting toward the mouth of the alley. The sirens grow louder, and adrenaline surges through my veins, propelling me forward. I can hear him cursing behind me, his voice laced with frustration and surprise. For a fleeting moment, I allow myself to feel the thrill of the chase, the promise of freedom just within my grasp.

I burst onto the bustling street, the neon lights flashing and reflecting off the wet pavement, casting an otherworldly glow over everything. I blend into the crowd, heart racing, as I maneuver through the throngs of people, each face a potential ally or enemy. Panic mingles with exhilaration, and I can almost taste victory as I weave through the bodies, my escape seeming within reach.

But just as I allow myself to relax, a hand grips my arm, yanking me back into the shadows. My heart drops as I face my captor, the world around me blurring into insignificance. "What the hell do you think you're doing?" a voice hisses, low and urgent. It's a familiar voice, one that both comforts and terrifies me.

"Lucy? Is that you?" I stammer, recognizing my partner's fierce determination shining through her eyes. Her hair is tousled, as if she's been through a storm, and her presence is both a balm and a reminder of the precariousness of our situation. "I thought I was—"

"You thought you were what? Out for a stroll?" she interjects, glancing over her shoulder as if expecting the darkness to swallow us whole. "You're playing with fire, and I don't know how to pull you back if you get burned."

"I can handle myself," I insist, shaking off her grip and scanning the street. The sirens are closer now, a cacophony of chaos that mixes with the frantic pulse of the city. "But we need to move. He's coming."

Her brow furrows as she processes my words, a flicker of concern darting across her face. "You're not seriously suggesting we confront him, are you? He's dangerous, and you've already underestimated him once."

A shadow crosses my mind, the memory of his smirk and the weight of his threats. "We don't have a choice," I reply, urgency lacing my voice. "If we let him go now, he'll come for us again. We need to take the fight to him before he can disappear into the shadows."

Lucy hesitates, and for a moment, uncertainty hangs heavy between us. "What's the plan, then? Running in blind is one thing, but this is different."

"I have a lead," I confess, the words spilling out before I can stop them. "There's something bigger at play here, and I need you to trust me." Her eyes widen slightly, the gears in her mind turning as she weighs my proposal.

With a reluctant sigh, she nods, determination flashing in her gaze. "Okay, then let's make it count. But you owe me a drink after this. I could really use one." A wry smile breaks through the tension, a reminder that even in chaos, camaraderie can light the way.

Just as we prepare to step back into the fray, a voice echoes from the shadows, smooth and dripping with malice. "You really think you can run away from me?" The chill in his tone sends ice running through my veins, and I whip around to find him standing at the alley's entrance, a dark silhouette against the flickering lights.

"Too late for second thoughts," he taunts, his gaze locking onto me with an intensity that sends a fresh wave of fear crashing over me. "You're not getting out of this that easily."

In that heartbeat, the world narrows to a single point—the confrontation ahead, the danger looming like a storm on the horizon. My heart races, every instinct screaming at me to act, but as I glance at Lucy, I realize that this is no longer just my fight. It's ours, and the stakes have never been higher.

As I step forward, determination surging through me, the ground beneath us trembles, the looming threat pressing in from all sides. We're outnumbered and outmatched, but surrender is not an option. The battle lines have been drawn, and there's no turning back now. With a final glance at my partner, I brace for impact, knowing that the moment of truth has arrived, and the ghost of our enemy is about to show his true face.

Chapter 12: Tethered by Fate

I lean against the cool, crumbling wall of the abandoned building, gasping for breath, the stale air filling my lungs like a long-lost comfort. My heart races, still echoing the rhythm of our escape. The darkness that once felt so suffocating has receded, replaced by the flickering light of a half-broken streetlamp just outside. Shadows play tricks on my mind, twisting familiar shapes into grotesque caricatures, but I find solace in the steady presence beside me. He stands close, his silhouette cutting a sharp line against the dimness, a guardian forged from fury and resolve.

"You're safe now," he says, his voice a low growl that thrums through the silence like a drumbeat. I can't quite meet his gaze yet; there's too much swirling between us—a tempest of gratitude, fear, and something else I dare not name. The adrenaline still courses through my veins, blurring the edges of my thoughts. I swallow hard, attempting to untangle the knots in my mind while the heat from his body radiates warmth against the chill of the night.

"I should have known they'd come for me," I murmur, my voice barely above a whisper, as if saying it too loudly might summon the shadows back. "I didn't think they'd be so brazen."

He huffs out a short laugh, dark and rich, the sound wrapping around me like a cloak. "They're desperate. They'll do anything to get what they want. And now you're in their sights." There's a weight to his words, a gravity that makes the air between us thick with unspoken truths. I glance up at him, finally daring to meet those stormy eyes, and I see the flicker of a challenge buried beneath the surface—a warning to tread carefully, lest I fall into the abyss of our shared fate.

"What do you mean by that?" I press, curiosity igniting a spark of defiance in my chest. "I'm just an ordinary girl trying to survive. Why would they care about me?"

"Ordinary?" His brow arches, skepticism dripping from his tone. "You're anything but ordinary. You've got something they want—something they can't take." The intensity of his gaze pins me to the wall, and I can feel my cheeks flush under his scrutiny. "You're tethered to a power that's larger than both of us."

The idea hangs in the air between us, heavy with implications. It reverberates in my mind, tugging at the edges of memories I'd rather forget. The strange occurrences that have punctuated my life like scattered raindrops, each one falling in isolation yet somehow coming together to create a storm. I shake my head, dismissing the thought, though the pulse of something familiar flutters in my chest.

"But why help me?" The question escapes my lips before I can restrain it, and I sense the shift in the atmosphere. "You don't owe me anything. You didn't have to pull me out of that mess."

"Maybe I'm a sucker for a damsel in distress," he quips, his lips curling into a smirk that dances along the edges of seriousness. But then the smile fades, and his expression hardens. "Or maybe I see something in you that you don't yet understand. You're stronger than you think, and you're going to need that strength to face what's coming."

A silence stretches between us, thickening with the weight of expectation. I can feel the flicker of uncertainty in my chest, the nagging voice that questions everything I know. Am I truly strong enough to face this? To confront the shadows that threaten to engulf me? I bite my lip, wrestling with the fear that clings to me like a shroud, but there's an ember of something else—a flicker of courage ignited by his presence.

"Tell me what I need to do," I finally say, my voice steadier than I feel. "If I'm going to get through this, I need to know what's at stake."

He studies me, his expression unreadable, and I catch a glimpse of something vulnerable beneath the bravado—a fleeting shadow that reminds me that he, too, is human, scarred by battles fought in the dark. "First, we need to get you out of this city. It's too dangerous. They'll be hunting for you, and I can't protect you here."

"Where will we go?" I ask, intrigued and terrified. The thought of leaving everything I know behind sends a shiver through me, but deep down, I feel the thrill of adventure stir.

"A safe house. Somewhere they won't think to look." He steps closer, the light catching the sharp angles of his face, illuminating the determination etched into his features. "But I can't do this alone. I need you to trust me."

His plea strikes a chord deep within me. Trust. The word feels foreign on my tongue, but something in his gaze promises safety, a lifeline in a world turned upside down. I nod slowly, my heart racing with the decision. "Okay. I'll trust you."

"Good." A hint of relief washes over his expression, and for the first time, I see the flicker of warmth beneath his guarded exterior. "But remember, it's not just about running. You have to fight, too."

"Fight?" The word hangs in the air, heavy with meaning. I'm no warrior; I've spent my life avoiding conflict, retreating from confrontation. But the stakes are high now, and the thought of standing my ground ignites a fire within me that I didn't know existed.

"Fight," he repeats, his voice low and steady. "For yourself. For the power that resides within you. And for those who can't fight for themselves."

His words ignite something deep within me, a flicker of resolve that whispers of potential I've yet to explore. The night holds countless uncertainties, but alongside him, I feel ready to face whatever awaits. Together, we step out of the shadows, into the unknown, bound by a shared purpose that resonates with the pulse of the city around us.

The air shifts as we step into the world outside the derelict building, a murky twilight descending around us like a velvet curtain.

A chill grazes my skin, but it isn't just the cold; it's the weight of uncertainty that lingers in the atmosphere. With every step, the streetlights flicker to life, casting long shadows that stretch across the pavement like ghostly fingers reaching out from the darkness. I can feel his presence beside me, a steady anchor amidst the chaos swirling in my mind.

"I hope you know how to navigate this city," I say, trying to keep the tremor from my voice. "Because I'm pretty sure I just took a wrong turn into a nightmare."

He chuckles softly, a sound that lightens the air even as it echoes with the tension of our reality. "You'd be surprised how often I've made wrong turns myself. This city's a labyrinth; the key is knowing which shadows to avoid."

I shoot him a sidelong glance, curiosity piqued. "And you think you're the expert in shadows?"

"Let's just say I've danced with enough of them to know their steps." His eyes glimmer with mischief, but the underlying seriousness is undeniable. "But don't underestimate the light either. Sometimes it's the most blinding moments that reveal the clearest paths."

The notion settles in my mind like a riddle I can't quite solve. Light and shadow, a metaphor for the tumultuous emotions swirling between us. I open my mouth to respond, to challenge his wisdom, but the echo of distant voices halts my breath. They cut through the night like shards of glass, igniting a flicker of panic in my chest.

"Do you hear that?" I murmur, gripping his arm instinctively. His muscles tense under my touch, a reminder of the strength he possesses, yet the urgency in my voice betrays my growing fear.

He nods, his demeanor shifting to one of alertness. "We need to keep moving." With that, he breaks into a jog, his long strides eating up the ground as I scramble to keep pace. The shadows twist around us, as if the city itself is alive and aware of our flight.

We navigate the twisting alleys, the echoes of laughter and music wafting from hidden bars and homes, the warmth of life a stark contrast to the dread threading through my veins. I can't shake the feeling that we are being hunted, like prey with the predator close behind. I glance back, half-expecting to see the darkness spill forth, but it remains just that—darkness.

"Why me?" I blurt out, the question tumbling from my lips in a moment of reckless vulnerability. "Why save me from them? What do you get out of it?"

He slows, turning to face me, his expression serious. "I'm not some knight in shining armor, you know. I've got my reasons, and they're not all altruistic." His gaze pierces through the dimness, and I can sense the weight of his past pressing down on him. "But I believe you're more than you realize. And that means something in this fight."

"That sounds suspiciously like a 'we're in this together' speech," I tease, trying to mask the flutter of my heart at the thought. "Do you also have a cape hidden under that jacket?"

His lips quirk up at the corners, and for a moment, the gravity between us lifts. "Only if it's the kind that matches my eyes. But seriously, we've got to stay focused. This isn't a game, and it's not just my neck on the line."

"Then what's your plan, oh wise shadow-dancer?" I ask, my bravado masking the knots in my stomach.

"I've got a contact who can help us. He's... resourceful," he says, a flicker of hesitation crossing his face. "We'll need to find him quickly, before they realize we're gone. His name's Jasper, and he runs a bar on the edge of town."

"Of course, a bar. Why does that not surprise me?"

"Because it's always the bar, isn't it?" he replies, a hint of humor lighting his voice. "I swear every city has one. It's where secrets flow as freely as the drinks."

With that, he leads me deeper into the labyrinthine streets, each turn a new adventure wrapped in uncertainty. The atmosphere shifts again as we near the bar, the vibrant pulse of music growing louder, spilling into the streets like a siren's call. My pulse quickens, a mix of excitement and apprehension swirling within me.

As we approach, the bar reveals itself, a quirky establishment adorned with twinkling fairy lights and a rickety sign that sways gently in the breeze. The doorway is framed by an assortment of potted plants, their leaves shimmering under the dim lights. It looks inviting, a stark contrast to the chaos of the night outside.

"Stick close," he murmurs, his tone a blend of caution and reassurance as he pushes the door open. The sudden rush of warmth envelops us, the scent of aged wood and spiced cocktails wrapping around me like a comforting embrace.

Inside, laughter and chatter mingle with the melodies drifting from a small stage where a local band strums a lively tune. Patrons are scattered across the bar and tables, their faces animated in conversation, blissfully unaware of the turmoil lurking just beyond their doors.

He weaves through the crowd, his presence commanding attention without a word, and I follow, my heart thrumming with the rhythm of the music and the flickering hope that maybe, just maybe, we'll find the answers we're seeking. As we approach the bar, I catch sight of the bartender, a burly man with a bushy beard and a twinkle in his eye, polishing a glass with practiced ease.

"Hey, Jasper," he calls out, his voice slicing through the din. The man looks up, and his smile widens as he recognizes the face that's all too familiar to him.

"What brings you here, my elusive friend?" Jasper asks, leaning on the bar with an air of casual confidence.

"Need a favor," he replies, the weight of urgency underscoring his tone.

Jasper's expression shifts, curiosity piqued. "You've got that look—trouble's found you again, hasn't it?"

I glance between the two of them, sensing an unspoken history steeped in loyalty and shared experiences. "Is that a question or a statement?" I interject, trying to sound nonchalant despite the butterflies taking flight in my stomach.

"Both, actually," Jasper says with a grin, his gaze assessing me as though weighing my worth. "So, what's the situation?"

"We're on the run, and we need a safe place to regroup," he explains succinctly, the gravity of our predicament clear in his voice.

Jasper's brow furrows slightly, and the air thickens with unspoken possibilities. "Safe places are hard to come by these days, but I might have something in the back. You'll have to trust me, though."

Trust. The word echoes again, a haunting refrain as I glance at the man who's become my unlikely savior. In this moment, surrounded by the chaos of a bar full of life, I realize how entwined our fates have become, how tethered we are to this unfolding story that stretches far beyond the shadows and into the light.

Jasper studies us both for a moment, his brow furrowing deeper as if measuring the stakes. "Trouble's become a bad habit for you, hasn't it?" He gestures toward the back of the bar, a silent invitation to follow. "Come on, then. I've got a place that'll be off the radar."

We push through the crowd, the music vibrating through the floor beneath our feet, a living pulse that seems to thrum in time with my racing heart. The atmosphere shifts as we follow Jasper through a narrow hallway lined with eclectic artwork and mismatched photographs—snapshots of lives intertwined, faces frozen in joy or contemplation. I glance at the faces, wondering about their stories, their shadows.

"This place is like a secret club," I murmur, half to myself.

"It is," Jasper replies, a sly grin breaking across his rugged features. "Only the right people know how to get in. And trust me, most of them are best left out of the light."

We step into a small room at the back, dimly lit and cluttered with mismatched furniture that tells its own tale of forgotten conversations and whispered secrets. A thick carpet muffles our footsteps as we enter, and a worn couch sits against the wall, its cushions inviting yet weary. A small table stacked with well-loved books occupies one corner, while an old radio hums softly in the background, its frequency crackling.

"Make yourselves comfortable," Jasper says, motioning to the couch. "I'll grab some drinks. You look like you could use a little liquid courage."

"Or just something to drown the inevitable chaos," I reply, unable to resist the urge to joke, even as tension coils in my stomach.

Once we're settled, I take a deep breath, letting the warmth of the room wrap around me like a blanket. "So what now?" I ask, turning to my savior, who remains steadfast, eyes scanning the room as if weighing every potential danger.

He leans forward, elbows on his knees, the light casting sharp shadows on his face. "We need to lay low, at least for the moment. Jasper's got connections. He'll know if they're onto you, and if there's a way to get you out of here safely."

"And then what?" I ask, the weight of the question pressing down on me. "Just run forever? I can't live like this, always looking over my shoulder."

"There's no running, not if they want you," he replies, his voice steady, laced with a harsh reality. "But that doesn't mean we can't fight back. We just need the right resources, the right allies."

I watch him closely, trying to catch a glimpse of the man behind the façade—the knight in the darkness who had risked everything to save me. "You make it sound so simple. But you know better than anyone that this isn't a fair fight."

"It's never been fair," he agrees, his tone turning serious again. "But it's not about fairness; it's about survival. And right now, you're the key to a lot more than you realize."

Before I can probe further, Jasper returns with two glasses in hand, the amber liquid sloshing gently against the sides. "Here we go—liquid courage for the battle ahead." He sets one glass in front of me and the other in front of my companion, raising his glass. "To surviving another day in this lovely city of shadows."

"Cheers," I murmur, lifting my glass, though the words feel hollow against the impending threat looming over us.

We clink glasses, the sound a brittle reminder of the fragility of our situation. I take a cautious sip, the warmth of the liquor sliding down my throat, igniting a fire in my belly. It offers a momentary reprieve from the swirling uncertainties, but it doesn't last long.

"Tell me more about this power you mentioned," I say, the question hanging heavily in the air. "What exactly do they want from me?"

His gaze sharpens, the casualness fading. "You have a gift, one that they believe could tip the scales in their favor. It's tied to something ancient, something that's been lost for a long time. They think if they capture you, they can control it."

"Control me?" I scoff, though the words don't sit well with me. "Good luck with that. I'm not exactly the submissive type."

His lips curl into a faint smile, but it doesn't reach his eyes. "That's precisely what they underestimate. The more they push, the more you'll fight back. It's in your nature."

"Maybe," I reply, my mind racing with the implications of his words. "But how do I even begin to understand something that's buried inside me?"

"First, you need to trust yourself," he says firmly. "And then, we'll find a way to unlock it. But right now, we need to focus on the immediate threat."

The gravity of his statement lingers in the air, a palpable reminder of the danger encroaching on us. Suddenly, a loud crash resonates from the front of the bar, followed by a cacophony of startled voices and the unmistakable sound of glass shattering.

My heart lurches. "What was that?"

"Stay here," he commands, rising to his feet, his posture shifting into one of readiness.

"I'm not some damsel waiting to be rescued again!" I protest, my voice sharper than intended as I leap to my feet, the adrenaline coursing through my veins igniting a fire I didn't know existed.

"Then prove it," he snaps back, eyes flashing with intensity. "Stay low, and keep quiet. I'll handle this."

He slips out of the room, his figure blending into the shadows, leaving me standing alone, heart hammering against my ribs. I can hear the murmur of confusion and rising panic from the patrons outside, their laughter replaced by a growing unease that prickles my skin.

I pace the small room, my thoughts racing. What if this was the moment everything collapsed? What if they found us here, in this hidden sanctuary? I try to breathe deeply, but every inhale fills me with dread.

Then I hear a voice, deep and commanding, rising above the chaos. "I know you're in here! Come out and face your fate!"

My heart sinks. The voice is familiar—an echo from my past, a remnant of shadows I thought I'd left behind. The door swings open abruptly, and the figure silhouetted in the light is one I'd hoped never to see again.

"Surprise, surprise," he smirks, his presence heavy with menace. "Looks like fate has a funny way of bringing people together, doesn't it?"

Every instinct screams at me to run, to hide, but the icy grip of fear roots me in place as I realize I'm cornered. I glance around the room, seeking a way out, but the walls feel like they're closing in, and I know in that moment that I have to fight, to confront this looming shadow from my past.

Before I can decide what to do next, he steps further into the room, his intentions clear, and my world tilts once more, caught in the web of fate, tethered to a darkness I can no longer ignore.

Chapter 13: Embers of Truth

The hideout felt like a living entity, its walls thick with whispers and shadows, the air dense with a palpable tension that could suffocate even the bravest soul. I settled deeper into the worn, leather couch, the smell of musk and a hint of sandalwood wrapping around me like an old blanket, both comforting and foreboding. The flickering light from the single bulb overhead cast erratic patterns on his face, illuminating his features in sharp relief. As he began to speak, each word fell like stones into the silence, heavy and deliberate.

"It wasn't always like this," he said, his voice barely above a murmur, each syllable dripping with a sorrow that cut through the stillness. His gaze drifted to the far wall, as if searching for the ghosts of his past amidst the peeling paint and fading memories. "We were once... something else. Friends, brothers in arms. But loyalty has a way of unraveling when the truth is too painful to face."

His story unfolded like a tapestry, thread by thread revealing a complex history woven with betrayal and loss. I leaned in closer, my heart thudding in my chest, feeling the weight of his secrets as if they were my own. It was a strange intimacy, the kind that sneaks up on you in the most unexpected of places, filling the gaps where trust had once flourished. I could see the boy he used to be behind the hardened facade of the man before me—wide-eyed and full of hope, now dimmed by the harsh realities of a world that had demanded too much from him.

I reached for his hand, fingers brushing against his calloused skin, the warmth igniting something within me. For a fleeting moment, he didn't pull away. I felt the unguarded connection, a delicate thread weaving between us, fraying but not yet broken. His eyes flicked down to our hands, and in that heartbeat, I thought he might let me in, share the burdens he carried so fiercely. But just as quickly, the moment shattered; he recoiled, slipping back into the shadows that cloaked him like a second skin.

"It's complicated," he said, his voice now edged with an emotion I couldn't quite place. Was it fear? Regret? "You don't understand what they did to us." The defensiveness in his tone was a sharp knife, cutting through the softness of the moment, and I felt the walls he had erected once again spring up, brick by brick.

"No, maybe I don't," I replied, frustration threading through my words. "But I want to. I want to understand you. What happened to your—our—lives?" I leaned back, folding my arms tightly against my chest, feeling suddenly exposed. It was ridiculous, really, this push and pull we found ourselves in, like a game of chess where each move was laced with anxiety.

He let out a shaky breath, eyes narrowing as he weighed my words. "You think you can handle it? You think knowing will change anything?" There was a challenge in his gaze, and I felt a spark of defiance flare within me. I wasn't here to cower, to run from shadows.

"Try me," I shot back, my heart pounding with the thrill of confrontation. "You don't get to decide what I can or cannot handle."

The silence that followed was thick with tension, the kind that could snap like a taut string at any moment. Finally, he sighed, the fight slipping from his shoulders like water from a leaky bucket. "It all started with the incident," he said, his voice lowering again, almost as if he were afraid of being overheard by the walls themselves. "The one that turned everything upside down."

I leaned closer, my pulse racing. "Tell me."

"There was a mission," he began, his words more guarded now, careful as if navigating a minefield. "A covert operation. It should have been simple. But it went wrong. Lives were lost. Friends were lost." His gaze hardened, a storm brewing behind his eyes. "And then, the blame. It fell on us. The ones left standing. No one cared about the truth. Just the fallout."

As he spoke, I felt the chill of betrayal seep into the room, wrapping around us like a fog. The air crackled with unspoken pain, each word he uttered acting as a reminder of the shattering consequences of loyalty gone awry. I wanted to reach out again, to reassure him that he wasn't alone in this, but fear gripped my heart—a primal instinct that whispered he would only retreat further into his shell.

"Why did you stay?" I asked, my voice softer now, almost tentative. "If it hurt so much?"

"Because some things can't be escaped," he replied, eyes darkening. "And because walking away means giving up on those who couldn't."

His admission hung in the air, raw and poignant, a fragile thread binding us together in this moment. I saw the depth of his struggle, the weight of his choices pressing down like a physical burden. It dawned on me that the man before me was not just a warrior; he was a survivor, navigating the wreckage of his own heart.

"I'm here," I said, a vow wrapped in sincerity. "You don't have to face this alone."

He turned to me, eyes wide with surprise, and for the first time, I caught a glimpse of the vulnerability lurking beneath his stoic exterior. Just as quickly, the shutters fell back into place. "I don't know if I can let you in. Not when I'm not even sure what's left of me."

"Then let me help you find out," I urged, my voice firm despite the tremor in my chest. "Let's piece it together."

In that charged silence, I could almost hear the gears turning in his mind, the battle between fear and hope raging within him. There was a flicker of something in his eyes—perhaps a longing for connection, for understanding—before the shadows swallowed it whole. I was prepared for anything, but the anticipation of what he might reveal next electrified the air between us, each moment heavy with the promise of revelation.

The tension in the room hung like a thick mist, curling around us as I waited, breath held tight in my chest, hoping he might break the silence that clung to the air like cobwebs. I could see the wheels turning behind his eyes, the way they flickered with indecision. "There are things I can't change," he finally said, his voice a gravelly whisper. "Things that haunt me, that wake me up in the middle of the night, drenched in sweat and regret."

I shifted, feeling the weight of his words settle heavily on my shoulders. "I know it's not easy," I replied, my voice steady, emboldened by the raw honesty he'd shared. "But holding it all in doesn't do you any good either." I wished desperately that I could reach through the barrier he had built, dismantling each wall with a gentle touch until we were standing side by side, unguarded and honest.

He met my gaze, his expression unreadable, and for a moment, I thought I might see the truth reflected back at me. But then he looked away, running a hand through his hair in frustration. "It's easier to keep everything buried," he admitted. "Easier than dragging someone else into this mess."

I couldn't help but let out a short laugh, the sound surprising even myself. "Easier? Is that really your excuse? Because from where I'm sitting, it seems like a recipe for disaster. You're not just a solitary island in this storm; you're part of a much bigger sea."

He turned back to me, a hint of amusement dancing in his eyes, though the darkness lingered. "Is that so? A larger sea, you say? Well, then consider me a very reluctant sailor."

"Maybe all you need is a better ship," I shot back, my tone teasing but earnest, the playful banter igniting a spark of warmth between us. "One that can weather the storms without capsizing."

His chuckle was like a balm, easing the tension that had settled so heavily around us. "And who's going to captain this ship?"

"I can't believe you're questioning my nautical abilities." I leaned back, crossing my arms with an exaggerated huff. "I'll have you know I've captained many a make-believe ship in my day."

He raised an eyebrow, a smirk playing on his lips. "Oh really? And what makes you a qualified captain, then?"

"The ability to throw an excellent tea party on the high seas," I replied, grinning back at him. "And the knack for keeping the crew entertained while avoiding the kraken."

"Sounds impressive," he said, laughter softening the harsh lines of his face. "But I'm still not convinced. What if the waters get too choppy?"

"Then we adapt. We figure it out together," I said, my heart pounding at the thought of really partnering with him—not just in this moment but in all the chaos life had thrown at us. "That's what good crew members do. We keep each other afloat."

There was a pause as he considered my words, the laughter in his eyes dimming slightly as the reality of our circumstances crept back in. "And what if I drag you under?"

"Then I'll swim," I declared, feeling bold. "I won't let you sink. Not without a fight."

He studied me, something unspoken swirling in the space between us, an intensity that made the room feel even smaller. I held his gaze, refusing to flinch as he leaned closer, the distance between us shrinking until I could feel the warmth radiating from him. "You have no idea what you're asking for," he said, a warning lacing his tone.

"Try me," I replied, undeterred, my heart racing. "I might surprise you."

With a resigned sigh, he leaned back, running a hand through his hair again, this time with an air of contemplation. "Alright then,

Captain. If you're serious about this, about learning what I carry... I'll share my truth. But know that it's messy, and it won't come neatly wrapped."

"I wouldn't want it any other way." I braced myself, feeling a surge of anticipation.

His eyes darkened as he drew in a deep breath, the air between us thickening once more. "It was the night of the ambush. We were caught off guard, blindsided by a betrayal that felt like a dagger to the heart." He paused, his expression twisting with the weight of memory. "A close friend turned informant, feeding information to the enemy. We lost everything that night—our team, our sense of security. I've never been able to shake that feeling of helplessness."

I felt a chill creep through me, the gravity of his words sinking in like a stone. "You didn't fail anyone," I said gently, reaching out to touch his arm. "You can't control what others choose to do."

He shook his head, an almost imperceptible tremor running through him. "But I was the leader. It was my job to keep everyone safe, and I failed."

"Failure doesn't define you," I insisted, my heart aching for the pain etched in his features. "What matters is how you move forward from it."

"Moving forward is harder than it sounds," he replied, his voice cracking slightly. "Every day feels like a reminder of what I lost."

I could see the vulnerability in him, a raw openness that stripped away the bravado he wore like armor. "Then let me help you carry that weight. You don't have to do it alone."

He looked at me, and for a moment, I thought he might break, the walls crumbling under the pressure of his pain. But then, just as suddenly, his resolve returned, a flicker of determination igniting behind his eyes. "You don't know what you're asking," he warned softly, the edge of his voice cutting through the air.

"Then let me find out," I challenged, feeling the energy between us shift again, a current of something powerful and undeniable. "Let me choose this. Let me choose you."

He hesitated, a battle of emotions playing out in his gaze, and I felt my breath catch, waiting for him to either step forward or retreat into the shadows once more. In that charged moment, I knew that whatever lay ahead, it would demand more than just courage—it would require an unwavering trust, one that had yet to be forged in the flames of our shared struggles.

The air between us crackled with an intensity that felt almost tangible, like electricity building before a storm. I could sense the weight of his past pressing down on him, but the defiance in his eyes sparked something within me. I was determined to break through his defenses, even if it meant stepping into the tempest of his memories.

"Tell me about that night," I urged softly, my heart racing at the thought of the secrets he held. "The ambush. What did it feel like?"

His gaze darkened, and I could see the muscles in his jaw clench as if bracing against the flood of emotions threatening to spill over. "It felt like betrayal," he said, the words laced with bitterness. "Like being stabbed in the back by someone I thought I could trust. I should have seen the signs."

"Sometimes, trust blinds us," I replied, the ache in my chest deepening. "It's the people we least expect who hurt us the most."

He nodded slowly, and for a moment, I thought I saw a flicker of understanding in his eyes. "And sometimes it's easier to build walls than to risk being hurt again."

"True, but what's the point of living like that?" I pressed. "A life behind walls is no life at all."

The corner of his mouth twitched upward, a hint of a smile teasing his lips. "Is that your way of saying you want to tear down my walls?"

"Only if you promise to help me rebuild something better," I replied, a challenge lacing my tone. "Because I refuse to let you hide from me any longer."

He chuckled, the sound low and rich, and for a moment, the weight of the past seemed to lift slightly. "You're stubborn, aren't you?"

"Stubbornness is my middle name," I shot back, and we both laughed, the moment breaking the tension like a breath of fresh air. But as the laughter faded, the gravity of our conversation returned, heavier than before.

"Alright," he said, shifting in his seat as he gathered his thoughts. "That night... it was chaos. We were ambushed in the middle of what should have been a routine patrol. No warning. Just gunfire and screams." His voice faltered, and I could see the memory etched on his face, raw and agonizing. "I lost men that night. Friends. I still hear their voices sometimes, calling out for help."

"I can't imagine," I murmured, my heart aching for the burden he carried. "But you didn't lose them because of you. You didn't ask for any of this."

He met my gaze, and for the first time, I saw a glimmer of the vulnerability he had tried so hard to hide. "You think that makes it easier? Knowing it wasn't my fault? It doesn't change the fact that they're gone. I still see their faces in my dreams."

"I know you can't forget," I said gently. "But maybe you can start to forgive yourself."

He exhaled, the tension in his shoulders easing ever so slightly. "That's a lot to ask, you know."

"I know," I replied, my voice unwavering. "But I believe you're stronger than you think. You've survived this long, and that says something about your spirit."

A soft smile broke through the shadows of his expression, and I felt warmth unfurl in my chest. "You have a way of seeing the light, even in the darkest of places."

"That's because I've had my fair share of darkness," I admitted, my eyes narrowing thoughtfully. "And I've learned that sometimes, the light comes from the most unexpected sources."

He leaned in closer, his expression shifting from somber to contemplative. "What about you? What's your story?"

I hesitated, the question hanging heavy in the air between us. It felt too personal, too vulnerable to share. "It's not as thrilling as yours," I finally said, trying to deflect. "Just a regular girl trying to find her place in a world that seems intent on throwing curveballs."

"Regular doesn't exist in my world," he replied with a wry smile. "So I'm intrigued."

I took a breath, gathering my thoughts like a storm cloud. "I grew up in a small town where everyone knew everyone else's business, and privacy was a luxury I could never afford. My dreams were bigger than the borders of that town, but I felt trapped, like a bird in a gilded cage."

He listened intently, the sharp focus of his gaze urging me on. "I thought leaving would bring freedom, but it only opened the door to new problems—ones I hadn't anticipated. I faced challenges that made me question everything I believed about myself."

"Did you find what you were looking for?" he asked softly, a hint of something deeper lurking behind his words.

"I found pieces," I said, a smile tugging at my lips. "But I think the search for yourself is never truly over. It's a journey, not a destination."

His expression softened, and I could sense the unspoken connection growing between us, threads of understanding weaving us closer. But just as I began to feel the warmth of that bond, a distant sound shattered the moment—an ominous thud echoing through the hideout.

We both froze, the laughter and confessions hanging in the air as reality crashed back in. I turned to him, heart racing. "What was that?"

His face hardened, the warmth fading as he shifted into a more alert stance. "I don't know, but it doesn't sound good."

Panic gripped me, twisting my stomach into knots. "We need to check it out."

"Stay here," he ordered, but I could hear the underlying tension in his voice, the urgency that crackled like static between us.

"No way," I shot back, my pulse quickening. "If there's trouble, I'm not hiding while you go out there alone."

He hesitated, searching my eyes for something, maybe reassurance, or perhaps the strength to convince me to stay put. "It could be dangerous."

"Maybe. But I'd rather face it together than cower in fear," I insisted, adrenaline coursing through me. "Whatever it is, we handle it together."

He opened his mouth to argue, but then, just as quickly, he closed it, nodding sharply. "Alright. But stay close."

We moved cautiously toward the door, the world beyond feeling more foreboding with each step. The thud reverberated again, louder this time, a deep echo that sent shivers skittering up my spine. He reached for the handle, his body tense, and I could feel the air thick with anticipation.

As he opened the door, the darkness beyond yawned like a hungry beast, and I strained to hear any signs of life, my heart hammering in my chest. A flicker of movement caught my eye, and I glanced up to see a shadow dart across the far side of the alley, barely visible in the dim light.

"Did you see that?" I whispered, my voice barely above a breath.

He nodded, his face pale as he stepped outside, the night air chilling my skin. "Stay behind me."

As we ventured out, the weight of the silence pressed down around us, an oppressive force that seemed to throb with danger. The thud returned, more urgent now, followed by a low rumble that felt like the earth itself was trembling beneath us.

"Something's coming," he murmured, tension coiling between us like a spring ready to snap.

"Then we're ready," I replied, adrenaline spurring me on, determination igniting the fire within. But just as we moved deeper into the darkness, the ground beneath us shook violently, and a deafening roar echoed through the night, sending a shockwave of fear coursing through my veins.

"What the hell was that?" he shouted, eyes wide with alarm as the shadows shifted around us, dark shapes merging and breaking apart in a dance of chaos.

And just like that, our moment of connection dissolved, replaced by the urgent need for survival. In that heartbeat, I knew the world had shifted once again, and everything I thought I understood was about to be tested in ways I could never have anticipated.

Chapter 14: The Unbreakable Bond

The sun dipped low on the horizon, casting long shadows across the courtyard of our makeshift stronghold. I could hear the distant echo of clashing metal, a sound that had become almost comforting in its familiarity. It was a reminder that I was not alone, that I had a purpose, a place in this world of chaos. With every lesson, every skirmish, I felt myself evolving—no longer the naive girl who had stumbled into this life, but a warrior in my own right, molded by the hands of my unlikely teacher.

His name was Cade, a man of contradictions, fierce yet tender, his presence both a shield and a flame that drew me closer even as it cautioned me to keep my distance. Each day spent training with him, I uncovered layers of his character, like peeling back the petals of a flower to reveal the heart hidden within. Cade was not just a fighter; he was an artist of combat, moving with a grace that belied his strength. Under his tutelage, I learned to wield my blade not just with brute force, but with finesse, to dance around my opponents as if we were caught in a deadly waltz.

Today, the air was thick with the scent of earth and sweat, the lingering taste of adrenaline buzzing on my tongue as I faced off against him. My heart pounded in my chest, not just from the exertion, but from the way his gaze held mine, a fierce intensity that set my skin alight. "Again," he instructed, his voice a low growl that vibrated through me.

I lunged forward, the tip of my sword aimed at his heart, and he countered effortlessly, his blade a flickering extension of his will. We clashed, the metal ringing out in the quiet afternoon, each strike a testament to our growing bond. As we moved, I couldn't help but notice the way the sunlight caught in his dark hair, illuminating the determined line of his jaw. In those moments, the world outside faded away, and it was just the two of us—an unbreakable alliance forged in fire.

But as I drew back to catch my breath, something shifted in the atmosphere. I could sense it—a prickling at the back of my neck that spoke of impending danger. Cade's expression darkened, a storm brewing behind those deep-set eyes. "We should wrap this up," he said, the warmth in his voice evaporating like mist in the sun. I nodded, a tightness forming in my chest. It was a familiar feeling, that intertwining of excitement and dread.

The shadows stretched longer as we made our way back into the fortress, the stone walls thick with history and secrets. We passed through the narrow corridors, the air heavy with whispers of those who had come before us. It was a place steeped in a legacy of battles fought and friendships forged, and it felt as though the very stones were alive with stories waiting to be unearthed.

I could sense Cade's unease as we entered the common area. The others were gathered around, their faces grim. An urgent tension hung in the air, palpable and suffocating. I caught snippets of conversation—rumors of a new faction rising in power, a group ruthless enough to threaten everything we had fought for. My stomach twisted at the thought. "What's going on?" I asked, my voice barely a whisper, but Cade's hand found mine, a reassuring squeeze that sent warmth flooding through me.

"The Council has received reports of an approaching army," he said, his brow furrowed. "They're unlike anything we've faced before."

My heart sank. I had hoped our days of constant conflict were behind us, but as the stories of violence unfurled like dark smoke in my mind, I felt the weight of our situation. "What do we do?" I asked, my voice steadier than I felt.

"We prepare," he replied, a steely determination lining his features. "We train harder. We gather allies."

As the group began to strategize, my thoughts whirled, a tempest of fear and resolve. I could feel the threads of fate tightening around us, weaving our lives together in a tapestry that was as beautiful as it was treacherous. Cade was at my side, his presence a solid anchor in the chaos, and as we plotted and planned, I realized that the bond we had forged was more than just a partnership; it was a lifeline.

In the days that followed, our routine transformed. Training sessions intensified, fueled by a new urgency. I pushed myself harder, my muscles aching with the strain, but every bruise felt like a badge of honor. With each clash of swords, I caught glimpses of Cade's admiration, and despite the chaos looming outside, I felt a flicker of hope ignite within me. The moments we shared, brief glances and whispered encouragement, spun a delicate thread of connection that drew us closer. Yet, with every stolen moment, I was reminded of the fragility of our situation.

One evening, as the sun dipped below the horizon, casting the world in hues of amber and violet, Cade and I found a rare moment of peace. We sat on the roof of the fortress, legs dangling over the edge, watching the stars emerge one by one. It was a fleeting sanctuary amidst the storm. I turned to him, wanting to capture this moment forever, and there it was—a softening in his eyes, an openness that made my heart leap.

"Do you ever wonder what it would be like... if things were different?" I asked, my voice barely above a whisper.

He glanced at me, his gaze piercing and full of understanding. "All the time."

And in that simple exchange, the weight of our shared struggles felt lighter, a balm against the uncertainty of our future. But as laughter bubbled between us, shadows flickered in the distance, an ever-present reminder that our fragile bond was just beginning to be tested.

The nights were becoming colder, the chill creeping into our bones as autumn tightened its grip on the land. The air was crisp, carrying the scent of damp earth and decaying leaves, an intoxicating reminder that change was upon us. It was during one such evening, beneath a sky blanketed with stars, that I found myself in a world both beautiful and dangerous, walking the line between the two with Cade at my side.

We had taken to the roof again, where the fortress felt like our own little kingdom, the chaos of the world below a distant murmur. I wrapped my arms around my knees, gazing out at the horizon where the last traces of daylight faded into night. Cade settled beside me, his shoulder brushing against mine, a warmth that made the air around us feel a little less biting.

"You know," he began, his voice a low rumble, "there was a time when I thought I'd never see the stars again."

I turned to him, curious. "What changed?"

His gaze remained fixed on the sky, but I could see the shadows flitting across his face, memories he chose not to share. "I learned to keep my head down and focus on survival. But sometimes, you have to look up to remember what you're fighting for."

His words hung in the air, heavy with meaning. In that moment, I understood something profound: survival wasn't just about living through each day; it was about finding moments of beauty even when the world threatened to consume you whole. "And what are you fighting for?" I asked, emboldened by the intimacy of the night.

Cade finally turned to meet my gaze, and the intensity of his eyes sent a shiver through me. "You, I think. This." He gestured broadly, encompassing the fortress, the stars, and perhaps even me. My heart swelled at his admission, the warmth spreading like wildfire through my veins, but before I could respond, a distant horn sounded, sharp and urgent, slicing through our moment like a dagger.

"What was that?" I asked, my heart racing. Cade was already on his feet, tension radiating from him as he scanned the darkened expanse before us.

"Trouble," he replied, his voice clipped. "Stay close."

We rushed down the stairs, the weight of dread heavy in my stomach. As we reached the common area, chaos erupted. The other members of our group were already gathering weapons, faces taut with fear and determination. I could feel the air thickening with anticipation, like the moment before a storm breaks.

"The scouts have spotted them!" one of our leaders shouted, his voice ringing out above the clamor. "An army is marching toward us. We need to prepare for a siege."

My heart sank. The gravity of our situation wrapped around me like a shroud, but I steeled myself, adrenaline coursing through my veins. This was it—the moment we had feared was finally upon us. I felt Cade's presence beside me, a steady force in the rising storm.

"Gather the archers," Cade commanded, his voice slicing through the noise. "We need to set up defenses and prepare for an ambush."

I followed his lead, adrenaline sharpening my focus as we worked alongside our allies. The camaraderie that had blossomed in our training sessions now transformed into a fierce determination, each of us knowing what was at stake.

Hours passed in a blur of activity, the night air thick with tension. We constructed barricades, distributed weapons, and strategized our defenses, each heartbeat echoing the urgency of our situation. As we worked, I caught glimpses of Cade amidst the frenzy, his movements purposeful and precise, an unyielding leader who inspired loyalty in those around him.

At one point, I found myself at his side, a quiver of arrows slung across my back. "What's the plan?" I asked, trying to keep my voice steady despite the whirlwind of anxiety churning in my chest.

"We draw them in, create the illusion of weakness," he explained, glancing at me with a fierceness that made my stomach flip. "When they least expect it, we strike. But we need to stay one step ahead."

"Sounds like a gamble," I said, trying to inject a hint of levity into the situation. "Are you sure you want to put your faith in my archery skills?"

Cade's lips curved into a half-smile, a flicker of warmth that made my heart skip. "If we're going to survive this, we need everyone's best. And I have a good feeling about you."

"Good feelings can be dangerous," I shot back, trying to maintain the banter despite the tension thrumming through me.

His expression turned serious again. "Just stay sharp. I need you focused."

The night deepened, and as the stars twinkled overhead, an eerie silence descended upon us. It was the calm before the storm, and I felt every nerve in my body sharpen, every instinct screaming at me to be ready. Then, just as the moon peeked out from behind the clouds, the ground trembled beneath our feet, a herald of the approaching enemy.

The sight that met my eyes was both terrifying and awe-inspiring. A wave of dark figures moved like a relentless tide, their numbers seemingly endless, a living shadow creeping toward our fortress. The air crackled with anticipation as I stood shoulder to shoulder with my comrades, hearts pounding in unison.

"Get ready!" Cade shouted, his voice cutting through the heavy stillness. I nocked an arrow, my fingers steady despite the chaos in my mind. I could feel the pulse of the fortress beneath my feet, a shared heartbeat of defiance against the storm that threatened to engulf us.

The first horn sounded, a deep, resonant call that echoed through the night, and the enemy surged forward, a dark wave crashing against our walls. I took a deep breath, my focus sharpening, and as the chaos erupted around me, I knew that this was it. We would either rise together or fall apart, and I was determined to fight for every heartbeat, for every precious moment of light we had forged in the darkness.

The air was electric, charged with the tension of impending battle as the enemy surged toward us. I could hear the heavy thud of boots on the ground, the rallying cries of men ready to seize what they believed was rightfully theirs. Each heartbeat echoed like a war drum, a reminder that we were no longer just a band of survivors; we were fighters, standing resolutely against an overwhelming tide.

Cade's voice cut through the chaos as he barked orders, his presence a beacon of strength amidst the rising storm. I clutched my bow, fingers trembling slightly as I felt the familiar weight of responsibility settle on my shoulders. This was not just about defending our home; it was about preserving the fragile thread of connection that bound us all together, a delicate tapestry woven from trust and camaraderie.

"Focus!" Cade's command snapped me back to the present, and I nodded, my heart racing as I steadied my breath. I drew an arrow from the quiver, the smooth wood warm against my palm. The battlefield was unfolding before me, a chaotic dance of shadows and light, and I was determined to find my place in it.

As the enemy drew closer, I released the first arrow, the sound of it slicing through the air like a promise. It struck true, the figure stumbling back with a pained grunt. A surge of exhilaration coursed through me. This was my fight, too. My resolve solidified with every arrow I loosed, a fierce fire igniting within me.

"Nice shot!" Cade shouted, his voice ringing with encouragement as he took down another opponent with a swift, decisive movement. I caught a glimpse of him in action—his body fluid and powerful, moving with a confidence that made my heart stutter. In that moment, I felt a surge of pride mingling with the adrenaline, a connection that spurred me onward.

The enemy, relentless as the tide, pressed forward, their numbers overwhelming but not insurmountable. We were trained, prepared for this moment, and yet, doubt lingered like a specter in the corners of my mind. Just as I was finding my rhythm, chaos erupted around us. A loud crash echoed, and I turned just in time to see one of our barricades shatter, splintering under the weight of the oncoming force.

"Fall back!" Cade shouted, his voice laced with urgency as he fought his way toward me, cutting down foes with a calculated precision. My heart raced, and I barely had time to process the danger before I felt a sharp pull at my shoulder. A hand grasped my arm, yanking me to safety just as an enemy soldier barreled past, their weapon glinting ominously in the dim light.

"Stay close!" Cade urged, and I nodded, heart pounding, as we maneuvered through the fray together. It was a whirlwind of sound and motion, the cries of battle mixing with the clatter of weapons and the heavy thrum of my own heartbeat.

We fought side by side, a rhythm that felt both exhilarating and terrifying. I could feel the heat radiating off Cade's body, the strength in his movements, and I marveled at how he seemed to anticipate my actions, weaving seamlessly into my defenses. With each passing moment, we pushed back against the encroaching wave, holding our ground.

But then, in the midst of our small victories, a new figure emerged from the chaos—a tall, menacing presence cloaked in dark armor, a banner of a twisted serpent emblazoned on his chest. My breath caught in my throat as I recognized him from the whispers of our scouts. The Wraith—a name spoken in hushed tones, a man who commanded fear and respect in equal measure.

He surveyed the battlefield with an unsettling calm, his eyes glinting with malice as they locked onto Cade. "There he is," he called, his voice smooth and mocking. "The great Cade, champion of the weak. You think you can protect them? You're a fool."

Cade's jaw tightened, the tension in his body palpable. "You don't belong here," he growled, stepping forward, every muscle coiled as if ready to spring.

"Ah, but I do," the Wraith replied, a twisted smile stretching across his lips. "This land will fall, and with it, your precious little band of misfits."

Without warning, he raised his hand, and a wave of dark energy pulsed through the air, crackling like electricity. It twisted and writhed, a malevolent force that set my skin on fire. I barely had time to react before it surged toward us, a black tide that threatened to engulf everything in its path.

"Cade!" I shouted, desperation spilling from my lips as I reached for him. But he was already moving, stepping into the oncoming darkness, his blade drawn, a fierce determination etched into his features.

"Get back!" he commanded, voice sharp as steel. But it was too late; the dark energy enveloped him in a swirling mass, and I felt my heart drop into the pit of my stomach.

"No!" I screamed, my body moving on instinct as I surged forward, adrenaline propelling me into the chaos. I fought through the fray, determined to reach him, to pull him back from the brink of whatever malevolent force sought to claim him.

The Wraith's laughter echoed around me, a chilling sound that cut through the chaos. "You think you can save him? You're too late," he taunted, his eyes glimmering with triumph.

As I reached the edge of the darkness, a fierce light flared within me—a burning resolve that surged through my veins. "I won't let you take him!" I shouted, drawing an arrow back, aiming straight for the heart of the Wraith.

But just as I released, a violent explosion of energy erupted, knocking me off my feet. I hit the ground hard, the world spinning around me as the darkness surged, swallowing the battlefield in its malevolent grasp. The last thing I saw before the shadows consumed me was Cade, fighting against the dark energy, his expression a mix of defiance and desperation.

And then, everything went black.

Chapter 15: A Twist in the Darkness

The shadows clung to us like a shroud, thick and suffocating, as we slipped deeper into the heart of the enemy's lair. I could feel the pulse of the night echoing in my veins, each heartbeat a reminder that the world outside was slipping away. The air was heavy with the scent of damp earth and distant smoke, underscored by the sharp tang of adrenaline. My senses were heightened, every sound amplified: the rustle of leaves, the low hum of distant voices, and the unsettling silence of the path ahead.

He moved with a grace that belied the danger surrounding us, his dark silhouette cutting through the gloom. I found myself stealing glances at him, drawn not only by his physical presence but by the magnetic aura of confidence that surrounded him. There was an intensity in his gaze that seemed to ignite the darkness around us. It was a fire that warmed my core, battling the chill of fear that wrapped itself around me. "Stay close," he murmured, his voice a low growl that sent a thrill through me. I nodded, my heart racing—not just from the peril we faced, but from the thrill of being so near to him, so utterly enmeshed in this shared danger.

The path narrowed, overgrown with brambles that snagged at our clothes, but we pressed on, determined. I could hear the distant sound of laughter—insidious and mocking—carried on the night air. Each chuckle and shout felt like a taunt, a reminder of how easily we could be ensnared. But he was steadfast, his grip on my arm firm yet reassuring as we navigated the twisted underbrush. "If we can just reach the ridge," he said, his brow furrowing in concentration, "we'll have the high ground. They won't expect us to flank them from above."

As we moved, I couldn't help but admire how the moonlight danced upon his features, illuminating the sharp angles of his jaw and the determined set of his mouth. It was intoxicating and terrifying all at once. I was acutely aware of every brush of his arm against mine, every fleeting glance shared between us, laden with unspoken promises and unacknowledged fears. "You really think we can pull this off?" I asked, trying to keep my voice light, masking the tremor of uncertainty that threatened to break through.

He paused, turning to face me, the intensity in his gaze unyielding. "If I didn't believe it, I wouldn't be here with you." The sincerity in his words wrapped around me like a warm blanket, pushing back the chill that had settled in my bones. "We'll get through this. Together."

We pressed on, the landscape shifting around us as we approached the ridge. The laughter grew louder, a cacophony of chaos that seemed to beckon us closer. But we had no intention of surrendering to that chaos. Instead, we were drawing strength from it, using the enemy's hubris to fuel our determination. As we crested the ridge, I could see their camp below, a sprawling mess of tents and flickering campfires, the flickers of light revealing faces in shadow, oblivious to the storm gathering above them.

My heart raced as we surveyed the scene. "There's a path down that way," I whispered, pointing to a steep slope that would lead us closer to the chaos without being seen. "If we can get close enough, we might be able to disrupt their operations."

"Good eye," he said, a smirk playing at the corners of his mouth. "You're learning quickly." The tension between us crackled like a live wire, an electric undercurrent that both excited and terrified me. I felt alive, acutely aware of every shift in the atmosphere, the way the wind whispered secrets through the trees.

But as we made our descent, a sudden rustling in the brush sent a jolt of alarm through me. I barely had time to register the sound before a figure emerged, blocking our path. He was tall, with a wild mane of hair that fell across his forehead, eyes gleaming with malice in the dim light. "Well, well, what do we have here?" he sneered, brandishing a weapon that glinted ominously. "Intruders in our midst."

My heart plummeted, fear surging through me like ice water. "We're not here to fight," I started, but the words felt hollow in my throat. The figure laughed, a dark, sinister sound that sent chills racing down my spine.

"Of course you are," he said, stepping closer, his confidence radiating like heat from a flame. "And you're not going anywhere."

In that instant, my mind raced. We were trapped, the net tightening around us, and the weight of our impending doom loomed heavy. But before I could fully process our predicament, I felt his hand tighten around mine, his thumb brushing against my knuckles in a gesture that steadied me.

"Let's make this interesting," he said, his voice calm and dangerously smooth. "You want a fight? Let's give them a show."

With a surge of resolve, he pulled me back, our bodies aligning as he positioned us to face our adversary. My heart pounded, a chaotic rhythm of fear and exhilaration as we stood united against the dark, the shadows of our past battles looming behind us. I realized then that I was not merely a pawn in his game—I was an equal partner, ready to face whatever came next. The unexpected turn of events ignited a spark of defiance within me, igniting a fierce desire to stand my ground. The path ahead may be riddled with obstacles, but with him by my side, I felt a renewed sense of purpose. Whatever awaited us, we would face it together, and I wouldn't have it any other way.

The tension hung in the air, taut and electric, as we squared off against the looming figure. His weapon gleamed in the firelight, a menacing reflection of our predicament. I could feel my pulse thrumming in my ears, but beneath the rush of fear was an undeniable exhilaration. This was it—no more hiding in the shadows. I glanced at him, his face set with fierce determination, and suddenly, I wasn't afraid anymore. "So, you think you can take us on?" I challenged, my voice steadier than I felt.

The intruder's lips twisted into a sneer, but I could see the surprise flicker in his eyes. Perhaps he hadn't expected a reaction from me. "Oh, feisty, are we?" he shot back, stepping closer. "But you're just a girl playing at heroics."

"Better a girl than a coward hiding behind a sword," I retorted, my courage swelling as I stood my ground. I could feel the warmth of his presence beside me, a steadying force, and I drew strength from it.

"Enough!" Our enemy snarled, raising his weapon. Just then, the crackle of underbrush erupted behind us as more figures emerged from the shadows, surrounding us with predatory intent. My stomach dropped; we had underestimated their numbers.

"Time to improvise," he said, his voice low but urgent, and before I could respond, he lunged forward, surprising our attacker with a swift kick that sent the man reeling back. Seizing the moment, I grabbed a nearby branch, wielding it like a weapon, feeling a surge of adrenaline. We were not going down without a fight.

The ensuing chaos felt surreal, the world blurring into a frenzied dance of shadows and flashes of steel. I swung the branch, feeling the satisfying thud as it connected with someone's shoulder. "I thought you said you'd keep me safe!" I shouted over the commotion, a wild grin breaking through my fear.

"I didn't think I'd need to protect you from yourself!" he shouted back, dodging a blow and retaliating with a well-placed jab. The banter felt absurd against the backdrop of danger, but it kept us grounded, tethered to each other amidst the chaos.

As we fought, I caught glimpses of the camp—firelight flickering like a heartbeat, the chaos igniting around us. The laughter I had heard before transformed into shouts of surprise and anger as they realized the intruders were fighting back. In that moment, I felt invincible. We were not just players in their game; we were rewriting the rules.

But just as victory began to seem within reach, the tide turned. A heavyset man barreled toward us, his presence more intimidating than the others, eyes narrowed like a predator's. He was too close, too powerful, and as he reached for me, I felt a pang of fear shoot through my gut. "Get back!" I yelled, swinging the branch again, but this time, he didn't flinch. He grabbed my wrist, yanking me toward him.

"Stop struggling, girl. You're outnumbered." His voice was a growl, dripping with contempt.

In that moment, everything slowed. I could feel my heart pounding in my chest, the heat of panic flooding my veins. But then, from the corner of my eye, I saw him—a flash of movement as he charged, tackling the man with a ferocity that shocked me. They crashed to the ground, a tangle of limbs and fury.

"Run!" he shouted, his voice strained as he fought to gain the upper hand. I hesitated, torn between my instinct to help and the desperate urge to escape. But my decision was made for me when I felt another set of hands grab me from behind.

"No!" I screamed, twisting and kicking, my branch forgotten. Just as I was about to succumb to despair, a sudden explosion rocked the camp, sending a plume of smoke into the air. The chaos erupted anew, the enemy momentarily distracted by the sudden commotion.

"Now!" he roared, scrambling to his feet and grabbing my arm. "This way!" We dashed toward the tree line, adrenaline coursing through my body as we slipped into the safety of the underbrush. The shouts of confusion faded behind us, swallowed by the night.

We didn't stop running until the sounds of chaos were a distant echo, our breaths mingling with the rustle of leaves in the night air. When we finally halted, my chest heaved with exhaustion, and I leaned against a tree, heart racing, trying to catch my breath.

"You okay?" he asked, his voice laced with concern as he stepped closer, brushing a strand of hair away from my face. The gesture sent a warmth through me that contrasted starkly with the cold sweat of fear.

"I think so," I replied, my voice shaky but tinged with exhilaration. "That was... insane."

A smirk tugged at his lips, and I couldn't help but smile back. "You handled yourself pretty well. I'd say you surprised me."

"Don't sound so shocked," I teased, trying to mask the tremor in my voice. "I can hold my own, you know."

"I do know," he said, his gaze unwavering. "And I like that about you." His words hung between us, rich with unspoken meanings and promises. For a heartbeat, the world around us faded, leaving only the two of us in the enveloping darkness.

But then, the reality of our situation crashed back in, and I straightened, the thrill of battle still surging through my veins. "What now? We can't just wander around in the woods forever."

He nodded, shaking off the tension that had built up around us. "We need to regroup, find a place to lay low for a while. If they find us again—"

"They will," I interjected, the dread creeping back into my mind. "They'll be looking for us."

"Then we need to be ready." He took a deep breath, his expression turning serious. "But first, we need to get our bearings." He scanned the trees, the shadows shifting with the wind. "Follow me."

As we made our way deeper into the forest, the atmosphere shifted, the air thick with mystery. The trees loomed like ancient sentinels, whispering secrets in the night. Each crack of a twig underfoot sent jolts of adrenaline through me, but the comfort of his presence reassured me. We were in this together, two unlikely allies navigating a world fraught with danger and uncertainty.

Suddenly, a flicker of light caught my attention—a soft glow weaving through the trees like a firefly's dance. "What's that?" I whispered, instinctively drawing closer to him.

"Let's check it out," he replied, his voice low and cautious. As we crept toward the light, curiosity replaced our caution, urging us forward. My heart raced—not just from the fear of what might lie ahead, but from the thrill of the unknown. Whatever awaited us could change everything, and as much as I wanted to keep my distance from danger, I was drawn to the adventure unfolding before us.

With each step, I felt the weight of uncertainty lift, replaced by a rush of exhilaration. The world was ours to explore, and as long as we faced it together, I was ready for whatever came next.

The flicker of light danced in the distance, beckoning us closer with an otherworldly glow. We moved cautiously, the underbrush crackling beneath our feet, each sound amplified in the hushed night air. I could feel the anticipation coiling in my stomach, a mix of excitement and apprehension. What awaited us just beyond the next cluster of trees? As we drew nearer, I noticed that the light was not merely a fire—it pulsed rhythmically, almost like a heartbeat, illuminating the surrounding foliage with an eerie brilliance.

"Are you sure this is a good idea?" I whispered, glancing sideways at him. He looked as intrigued as I felt, a slight smile playing on his lips that made my heart flutter.

"I live for bad ideas," he quipped back, the twinkle in his eye suggesting he found this thrill as intoxicating as I did. "Besides, I can't resist a good mystery."

His words made me chuckle, easing some of the tension that had built up within me. With every step, my initial fear melted into a sense of adventure. Together, we were explorers in a world that seemed to shift and shimmer with possibilities.

As we stepped through the last of the trees, the light revealed itself fully—a shimmering pool, its surface smooth like glass and glowing from within. The illumination came from bioluminescent plants that surrounded it, their soft hues casting ethereal patterns on the ground. My breath caught at the beauty, the way the light played on his face, softening the rugged lines of his features. "Wow," I breathed, captivated. "It's like something out of a fairy tale."

He stepped closer to the water's edge, his gaze intense as he peered into the depths. "Or a trap," he cautioned, always the realist. "Let's not jump in just yet."

"Right," I replied, though my curiosity battled with caution. "But what if it holds answers? Or—"

"Or it could be a way to get us killed." His tone was playful, but there was an underlying seriousness that grounded my excitement. "Let's see if there's anything else we can find first."

We circled the pool, taking in the strange plants and the whispering sounds of the night. The atmosphere was thick with magic and mystery, as if the very air was charged with stories waiting to be uncovered. I spotted a small clearing nearby, a perfect spot to gather our thoughts and maybe even plot our next move.

"Over here," I called, leading him to the clearing where the moonlight spilled down in silvery beams. It was a sanctuary, far removed from the chaos we had just escaped. We settled onto the cool grass, the tension of the night slowly unraveling like a tight knot.

"Do you think they'll find us?" I asked, wrapping my arms around my knees, feeling the weight of our earlier confrontation pressing against my chest.

"They might," he replied, resting his chin on his hand as he stared into the distance. "But we'll be ready for them. We've survived worse."

His confidence was contagious, and I felt a flicker of hope ignite within me. "You really think we can turn the tide?" I mused, my voice tinged with determination. "That we can actually outsmart them?"

"I know we can," he said, turning to meet my gaze. The intensity in his eyes was like a jolt of electricity. "We have each other. That makes us stronger."

The unspoken truth hung between us, heavy with possibilities. I wanted to believe him, wanted to embrace the idea of facing the world as a team. "You're not so bad for a brooding vigilante," I teased, nudging him playfully with my shoulder.

"Only for you," he shot back, a smirk breaking through his serious facade. The banter felt like a lifeline, pulling us both from the depths of uncertainty.

But before I could respond, the atmosphere shifted. A distant rumble echoed through the night, not unlike thunder but layered with an ominous undertone. My smile faltered, the shadows creeping back into my mind. "What was that?"

"Probably nothing," he said, though the tightness in his voice betrayed his own concern. We exchanged glances, an unspoken agreement passing between us. "Let's check it out."

We rose cautiously, the light from the glowing pool casting strange shadows as we made our way back through the trees. The air felt charged, alive with tension. The low rumble grew louder, more insistent, reverberating through the ground beneath our feet. I shivered, glancing over my shoulder, half-expecting to see dark figures emerging from the woods.

As we approached the edge of the clearing, we caught sight of flickering torches illuminating the path leading back toward the camp. A small group of figures was emerging, their forms becoming clearer as they moved with purpose. "They're coming," I whispered, my heart racing.

"Stay behind me," he instructed, his voice low and steady. I could feel the protective energy radiating from him, and it steadied my nerves even as my mind raced with possibilities.

We ducked behind a thick tree trunk, peering out at the approaching figures. They moved with a predatory grace, their faces obscured by hoods, but I could sense the menace emanating from them. "What do we do?" I whispered, adrenaline coursing through me.

"We wait and see," he replied, eyes fixed on the advancing group. "We need to gather as much information as we can."

I nodded, my mind racing with strategies, but the dread in my gut twisted tighter. There were too many of them, and as they drew closer, I caught snippets of their conversation, the malicious undertones sending chills down my spine.

"Did you see the way they fought?" one of them hissed. "They're stronger than we thought. We need to be prepared."

"Don't worry," another sneered. "They won't escape this time. We'll make an example of them."

A surge of fear washed over me, and I turned to him, panic rising in my throat. "What if they find us? What if we're too late?"

"We won't let that happen," he vowed, the conviction in his voice anchoring me even as the darkness threatened to close in around us.

But just as I felt a glimmer of hope spark anew, the ground beneath us trembled again, this time more violently. The trees shuddered, and a low growl reverberated through the air. It was as if the earth itself was responding to the gathering storm. My heart raced as I glanced at him, his expression a mixture of concern and determination.

"Did you feel that?" I asked, my voice barely above a whisper.

"Yeah," he said, frowning as he strained to listen. "We need to move—"

Before he could finish, the shadows around us erupted, and a massive creature burst from the underbrush, its form barely visible in the dim light. Panic surged through me, primal and electric, as the realization hit—this was no ordinary night, and we were not just battling against our enemies. Something far more sinister was awakening, and it was hungry for chaos.

The creature roared, a sound that echoed through the trees like a death knell, and I felt the air thicken with dread. We were standing at the edge of something monumental, and in that moment, the weight of uncertainty pressed down on us both. The fight was far from over, and we had just stepped into a darkness we could never have anticipated.

Chapter 16: The Veil of Betrayal

The air crackled with tension as I stood there, heart hammering in my chest, feeling as if I'd stumbled into a storm that had been brewing for far too long. The sun hung low in the sky, casting a golden glow over everything, but all I could see was the darkness lurking in his eyes—the flicker of a truth I had been blind to, concealed behind a charming smile and soft words.

"How could you?" I managed to choke out, my voice breaking, the accusation echoing like a bell tolling in the silence between us. I wanted to scream, to throw something, anything, to shatter the perfect illusion he had crafted around us. But instead, I stood frozen, rooted in a mixture of disbelief and fury. The truth clung to me like a heavy cloak, suffocating and unbearable.

He shifted, his gaze flickering away from mine, and in that moment, I saw him for what he really was—vulnerable, yes, but also trapped. He was a prisoner of his own making, ensnared in a web of deceit that stretched far beyond the walls of our little world. I took a step back, the distance between us suddenly feeling insurmountable. "All those moments... were they lies? Were you just playing a part?" The accusation hung heavy in the air, filling the space with an unbearable weight.

"I didn't want to hurt you," he said, his voice low, filled with a desperate urgency that made my stomach twist. "I thought... I thought I could protect you."

Protect me? I wanted to laugh, the bitter sound of it clawing its way up my throat. "Protect me from the truth? Is that it?" I could feel the heat rising in my cheeks, a mix of shame and anger flushing my skin. How had I allowed myself to be swept away by his charm, by the way his laughter had always danced like sunlight in a darkened room? "By keeping me in the dark?"

He ran a hand through his hair, frustration evident in the tightness of his jaw. "You don't understand! It's not that simple. I was trying to navigate a game that was never meant for us." His eyes bore into mine, dark and stormy, as if they held the answers I sought. But all I could see were the shadows, swirling like the impending night.

"Then make me understand," I shot back, crossing my arms tightly over my chest, a futile attempt to shield myself from the raw honesty of our situation. "Tell me everything. No more secrets." The words tasted like poison, bitter on my tongue, but they were necessary. If he truly wanted to salvage whatever remained of us, he had to lay bare the truth, no matter how jagged and sharp.

He hesitated, the weight of my demand pressing down on him like a physical force. I watched the play of emotions on his face—regret, fear, and a flicker of something else, something darker. Finally, he spoke, his voice a hoarse whisper that felt like a confession. "I'm caught in the middle of a conflict between two powerful forces. I thought I could manipulate the situation to our advantage, to keep you safe. But it's spiraling out of control, and now it's threatening everything we have."

His words wrapped around me, tightening like a noose. I felt my resolve waver, but the betrayal ran deep. "You should have trusted me enough to let me in," I said softly, the fight leaving my voice. "Instead, you turned me into a pawn in your game."

He stepped closer, desperation etched on his face. "I never wanted that! I wanted to protect you, to keep you out of the crossfire. But now..." His voice trailed off, and the silence stretched between us, thick and suffocating. "Now, I don't know if I can."

I swallowed hard, the lump in my throat threatening to choke me. "Maybe you should have thought of that before," I said, turning away from him, the weight of his gaze like a physical blow. The shadows of betrayal curled around me, a cloak that felt both familiar and terrifying. My heart raced as I considered the distance I would need to put between us—how I would have to rebuild the walls I had let crumble, fortifying my defenses against the very man who had once made me feel invincible.

But as I walked away, my heart ached with a confusing blend of anger and sorrow. I wanted to believe there was still a path forward, but the ground felt shaky beneath my feet, every step echoing with uncertainty. The vibrant world around me—the colors, the sounds, the very essence of what had once been a sanctuary—now felt tainted, as if the sun itself had dimmed in response to the shadows that loomed over us.

Each corner I turned only deepened the divide, the air heavy with unspoken words and unresolved emotions. I could feel him behind me, a dark presence, but I didn't dare look back. To do so would mean admitting that the bond we had forged was not just a fragile illusion but something real, something worth fighting for. Yet, in that moment, all I could think about was the sting of betrayal, the shattering of trust, and the bitter taste of what could have been.

I stepped out into the evening air, the chill biting at my skin, the night sky a sprawling canvas dotted with stars, each one a reminder of the vastness of the unknown ahead. I took a deep breath, determined to find my footing, to reclaim my strength. I would not be a pawn. I would rise, stronger and wiser, even if it meant navigating this labyrinth alone.

The chill of the evening air wrapped around me like a forgotten blanket, heavy and oppressive, as I made my way down the familiar cobblestone streets that seemed to mock me now with their whimsical charm. Each step echoed with the rhythm of my heart, pounding a frantic beat of anger and confusion. Lanterns flickered overhead, casting soft pools of light that barely penetrated the growing shadows, a reminder of the warmth I once felt in this town—the laughter shared over steaming mugs of cocoa, the playful banter with friends under the stars. Now, those memories felt like shards of glass, glinting dangerously in the dark.

As I reached the corner café, the scent of freshly baked pastries wafted through the open door, mingling with the heady aroma of coffee. I hesitated, torn between the allure of comfort and the gnawing feeling of betrayal. This was our place, where we had shared secrets and dreams, and yet it now felt tainted. With a deep breath, I pushed through the door, the chime of the bell sounding like a cruel reminder of what had been.

The café was cozy, filled with the murmur of conversations and the soft clinking of cutlery. I spotted a corner table by the window, the one where we had laughed until our sides hurt over too many mugs of hot chocolate. I settled in, absently tracing the outline of the chipped table with my finger, the rough wood grounding me even as my thoughts whirled.

A few moments later, the waitress approached, her smile warm and welcoming. "The usual?" she asked, her eyes sparkling with a familiarity that made my heart ache.

I forced a smile, a weak imitation of my usual cheer. "Actually, I'll have a coffee, black. And a slice of that lemon tart, please."

As she moved away, I glanced outside, watching the people pass by, oblivious to the storm that raged within me. The world continued to turn, and I felt like a ghost, hovering on the edges of my own life. My phone buzzed on the table, the screen lighting up with a message from him. I couldn't bear to look, the ache of my heart amplifying with every passing second. Instead, I pushed the device away, as if that simple action could shield me from the chaos of my emotions.

Minutes later, my coffee arrived, steaming and dark, a stark contrast to the sweetness of the lemon tart that followed. I took a tentative sip, the bitterness settling against my tongue, a reflection of the turmoil swirling inside me. Just then, the door swung open, a rush of chilly air announcing the arrival of a figure I recognized too well. He walked in, the sunlight outside casting a halo around him, but in my eyes, it only illuminated the shadows of deceit that clung to him.

My breath hitched in my throat as he scanned the room, and for a moment, I dared to hope he wouldn't see me. But our gazes locked, and the intensity of his stare sent a shockwave of emotions racing through me—anger, longing, confusion. He approached, a determined set to his jaw that spoke of resolve, and I braced myself for the confrontation I had been avoiding.

"Can we talk?" His voice was low, laced with an urgency that tugged at my heart even as my mind screamed for distance.

I shook my head, the impulse to turn away battling against the pull of familiarity that had once been so comforting. "What's there to talk about? You've said enough already."

"Please." He sighed, the weight of the word pressing heavily between us. "I need you to understand. I never wanted to keep you in the dark. I thought I could handle it. I thought I could shield you from all this." He gestured vaguely, as if the chaos of the world could be contained by mere hand movements.

I rolled my eyes, unable to help the sharp retort that slipped from my lips. "And how's that working out for you? You're a terrible shield, it turns out."

"Not a shield, a strategy," he corrected, the corners of his mouth twitching as if trying to suppress a smile. "And maybe my strategy was flawed. But I thought—"

"Thought what? That you could protect me by lying?" My voice was a whisper now, heavy with the weight of betrayal. The warmth of the café felt stifling, the distance between us collapsing under the intensity of our emotions.

"By trying to keep you safe from the dangers I've entangled myself with." His eyes were earnest, filled with a desperation that tugged at the remnants of my resolve. "There's a lot at stake here. I didn't realize how deeply I'd gotten in over my head until it was too late."

"And now?" I challenged, leaning forward, searching for the truth hidden in the depths of his gaze. "What do we do now?"

He took a deep breath, the tension between us palpable. "I need your help. I know it sounds insane, but I can't unravel this without you. You're the only one who can see the pieces clearly."

I stared at him, incredulous. "You want me to help you with this mess? You're asking me to dive headfirst into the very chaos you tried to protect me from?"

"Yes! Because together, we might just have a chance." His voice was urgent, filled with a fire that made my heart race. "I can't do this alone. We can't keep running from this."

I felt my heart begin to thaw at his words, the protective walls I had tried to build around myself cracking under the heat of his plea. Part of me screamed to walk away, to hold on to my anger and self-preservation. But another part—a part that had loved him fiercely, despite everything—was drawn to the challenge, to the idea that we could fight this together, whatever "this" entailed.

"Fine," I said, the word slipping from my lips before I could think better of it. "But if we're doing this, there are no more secrets. You tell me everything."

His relief was palpable, a weight lifting from his shoulders as he nodded vigorously. "Absolutely. No more secrets. I promise."

As we sat down together, the warmth of the café enveloping us once more, I felt a flicker of hope igniting in the midst of the chaos. The path ahead was uncertain and fraught with danger, but perhaps, just perhaps, we could navigate it together.

The café buzzed around us, the comforting hum of life contrasting sharply with the turmoil brewing in my chest. I sat across from him, my heart thumping a nervous rhythm that was both familiar and foreign, as if the very air between us had thickened with unsaid words and tangled feelings. Each sip of coffee was a bitter reminder of the stakes we now faced. I had thought I could walk away, sever the ties that bound us, but now I was tethered, the gravity of our shared choices pulling me back into a turbulent orbit.

"So, what's the plan?" I asked, forcing the words out with a bravado I didn't quite feel. "Are we just going to dive into this mess together, hand in hand, like it's some sort of twisted fairy tale?"

He chuckled, the sound low and a little strained, as if he were trying to mask the seriousness of our predicament with humor. "If you want a fairy tale, I might need to borrow a magic wand. Preferably one with a very long reach."

"Right," I said, rolling my eyes. "Because a flick of the wrist will fix everything. You've got the plan, or are we improvising this whole thing?"

His expression turned serious, the lightness fading from his eyes as he leaned forward, elbows on the table. "There's a meeting tomorrow night. It's where everything happens—the deals, the betrayals, all of it. I need you there."

"Why? So I can hold your hand while you make backdoor deals? I'm not some damsel waiting for her knight to save her," I shot back, my heart racing with a mix of anger and a flicker of excitement. "You need to be more specific."

"Because I believe in you. You see things I don't," he replied, an earnestness in his voice that sent a ripple of warmth through me. "You're clever, resourceful. If things go south, I need someone who can think on their feet."

The compliment caught me off guard, and I felt a blush creep up my cheeks despite the circumstances. "I can think on my feet, sure, but I also have a habit of tripping over my own shoelaces. Not exactly ideal for a high-stakes showdown."

"Then wear better shoes," he said, a grin breaking through the tension, and for a moment, I could almost forget the weight of our reality. But laughter was a fragile thing, and the seriousness of our situation loomed just behind it, a dark cloud threatening to rain on our fragile moment.

I hesitated, torn between the thrill of the unknown and the caution that kept me anchored. "And if I say no? What happens then?"

"Then we both end up in over our heads," he replied, his tone steady, but his eyes flickered with the fear of what lay ahead. "You might not be directly in the line of fire now, but you will be. They don't take kindly to loose ends."

A chill ran down my spine at his words, and I clenched my fists, the nails digging into my palms as I weighed my options. "You're asking me to jump into a war zone. What do I get in return?"

His gaze softened, sincerity washing over his features like a warm tide. "You get the chance to fight back. To be part of something bigger than us, to reclaim the narrative instead of being a victim of it. Isn't that worth it?"

I took a moment to absorb his words, the complexity of our situation unfolding in my mind like an intricate tapestry. It wasn't just about us anymore; it was about power, control, and a fight for something I had once believed was safe and ordinary. A chance to rewrite the story we'd both stumbled into, one fraught with peril but rich with potential.

"Fine," I said, determination seeping into my tone. "I'm in. But you better keep me in the loop. No more secrets. If I'm going to play this game, I need to know all the rules."

He nodded, the flicker of hope igniting in his eyes. "I promise. No more secrets."

We finished our coffee in silence, the weight of our decisions settling around us like a thick fog. As we stood to leave, a sense of purpose began to anchor me, threading its way through the confusion and anger. We walked side by side, our shoulders brushing, the electricity of shared determination sparking between us.

As we stepped outside, the evening air felt charged, as if the world held its breath in anticipation. The streets that had once seemed so inviting now felt like a labyrinth of shadows, each corner hiding potential danger. I looked at him, the man who had pulled me into this world of secrets and deception, and felt an unshakeable bond form between us. We were two pieces of a puzzle that had yet to reveal its true image.

"Tomorrow night," I murmured, anxiety and excitement dancing together in my chest. "We'll need to plan our approach."

He nodded, the seriousness of the moment reflected in his eyes. "We'll go in, blend in, gather information, and get out. No heroics, no reckless moves."

"Right," I agreed, my mind already whirling with possibilities. "So, we'll act like we belong. Got it. But let's just be clear: I'm not wearing anything that makes me look like a bouncer."

He laughed, and it was a sound that brought a hint of normalcy back to our chaotic evening. "Noted. You can wear that cute red dress that always turns heads."

"Now we're talking," I said, my spirit lifting at the prospect of reclaiming some semblance of normalcy amidst the chaos. "I could get used to this whole 'fighting the system' thing, especially if I look good while doing it."

As we walked along the street, the lanterns casting a warm glow on our faces, I couldn't shake the feeling that the night was only the beginning. But just as I felt the stirrings of hope, a figure emerged from the shadows, blocking our path. My heart lurched, instinctively stepping closer to him, my breath catching in my throat as the stranger's features sharpened in the light.

"Going somewhere?" the figure asked, a sly smile spreading across his lips, the glint of danger flickering in his eyes. "Because I think we need to talk."

A cold shiver crept down my spine as the realization hit. This wasn't a mere chance encounter. The game was about to change, and we were standing on the precipice of a decision that could alter everything.

Chapter 17: Echoes of the Heart

I moved through the crowded market with the precision of a dancer, weaving in and out of throngs of people, my mind racing faster than my feet. The air was thick with the aroma of spices and roasting meat, the vibrant colors of the stalls blurring into a kaleidoscope of life. Each shout of the vendors, their voices rising above the din, was a reminder of the world outside my own turbulent thoughts. I was on a mission, or so I told myself. But even as I forced my focus onto the tasks at hand, memories of him swirled in my mind like the dust that danced in the sunlight filtering through the awnings.

It was maddening. I caught glimpses of his smile in every stranger's face, heard echoes of his laughter in the rustle of the wind. Each time I closed my eyes, the warmth of his hand enveloping mine surged back, igniting a longing that sent sharp pangs through my chest. I shook my head, willing myself to concentrate. This was no time for reminiscing about a past that felt like it belonged to someone else. We were not just tangled in memories; we were caught in a relentless cycle of pain and hope that seemed to snare us with every turn. I was supposed to be moving on, not allowing myself to be weighed down by what could have been.

As I approached a vendor selling handwoven baskets, my thoughts spiraled further. His eyes, those deep pools of vulnerability, had once held the promise of everything I yearned for. I thought of the way he'd looked at me just before he vanished into the night, the rain cascading around him like a curtain drawn between us. It was that moment of despair that felt like a lifetime ago, yet the emotions were still raw, a tender wound that refused to close. I felt a strange mix of resentment and yearning; how could he make me feel so utterly alive and then disappear as if he never existed at all?

With a shake of my head, I forced myself to focus on the mission. The assignment loomed large in my mind, a dark shadow against the backdrop of my emotions. There was an enemy lurking, plotting in the shadows, and it was my job to uncover their schemes. But every time I envisioned the face of our foe, it morphed into his. I couldn't let my heart rule my head, even if it was proving to be the toughest battle of all.

The sun dipped lower in the sky, casting an orange glow over the bustling marketplace. My heart raced with the anticipation of what was to come, and I began to move toward the rendezvous point. It was a narrow alley, away from the chaos, where whispers could travel undetected. But as I turned the corner, my breath caught in my throat. There he was—standing there, soaked to the skin, as if he had emerged from the very rainstorm that had once driven us apart.

His dark hair clung to his forehead, and the contours of his face were illuminated by the waning light. There was an uncharacteristic vulnerability about him, a brokenness that stirred something deep within me. I wanted to scold him, to tell him he had no right to disrupt the fragile equilibrium I had constructed. Yet, as our eyes met, I felt the walls I had so carefully built begin to crumble.

"Why are you here?" My voice came out stronger than I felt, laced with a mixture of anger and relief. I wanted to shove him away, to pretend that the ache in my chest didn't exist, but the truth was far more complicated.

He stepped forward, the tension crackling between us like electricity. "I came to find you," he replied, his voice low and urgent, a balm to my stormy heart. "I've been searching everywhere."

"Searching for what? More broken promises?" I spat, the words tumbling out before I could filter them through the remnants of my heart. "You don't get to come back and expect everything to be okay."

But as I said the words, I felt the weight of them, heavy and laden with all the things I didn't want to admit. I didn't want to see him like this, lost and drenched, yet here we stood, the distance between us both a chasm and a thread.

"Please, just listen to me." He reached for my hand, the simple gesture igniting a firestorm of memories—the warmth of shared laughter, the comfort of whispered secrets. I felt the familiar tug of connection, but my resolve held firm, for I knew all too well how fragile that bond could be.

I pulled away, keeping my heart shielded. "You had your chance," I said, though my voice trembled slightly, betraying the turmoil within. "You can't just waltz back into my life like you didn't shatter it into a million pieces."

"Maybe I can't," he replied, his eyes searching mine, desperate and raw. "But I need you to understand. I didn't mean for any of this to happen. I was trying to protect you."

"Protect me?" The word left my lips like a bitter laugh. "You think disappearing was protecting me? You left me alone to deal with the mess you created!"

Yet even as I lashed out, I saw the hurt in his expression. It was a mirror of my own anguish, and in that moment, the walls I'd built began to tremble. Perhaps the truth was more complex than either of us wanted to admit, a web woven with threads of love, regret, and unspoken fears.

As the rain dripped from the awning above us, the world seemed to fade away. In that narrow alley, under the weight of our shared history, a flicker of hope ignited between us. I wanted to hate him, to push him away for all the heartache, but the bond we shared was undeniable, a tether that even the fiercest storm could not sever.

His hand found mine again, tentative yet insistent. "Let me explain," he urged, and I could feel the warmth of his touch seep into the coldness that surrounded me. Just for a moment, I hesitated, allowing myself to bask in the warmth of what could be—a warmth that could heal, if only I let it.

The warmth of his hand against mine was a fragile thing, like a thin strand of silk stretched tight, ready to snap at the slightest provocation. Yet, in that moment, it was everything. I drew in a shaky breath, the familiar scent of rain-soaked earth and his unmistakable cologne filling my lungs, grounding me in a reality that felt too surreal to be true. "You think you can just show up and fix everything with a few sweet words?" I challenged, feeling the heat of anger simmering beneath my skin.

"I'm not trying to fix it," he replied, his voice steady despite the storm brewing in my heart. "I just want you to know why I left, why I thought I had to."

The alley around us pulsed with life—a stray cat darting for shelter, the faint sound of music drifting from a nearby tavern, and the laughter of children splashing in puddles. Yet, here we stood, wrapped in a cocoon of tension, the world outside fading away. "Why you had to?" I echoed, my voice rising slightly as if I could pierce through the haze of doubt. "What were you protecting me from? Yourself? Your mistakes?"

He winced, and I could see the vulnerability in his eyes, the regret etched into the lines of his face. "I thought I was doing the right thing. I thought it would keep you safe." His words were raw, laced with a sincerity that made my heart flutter despite myself. "But the truth is, I was scared. Scared of what I felt for you and what it meant."

"Scared?" I laughed, a bitter sound that didn't quite reach my eyes. "You think that justifies leaving me in the dark? You abandoned me when I needed you most. Do you know how that feels?"

"Every day." His gaze pierced mine, unwavering, the rain cascading down his cheeks mingling with the raw emotion in his voice. "Every single day since I walked away, I've felt it. I thought I was sparing you from the chaos in my life, but all I did was create a different kind of chaos in yours."

The truth hung between us like a fragile glass ornament, waiting for the slightest breath to shatter it. I wanted to scream, to shake him until he understood how deeply he had hurt me. But I also felt the undeniable pull of the past, the warmth of our shared laughter, the comfort of our late-night talks that had woven us together in a way that felt impossible to unravel. "You should have trusted me to make that choice for myself," I said finally, the anger dissipating, replaced by a weary acceptance.

"I know," he admitted, stepping closer, the space between us narrowing until I could feel the warmth radiating from him. "And if you let me, I want to try to make it right. I need you to understand everything that's happened since then."

I hesitated, torn between the desire to cling to the past and the urge to protect myself from further pain. "What do you mean?"

He took a deep breath, his expression shifting from regret to determination. "There are things happening—things I didn't want to involve you in. The enemy we're both after, they're more dangerous than you know. I had to leave to keep you out of it. I thought I could shield you, but the truth is, I only made things worse."

My heart raced. The weight of his confession settled over us like a thick fog, stifling and heavy. "So this is about the mission? About the enemy? You think I'm just some damsel in distress?" I took a step back, feeling a surge of indignation. "I can handle myself. I've been fighting my battles long before you waltzed back into my life."

"Exactly." His voice softened, and he reached for my hand again, more gently this time. "You're stronger than anyone I've ever known, and that's why I couldn't let you get dragged into this. But now, it's bigger than either of us. You're already in danger just by being here."

My mind raced, processing the implications of his words. Danger? I had sensed it, felt it in the air, an unseen predator lurking just beyond the periphery of my awareness. The shadows had grown longer, whispers of betrayal had lingered, and now I was left to wonder how much of it was tied to the very man standing before me. "You should have told me," I insisted, the urgency in my tone demanding he understand the depth of my frustration. "I could have helped."

"I know," he replied, frustration edging into his voice. "But I thought it was too late. I thought I'd already lost you."

The air crackled with unsaid words, and I could feel the storm swirling around us—both outside and within. "So what now?" I asked, my heart pounding with both fear and anticipation. "What do you want from me?"

"I want to work together," he said, his grip on my hand tightening as if he feared I might slip away again. "There's a plan. A way to uncover the truth and stop whatever they're plotting before it's too late. But I need you with me. We can't do this alone."

The resolve in his eyes mirrored my own desperation to reclaim what we'd lost. I felt the spark of hope igniting deep within me, a flicker that promised a chance to mend the fracture between us. But with hope came trepidation, for I had seen too much to walk blindly into danger again. "If we're going to do this," I said, my voice steady despite the tumultuous emotions surging through me, "you have to be honest with me. No more secrets. No more running away."

He nodded, the sincerity in his gaze melting away the barriers I had so carefully constructed. "I promise," he vowed, and for the first time, I believed him.

Before I could second-guess myself, I squeezed his hand, feeling the warmth seep into my skin. "Then let's find out what we're really up against."

And with that simple agreement, we stepped into the storm together, ready to face whatever awaited us, the past lingering at our heels, but no longer dictating our path forward.

The rain continued to fall, a soft patter that enveloped us in its rhythm, muffling the world outside our little bubble. I squeezed his hand, grounding myself in the moment, aware that the stakes had shifted. We were no longer just two people caught in a cycle of hurt and hope; we were partners in a dangerous game, navigating a landscape riddled with shadows and uncertainty.

"Do you have a plan?" I asked, trying to summon the steely resolve that had always propelled me through the chaos of my life. "Or are we just winging it like last time?" My attempt at levity hung in the air, a faint smile flickering at the corners of my mouth, but it was overshadowed by the weight of the task ahead.

He met my gaze, his expression a mixture of determination and unease. "We need to meet with someone who has information on the enemy's next move. A contact I thought I could trust." He hesitated, his brow furrowing as if the thought of this person stirred some old unease. "But I'm not so sure now. Trust is a tricky thing."

"Then we'll go in with our eyes wide open," I replied, bolstered by the familiar thrill of the chase. "Let's not repeat past mistakes, shall we? I'd like to avoid any more 'oops, I disappeared' scenarios if possible."

His lips twitched, and I could see a hint of relief in his expression, as though he had needed that moment of levity as much as I did. "Deal. We'll do this together, and if I feel the urge to run, I'll resist the impulse—at least until you're safely away."

"Good to know I'm the one keeping you grounded," I shot back, playfully nudging his shoulder. "But let's focus on not getting ourselves killed first, okay?"

As we started down the alley, the rain lightened to a mist, swirling around us like the ghosts of our past. Every step felt laden with history, yet the path ahead shimmered with possibilities. The flickering streetlights cast long shadows, and the sound of our footsteps echoed in the quiet. I couldn't shake the feeling that we were walking into a trap, a realization that sent a shiver down my spine.

"Where's this contact?" I asked, pulling my jacket tighter against the cool air that wrapped around us like a shroud.

"There's a bar a few blocks away, hidden in plain sight," he explained, glancing around as if assessing the danger lurking in every corner. "It's a dive, but it's got a reputation for discretion. If anyone knows what's happening, it'll be there."

The idea of entering a bar felt strangely nostalgic, as if we were falling back into our old routines. Yet the stakes were higher now. The thought of facing an unknown enemy filled my stomach with a mixture of dread and excitement. "So we're back to hunting for information in dark corners?" I asked, half teasing, half serious. "What's next? A mysterious informant with a scar and a penchant for riddles?"

"Maybe a cryptic warning about a 'wolf in sheep's clothing'?" he quipped, and I felt a rush of warmth at his playful banter.

We turned a corner, and the bar came into view—a small, nondescript building that blended seamlessly with the urban landscape. A flickering neon sign buzzed overhead, casting a pale glow onto the pavement. The door creaked open as we approached, and I felt a twinge of apprehension. This was the kind of place where secrets were exchanged, and I knew well enough how dangerous they could be.

Stepping inside was like stepping into another world. The dim lighting cast shadows over the faces of patrons hunched over their drinks, a muted symphony of murmurs and clinks of glass filling the air. My eyes scanned the room, landing on a figure at the bar—a man with a rugged demeanor and an aura of quiet authority. He was the kind of person who seemed to command attention without trying, and I could feel the tension in the air as we approached him.

"Dylan," my companion said, his voice steady as he nodded at the man. "We need to talk."

Dylan turned, his eyes narrowing slightly as they flicked between us. "I didn't expect to see you again, especially not with... company." His gaze lingered on me, assessing, evaluating, and I felt a flash of irritation.

"Now's not the time for games, Dylan," I said, trying to project confidence. "We need information, and we need it fast."

"Information isn't cheap, sweetheart," he replied, leaning back against the bar with an air of casual indifference that belied the tension in the room. "What are you willing to offer?"

"We're not here to barter," my companion interjected, a low growl of frustration creeping into his tone. "We have a mutual enemy, and if you know what's good for you, you'll help us."

Dylan's lips curled into a sly smile, a glint of mischief in his eyes. "Ah, I see. The old 'the enemy of my enemy is my friend' routine. How quaint." He gestured toward an empty table in the corner. "Why don't you take a seat? I'll pour you both a drink. If I'm going to help you, I'll need something to take the edge off this... delightful reunion."

With a shared glance that spoke volumes, we made our way to the table. The atmosphere was charged, the air thick with uncertainty. I couldn't shake the feeling that we were stepping deeper into a web we might not escape. As we settled into our seats, I caught the fleeting look of concern in my companion's eyes, a silent acknowledgment that we were treading on dangerous ground.

"Do you trust him?" I whispered, leaning closer as Dylan prepared drinks at the bar, his back turned to us.

"Not for a second," he admitted, his voice low and tense. "But he's our best shot at getting what we need."

"Great," I said, rolling my eyes. "Trust issues and potential betrayal. This is shaping up to be an excellent evening."

He chuckled softly, the tension between us easing for a moment. "Just keep your guard up. We need to be ready for anything."

As Dylan approached the table with two drinks, the tension in the air thickened once more. "To new beginnings," he said, raising his glass with a smirk, his eyes glinting with something unspoken. I caught a hint of menace lurking beneath the surface, like a storm brewing just out of sight.

"Let's skip the pleasantries," my companion replied, his tone hardening. "What do you know about the enemy?"

Dylan leaned in, lowering his voice as if sharing a precious secret. "I know more than you think. But the information comes at a cost—"

The bar door swung open with a violent creak, and all eyes turned toward the entrance. A chill raced down my spine as a figure stepped inside, silhouetted against the rain-soaked street. My heart raced as I recognized the familiar shape—a tall man in a dark coat, his face obscured by shadows.

"Get down!" I shouted instinctively, but it was too late. A shot rang out, echoing through the bar like thunder, and everything around me exploded into chaos.

Chapter 18: The Rise of Shadows

I had never been one to embrace the chaos of war, yet here I was, standing shoulder to shoulder with him, the weight of the impending battle hanging heavily in the air. The crisp morning breeze carried the scent of damp earth, mingled with the faint traces of smoke from distant fires. It whispered promises of change, of an end to the shadows that had lurked in the corners of our lives for too long. As the sun broke through the clouds, casting golden rays across the field where destiny would unfold, I felt a flicker of hope ignite within me.

With every day that passed in our training, our bond deepened. We were no longer merely allies; we had become a force to be reckoned with, a symphony of strength and determination. The clashing of our swords during practice sessions echoed like a heartbeat, each strike and parry a testament to our unwavering commitment to one another. I watched him—his hair tousled and wild, a smudge of dirt on his cheek—fighting not just against the specters of our enemies but against his own doubts, as I battled mine. In those moments of shared exhaustion, I found my sanctuary, my refuge from the swirling chaos that threatened to engulf us.

Each evening, we would collapse onto the grass, breathless and laughing, the laughter peeling away the layers of tension that had accumulated throughout the day. I cherished these moments of levity as we recounted our training mishaps: the time I misjudged a lunge and ended up tumbling into a thorny bush, or when he, in a particularly zealous attempt to demonstrate a new technique, managed to trip over his own feet. He laughed harder at my embarrassing moments than I did, a teasing glint in his eyes that sent warmth flooding through me. It was in those gentle jests that I found solace, a reminder that even amidst the gathering storm, joy could be found.

As twilight descended upon our makeshift camp, we would sit close, sharing stories that blurred the lines between past and present. He would speak of his childhood, of days spent in the sun-dappled woods, forging friendships that felt as eternal as the towering trees around them. I would share tales of my own youth—of laughter echoing through bustling streets, of dreams woven from the bright threads of possibility. We spoke of everything and nothing, and in those quiet exchanges, we wove our own tapestry, a shared narrative that anchored us in the midst of uncertainty.

The nights were often sleepless, plagued by the distant echoes of a darkness that never seemed far away. I could feel its pulse, a malignant force stirring in the depths of the forest that loomed at the edge of our training grounds. It loomed large and ominous, casting a shadow over our resolve. The whispered warnings from the wind felt like a herald of doom, a reminder that our enemy was not just a faceless adversary but a cunning and relentless foe. And yet, every time the fear threatened to creep in, I would look at him, and the certainty in his gaze would anchor me. We were two halves of a whole, and together, we could face the abyss.

The day of reckoning approached with a relentless inevitability, each sunrise a stark reminder that our moment was drawing near. As the air thickened with tension, our training intensified. We worked until our muscles burned and our minds blurred, each session a fierce dance of aggression and strategy. Our instructors watched with keen eyes, their sharp words cutting through our fatigue, pushing us to exceed our limits. I welcomed the pain; it was a testament to our growth, our transformation from fledgling warriors to a formidable duo.

But amidst the fervor, I sensed an undercurrent of change, a twist in the narrative that was unfolding. Whispers among the ranks hinted at a betrayal lurking within our midst, shadows skirting the edges of our camp, growing bolder with each passing day. I watched as alliances shifted, faces that had once radiated camaraderie now marred by suspicion. The threat was not merely external; it breathed within us, a gnawing doubt that could unravel our unity from within.

One evening, as we sat before the flickering fire, I turned to him, the crackling flames casting dancing shadows across his face. "Do you ever wonder if we're prepared for what's coming?" My voice, usually steady, trembled as the question escaped my lips.

He looked at me, his expression unreadable. "Preparedness is a funny thing. You can train for a lifetime, but when the moment arrives, everything can change." There was a weight to his words, a depth of understanding that echoed my own fears.

I swallowed hard, allowing his words to sink in. "What if we're not enough?" The vulnerability felt raw, like a gaping wound laid bare.

His hand found mine, warm and reassuring. "Together, we are more than enough. The shadows may grow, but they cannot consume what is forged in light." His confidence wrapped around me like a protective shield, igniting a flicker of determination within my chest.

But as the last embers of daylight faded, a chilling howl echoed through the woods, a sound that sent a shiver down my spine. It was a cry steeped in malevolence, a harbinger of the chaos that lay just beyond the trees. We both froze, the flicker of warmth between us snuffed out by the encroaching dread. This was it—the rise of shadows.

In that moment, I realized the truth: our battle was not just against an external enemy but against the very darkness that threatened to seep into our souls. And I understood that while the stakes were higher than ever, we had forged a connection that might just be our greatest weapon. The uncertainty loomed before us, but as we prepared to face the night, I felt a surge of resolve. Whatever awaited us, we would confront it together.

The night crept in like a thief, stealing the last vestiges of warmth from the day. The once vibrant hues of sunset surrendered to a blanket of inky darkness, the air thickening with a tension that felt almost palpable. I stood by the fire, its flickering light casting long shadows that danced around me, mirroring the unease curling in my gut. The crackling flames were a comfort, but they did little to quell the sense of foreboding that loomed like a storm on the horizon.

As I glanced around our makeshift camp, I could see the others preparing for what lay ahead. Each face bore the weight of uncertainty, eyes darting toward the encroaching forest as if it might spring to life at any moment. My heart raced, matching the cadence of their hushed conversations. They exchanged nervous glances, a silent acknowledgment that the enemy was no longer a distant threat but a looming reality. It was as if we could feel the darkness curling around us, hungry and waiting, and yet, in that moment, my gaze found him.

He stood a few paces away, silhouetted against the firelight, a bastion of strength amidst the uncertainty. The shadows played across his features, highlighting the determined set of his jaw and the fierce glint in his eyes. He caught my gaze and, for a heartbeat, the world around us faded away. I offered him a tentative smile, one that felt like a lifeline tossed in a stormy sea. He returned it, a flicker of warmth piercing through the encroaching chill. "Ready for another round?" he asked, his voice teasing, an anchor against the tide of fear threatening to pull us under.

"Only if you promise not to trip over your own sword this time," I shot back, a playful spark igniting between us. We both knew that humor was our shield, our way of keeping the darkness at bay, if only for a moment. I could see the tension in his shoulders ease slightly at my banter, and for a fleeting instant, I dared to believe we could face whatever came our way.

But the laughter was short-lived. As night deepened, the atmosphere shifted, thickening like a fog rolling in from the sea. A distant howl sliced through the air, its mournful tone sending shivers racing down my spine. The camp fell silent, a collective breath held as we all turned toward the forest. Shadows danced just beyond the treeline, whispering secrets that curled like smoke, tantalizing and terrifying. "I think they're getting bold," one of our comrades murmured, his voice barely above a whisper.

The air felt electric, charged with unspoken fears and the reality of our situation. It was as if the darkness had eyes, watching, waiting for us to falter. "We need to stay sharp," I said, my voice cutting through the tension. "We can't afford any slip-ups."

He nodded, his gaze unwavering. "Together. We'll face it together." It was a mantra, our shared promise, and I clung to it like a lifebuoy.

The night wore on, and our small group gathered around the fire, sharing stories and strategies in hushed tones. I felt the camaraderie wrap around us, a fragile but comforting cocoon against the encroaching dread. We talked of our training, the battles we had faced, and those yet to come, each word building a bridge of solidarity. But beneath the laughter and bravado, I sensed a current of fear, a hesitation that lingered like a shadow refusing to be cast away.

As the fire burned low, I leaned closer to him, seeking warmth and solace. "What do you think will happen when we confront them?" I asked, my voice barely above a whisper, though the question felt thunderous in the stillness.

He considered this, his brow furrowing as if wrestling with his thoughts. "I think... we'll have to make choices. Hard ones. The kind that could define who we are, who we become."

I swallowed hard, his words resonating in the depths of my mind. The weight of our choices was a burden I had not fully comprehended until that moment. "You're right," I admitted, the reality settling like a stone in my stomach. "But we won't let it define us. We'll write our own story, no matter what."

He smiled at that, a hint of admiration in his eyes, and I felt a surge of determination. No matter what lay ahead, we would fight not just for survival but for a future we could claim as our own.

The night deepened, and the shadows drew closer, weaving in and out of the darkness like tendrils of smoke. I closed my eyes for a moment, focusing on the warmth of the fire and the steady rhythm of his breathing beside me. It was a grounding force, a reminder that I was not alone.

Yet as the embers faded, a sudden commotion erupted from the outskirts of our camp, shattering the fragile peace. Shouts echoed through the trees, urgency lacing every syllable. I leaped to my feet, adrenaline flooding my veins as he grabbed my arm, eyes sharp with concern. "Stay close," he instructed, his voice firm.

We moved swiftly toward the source of the noise, hearts pounding in sync. The camp was in chaos, soldiers scrambling to grab their weapons, eyes darting toward the forest as the howls grew louder, more insistent. "They're coming!" someone yelled, panic rising like smoke in the air.

The moment stretched like a taut wire, each second heavy with the weight of inevitability. I could feel the shadows coalescing at the edges of our camp, a dark tide rolling in, and my breath quickened with fear. "What do we do?" I asked, trying to sound more certain than I felt.

"We fight. We hold our ground." His grip tightened on my hand, a lifeline amidst the chaos. "Remember everything we've trained for. We'll stand together."

His resolve fueled a fire within me. I nodded, steeling myself for what lay ahead. We moved as one, our hearts beating a fierce rhythm that echoed in the silence. This was it—no turning back now.

The darkness surged forward, a tide of shadows ready to swallow us whole, but I felt a flicker of courage ignite within me. Whatever came next, we would face it together.

As the first wave of darkness broke against our defenses, I drew my sword, the familiar weight grounding me. I was ready. We were ready. And in that moment, with the chaos swirling around us, I knew we were about to write our own story, one that would be forged in the fire of battle and the strength of our unbreakable bond.

The clash of steel rang out, sharp and immediate, slicing through the night as we took our positions on the battlefield. The air crackled with tension, heavy with the scent of impending chaos. My heart thundered in my chest, each beat a reminder of the stakes, a reminder that we were on the precipice of something monumental. I stole a glance at him, and the determined fire in his eyes ignited a spark of courage within me. This was it—our moment to stand firm against the encroaching shadows.

The enemy surged forth, dark figures moving like smoke and shadow, eyes glinting with malice. They were a swirling mass, a living embodiment of our fears, and I could feel the energy shifting around us, a tempest building as we braced ourselves for the onslaught. My grip tightened around my weapon, the familiar weight a comfort, grounding me amidst the chaos. "No fancy footwork this time, okay?" I shot at him, my tone light despite the gravity of our situation.

"Only if you promise not to lead with your chin," he quipped back, a grin flickering across his face, momentarily easing the tension that threatened to consume us.

The first wave of shadows crashed against our line, and suddenly, we were engulfed in a whirlwind of movement. Swords clashed, a cacophony of metal and cries filling the air, but amidst the chaos, I felt the rhythm of the battle settle into something almost primal. Every strike, every parry felt instinctual, as if the very essence of combat flowed through my veins. I moved with purpose, every swing of my sword a defiance against the darkness that sought to overwhelm us.

As I fought, I caught glimpses of him, a warrior in his own right, weaving through the throng with grace and strength. He was a force of nature, and I marveled at the way he seemed to flow with the fight, his movements a fluid dance amidst the chaos. The shadows roared as they pressed against us, but he stood resolute, deflecting their blows with a confidence that bolstered my own resolve.

Yet, the enemy was relentless. They pressed in closer, their snarls echoing in the night, and soon the fight became a desperate struggle for survival. I felt the weight of fatigue settle in my limbs, but I refused to waver. "They're not just fighting us," I shouted over the din. "They're trying to break our spirits!"

"Then let's make sure they fail," he replied, his voice cutting through the chaos like a beacon.

In that moment, I caught sight of a shadowy figure lurking at the edge of our formation, watching with eyes that glowed with an unsettling intensity. The figure was unlike the others—more solid, more menacing, as if it were the embodiment of darkness itself. An icy tendril of fear curled around my heart. "We need to take out that one!" I yelled, my voice strained. "It feels different!"

He nodded, a flash of determination in his gaze. "I'll create a distraction. You flank them from the side."

Before I could respond, he surged forward, charging toward the shadowy figure with reckless abandon. I watched, a surge of adrenaline coursing through me as he drew the attention of several dark warriors, his movements a calculated blend of aggression and agility. I took a deep breath, steeling myself for the task ahead.

As I slipped into the fray, weaving through the chaos, I felt the adrenaline coursing through my veins, sharpening my focus. I ducked under a sweeping strike, feeling the air rush past me, and then countered with a quick thrust of my blade, finding purchase in the side of a shadowy form. It let out a shriek that resonated in the night, but I had no time to celebrate the small victory; I was moving forward, intent on my target.

I found my opening, slipping past the clashing bodies, closing the distance to the ominous figure. It turned toward me, a grin spreading across its shadowy visage, revealing a glint of sharp teeth that sent a jolt of fear spiraling through me. "You think you can defeat the darkness?" it hissed, its voice a chilling echo that seemed to reverberate within my very bones.

"Maybe I don't need to defeat it," I shot back, my voice steadier than I felt. "I just need to hold it back."

With a fierce determination, I lunged forward, swinging my sword with all the strength I could muster. The figure darted to the side, its movements impossibly swift, and I barely managed to avoid a retaliatory strike aimed at my throat. I stumbled, regaining my balance, but in that moment, I realized I was not just fighting for my life; I was fighting for our future, for every moment we had shared.

Just then, a deafening roar erupted from the depths of the forest, the sound shaking the very ground beneath us. The shadows paused, a momentary stillness enveloping the battlefield, as if the world itself held its breath. I felt a chill crawl down my spine. "What was that?" I asked, my voice barely above a whisper.

But before I could contemplate the implications, the air rippled around us, an unseen force surging forward. A wall of darkness erupted from the forest, crashing toward our camp like a tidal wave. The shadows pressed in, their forms twisting and writhing, merging into one colossal entity—a living embodiment of despair.

"Fall back!" he shouted, his voice cutting through the confusion as he rushed toward me, his expression a mix of urgency and fear. "We can't hold this line!"

As we began to retreat, the ground trembled beneath our feet, the darkness stretching and reaching for us like fingers of ice. My heart raced, a visceral panic rising within me as I fought against the instinct to flee. "We can't just abandon our post!" I argued, but I felt the weight of his hand on my shoulder, grounding me.

"We need to regroup, to find a stronger position!" he insisted, pulling me back as the shadows closed in.

Just then, a flash of light erupted from the edge of the forest, illuminating the dark mass for a fleeting moment. A figure emerged, cloaked in brilliance, wielding a weapon that glowed with an ethereal light. "Hold your ground!" the figure called, a voice that resonated with authority and courage.

My breath caught in my throat. Who was this stranger, and what hope did they bring against the encroaching darkness?

But before I could voice my thoughts, the ground beneath us shifted violently, and I stumbled, losing my footing. I glanced up just in time to see the dark mass engulfing the figure, swallowing them whole in a rush of shadows. "No!" I cried out, reaching for them instinctively, but the darkness surged back, a chaotic wave crashing over us.

As I struggled to regain my balance, the last glimmer of light flickered and vanished, plunging us back into the depths of night. The shadows roared with triumph, the sound echoing through the battlefield, and I felt a dread unlike anything I had experienced before clawing at my heart.

"We have to go!" he shouted, urgency thrumming in his voice, but I hesitated, staring into the void where the figure had stood. "What if they were our only chance?"

His gaze was fierce, his grip on my arm unyielding. "We can't save anyone if we're consumed by the darkness ourselves!"

In that moment, I knew he was right. As the shadows pressed in, threatening to overtake us, I took a deep breath, steadied my resolve, and nodded. Together, we turned, racing toward the flickering firelight that still flickered against the encroaching dark. But as we moved, I couldn't shake the feeling that something more sinister lurked within the shadows, waiting for the perfect moment to strike.

The roar of the darkness echoed behind us, and with every pounding heartbeat, the chilling realization settled in: the battle was far from over.

Chapter 19: The Sacrifice

The wind howled through the ancient trees, their gnarled branches twisting against the stormy sky like the desperate fingers of lost souls reaching for salvation. I stumbled through the underbrush, my heart racing, adrenaline coursing through my veins as I searched for him. The battlefield lay sprawled behind me, a maelstrom of light and shadow, as if the heavens themselves were torn apart. Echoes of clashing swords and anguished cries reverberated in my ears, but the cacophony faded into a dull roar as panic clutched at my chest.

"Where are you?" I shouted, my voice barely rising above the tempest. I could feel the weight of the world bearing down on me, the stakes rising with every passing moment. Each step felt heavier, as if the very ground beneath me conspired to keep me from reaching him. I had to find him.

Through the chaos, I remembered his laughter, warm and inviting like a beacon amidst the shadows. It had been a bright note in a world painted with gray, a sound that could ignite hope even in the bleakest of times. I could see his face in my mind—those deep, dark eyes filled with mischief and determination, a smile that could chase away my fears. But now, that laughter felt like a distant echo, swallowed by the storm.

As I pushed forward, branches whipped at my arms, and rain lashed against my skin, but I pressed on, propelled by sheer will. The air was thick with the metallic scent of blood and the acrid tang of magic, a reminder of the sacrifices made on this cursed ground. In the distance, I glimpsed a flicker of light through the trees, a glimmer that beckoned me closer. My heart leaped, hope igniting within me as I sprinted toward it, my boots squelching in the mud.

The moment I burst into the clearing, the scene before me stole my breath. There he was, crumpled against the base of an ancient oak, its roots twisting around him like a protective embrace. But the sanctuary it offered was a cruel illusion. His shirt was torn, dark stains blooming against the fabric like flowers in a dying garden, and his face—oh, his face—was pale and drawn, framed by dark strands of hair plastered against his forehead.

"Please," I gasped, rushing to his side, my heart clenching at the sight of him so vulnerable. "Stay with me."

His eyes fluttered open, and for a moment, recognition flickered across his features, warmth mingling with pain. "You found me," he said, his voice a fragile whisper, like the delicate breath of a dying star. "I knew you would."

"No," I choked out, my fingers trembling as I reached for him, brushing the hair away from his forehead. "You can't leave me. Not like this."

He smiled, a bittersweet curve of his lips that made my heart ache. "For you," he murmured, the words barely escaping his lips. "I would do it all again."

The world around us fell silent, the chaos retreating like a tide, leaving only the two of us in this moment—a fragile bubble against the storm. But I could feel the chill creeping into his bones, the life slipping away as surely as the sun sinks beneath the horizon.

"No! Don't say that. We can fix this!" I cried, desperation clawing at my throat. I could hear the distant sounds of battle echoing, but they felt far away, muted by the pounding of my heart. "You're going to be okay. Just hold on."

"Look at me," he said softly, a fierce intensity in his gaze that pulled me in like gravity. "You have to understand... it's not just about me." His breath hitched, and I felt the weight of his words settle around us like a shroud. "I chose this. For you. To protect you."

My chest constricted, anger bubbling beneath the surface. "You can't just give up! You can't leave me like this!"

He shook his head slightly, wincing at the movement. "I'm not leaving you. I'll always be with you."

I pressed my hands against the wound, as if sheer force could mend what was broken, but the warmth seeped away like sand slipping through my fingers. "You need to fight! Please, fight for us."

His gaze softened, a profound love shimmering in the depths of his eyes, but it was tinged with sadness, a knowing acceptance that twisted the knife deeper in my heart. "You are my fight," he breathed, and I felt the energy of his words wrapping around us like a blanket, binding us together even as the light in his eyes flickered.

The air thickened with an unseen weight, a pressure that made it hard to breathe. The world outside our little bubble faded, replaced by a quiet understanding that I didn't want to acknowledge. I felt my heart shatter, each piece piercing through me like glass. "You can't... you can't go," I whispered, tears spilling down my cheeks, mixing with the rain.

He reached out, his fingers brushing against my cheek, warm despite the coldness enveloping him. "Promise me," he said, his voice a mere breath. "Promise me you'll live. You'll find a way to carry on."

"No!" I shouted, rage and despair crashing through me. "I refuse to let you go!"

But deep down, I knew the truth, a truth that clawed at my insides. The shadows were encroaching, and I could feel his strength waning. In that moment, something within me shifted, a deep-seated resolve hardening like steel. "I'll save you," I declared, every ounce of my being igniting with the power of that promise. "I'll do whatever it takes."

His smile returned, fragile but fierce. "You are my light," he whispered, and in that heartbeat, everything changed.

With a surge of energy, I grasped his hand, intertwining our fingers. In that connection, I felt the depth of our bond, a love forged through trials and sacrifice. And in the storm, I swore to him and to myself that I would not let this be the end. I would fight for him, for us, no matter the cost.

The moment I clasped his hand, a current of energy surged between us, crackling like the first spark of a fire igniting in the dark. I could feel the weight of his pain pressing against me, but alongside it flowed a thread of hope—thin and fragile but bright enough to cast away the shadows that threatened to engulf us. The rain intensified, each drop a reminder of the world outside our bubble, yet inside, it was just him and me, the heartbeats echoing like a drum urging me forward.

"I'm going to get you out of here," I declared, my voice trembling with an emotion I could no longer contain. The wind howled around us, an uninvited guest, but I focused on his gaze, steady and reassuring. "You're going to live, and we're going to laugh about this one day."

"Laughing, huh?" His lips curled into a faint smile, but the moment was fleeting, dimmed by the shadow of pain that crossed his features. "What's the punchline? 'How I nearly bled out under a tree while my girlfriend played nursemaid?'"

I chuckled despite the gravity of our situation, shaking my head as I wiped away my tears with the back of my hand. "I'll think of something better than that. Give me time."

A brief silence fell between us, punctuated by the distant sounds of battle, but I could feel the current between us shifting. It was as if our shared laughter, light as air, was stirring something deep within the magic that pulsed in the air around us. I had no idea if it would work, but desperation is a powerful motivator, and my heart was a furnace of determination.

"I can't lose you," I said, squeezing his hand tighter. "Not now. Not ever."

"Then fight for me," he urged, his voice a mere breath, but filled with an urgency that made my heart race. "You have more power than you know. Channel it. Use it."

His words struck a chord deep within, resonating with a truth I had always felt but never fully embraced. I closed my eyes, centering myself, grounding my spirit in the chaos that surrounded us. The winds howled and the rain lashed at my skin, but in that moment, I felt as though the entire universe hinged on my ability to draw strength from within.

"Okay," I breathed, letting the air fill my lungs, finding the quiet within the storm. "Together, then."

As I opened my eyes, I could see the flickering lights around us intensifying, glowing with a warmth that felt almost alive. I drew upon every memory of joy, every moment of laughter we'd shared, and with it, I ignited the magic swirling around us, weaving it into a tapestry of hope and love. The very fabric of the world shifted, resonating with my intentions, the air shimmering with possibilities.

The moment the energy surged through me, I felt the connection between us flare to life. It was as if I had unlocked a door to a reservoir of strength that had lain dormant, just waiting for this moment. I focused on him, willing every ounce of my power into his being. "Stay with me," I whispered, the words more a prayer than a plea.

The light that enveloped us pulsed, dancing around us, and I could see the shadows retreating in its wake, drawn back by the brilliance of our bond. His face shifted from pain to something resembling relief, and I felt his fingers respond, squeezing mine as the warmth spread through him, filling the spaces the darkness had claimed.

"You're... you're doing it," he breathed, awe threading through his voice. "I can feel it."

"Of course you can. I told you I'd fight," I replied, determination pouring from my heart into my words. "Now just hold on."

And he did. With every beat of my heart, I felt him tethered to me, our lives intertwined like the roots of the ancient tree behind him. The chaos of battle faded, the cries of the warriors blending into a harmonious symphony that urged us forward. It was a dance of light and dark, and together, we were crafting a new rhythm, a melody woven from our shared dreams and defiance.

Yet, just as I dared to hope that our love might conquer even death, a piercing cry sliced through the air, yanking me back into the reality of our situation. My heart sank as I turned, drawn by the sound, only to see the dark shapes of figures emerging from the mist—a host of enemies, shadows cloaked in malice, their intent clear as they approached with malevolent grace.

"Stay close," I commanded, my voice steadying, a resolve building within me like a tidal wave. I could feel his heartbeat synchronize with mine, the warmth of his presence a reminder that I wasn't alone in this fight. "We're not done yet."

The figures advanced, their eyes gleaming like polished stones, cold and empty. It would have been easy to falter in the face of their cruelty, but there was a fire igniting in my chest, a fierce love that made me bold.

"Let's give them a show," I said, a wry grin tugging at my lips, and despite the gravity of our circumstances, I felt the familiar spark of mischief bubble up. "Shall we?"

"Always," he replied, his voice steadier now, an echo of the strength he had instilled in me.

As the first shadow lunged, I drew upon the light within, releasing it like a storm, a cascade of energy bursting forth. It wrapped around us, illuminating the clearing as I directed the power outward, surging toward our attackers. They recoiled, momentarily caught off guard by the unexpected brightness, and for a fleeting moment, hope flickered in my chest like a candle against the dark.

But as the shadows faltered, a darker force surged from their ranks—a figure cloaked in the deepest night, his presence a palpable void that seemed to suck the light from the air. My heart raced as he approached, a wicked smile spreading across his lips, a sinister gleam in his eyes that sent a shiver down my spine.

"Ah, what a touching reunion," he taunted, his voice smooth like silk but laced with venom. "But love, my dear, can only take you so far."

I steeled myself, every instinct screaming to protect him, to shield us from this encroaching darkness. "You don't understand," I shot back, my voice firm despite the tremor in my hands. "We've fought too hard to be torn apart now."

The shadowy figure merely chuckled, an unsettling sound that echoed through the trees. "Ah, but you underestimate the power of despair."

In that moment, I felt the world teeter on the brink. I could see the darkness swirling around us, threatening to snuff out the light we had just ignited. But within me, I sensed a flicker of resistance, a spark of our bond that would not be extinguished. I turned to him, meeting his eyes with unwavering resolve.

"Together," I whispered, and as we braced ourselves for the confrontation, I knew one thing with absolute certainty: whatever happened next, I would not let him face it alone.

The air crackled with tension, a thick, electric hum that resonated deep within me as I faced the looming darkness. It twisted around the shadowy figure like a cloak, a malevolent force that exuded a palpable dread, taunting us with its very presence. His eyes, two dark voids, glinted with amusement, a predator reveling in the hunt. I felt a surge of protectiveness wash over me, instinctive and raw, igniting my spirit like kindling in a fire.

"Love is sweet," he purred, his voice smooth as silk yet laced with malice. "But it makes you weak. You don't understand what you're up against."

"Please," I shot back, finding my voice, steady despite the quaking of my heart. "You don't know anything about love." I stepped forward, drawing strength from the warmth of my companion's presence beside me, the bond we'd forged shimmering like a shield against the encroaching shadows. "It's not a weakness; it's a weapon."

He laughed, a sound devoid of joy, echoing eerily against the surrounding trees. "How quaint. But let's see how you wield it."

As he spoke, the shadows behind him began to shift and coalesce, forming dark tendrils that lashed out toward us like serpents seeking to ensnare their prey. I felt the air grow thick with dread as they surged forward, curling around my ankles, pulling me down into the depths of despair. I could feel my heart racing, but amidst the chaos, a flicker of resolve ignited within me.

"Now!" I shouted, channeling everything I had into a surge of light that pulsed outward. It burst forth from my fingertips, illuminating the darkness with a radiant glow, pushing back against the tendrils that sought to bind me.

"Is that the best you can do?" the shadow figure sneered, his confidence unshakeable, but I could see the flicker of doubt in his eyes. My heart pounded as the tendrils recoiled, their advance halted momentarily by the sheer force of our connection.

"We can do better," my companion chimed in, his voice gaining strength as the light wrapped around us both, a cocoon of brilliance against the encroaching dark. "Together."

With a fierce nod, I concentrated harder, drawing upon the well of magic that surged within me, fueled by love and determination. The air shimmered with energy, swirling around us like a tempest. "Let's show him what love really means."

In that instant, we released a torrent of light, cascading outwards like a wave crashing against the shore, enveloping everything in its path. The shadow figure faltered, his confident smirk faltering, the tendrils dissipating as the light seared through the darkness like a comet streaking through the night sky.

But just as victory seemed within reach, a sinister grin stretched across his face, and I felt a sudden shift in the air, an unsettling chill that swept through the clearing. "Foolish children," he hissed, the shadows swirling around him like a storm, gathering force and intensity. "You think you've won?"

With a flick of his wrist, the darkness coalesced into a vortex, spiraling outwards with a vengeance. I could feel the energy shift, an oppressive force that bore down upon us, threatening to extinguish the light we had fought so hard to wield.

"Stay close!" I yelled, reaching for my companion, my fingers brushing against his in a desperate grip. Together, we formed an unbreakable line of defense, the warmth of our connection a lifeline against the encroaching shadows.

But as the darkness swelled, I could see the tendrils reforming, coiling around us with a vicious intent, their edges sharp as knives. "What is this?" I gasped, panic rising within me. "We can't let it take us!"

"Focus!" he urged, his voice steady even as the tendrils brushed against his skin, seeking to wound. "We have to push back harder!"

Gathering all my strength, I summoned the light again, but this time, I concentrated on the source of my power: the bond we shared, the laughter, the love that had ignited in the depths of our souls. "You will not take him!" I shouted into the maelstrom, channeling every ounce of my magic into the light, directing it toward the dark figure that loomed ahead.

The vortex roared, a cacophony of chaos that threatened to drown us, yet I felt the magic responding to my call, gathering around us in a brilliant explosion. The force erupted outward, striking the shadow figure directly in the chest, and for a moment, everything seemed suspended in time.

But just as victory was within my grasp, a bone-chilling scream pierced the air, echoing with the sound of shattering glass. I turned, my heart plummeting as I saw him, my companion, caught in the tendrils' grasp, a look of horror etched across his face.

"No!" I cried out, reaching for him, but the darkness clamped down, pulling him away from me, his body twisting like a marionette in the hands of a cruel puppeteer. "Let him go!"

"You think your love can save you?" the shadow figure spat, his voice dripping with disdain. "I will feast upon it, and your bond will only make me stronger!"

The tendrils tightened around him, squeezing as he struggled against their grip, his eyes locking onto mine, filled with both fear and fierce determination. "Fight!" he shouted, desperation lacing his words. "You can't give in! Don't let him win!"

The weight of his plea hit me like a tidal wave, and I felt something shift deep within me. A fierce protectiveness ignited in my heart, a flame that surged with an intensity I had never known. The shadows danced around me, but this time, they only fueled my resolve.

With a roar that echoed through the clearing, I channeled every ounce of power I possessed, summoning the magic of our bond, the warmth of every memory we had shared. "You will not take him from me!" I screamed, unleashing a burst of light that erupted from my core, enveloping the darkness in a brilliant explosion.

The tendrils recoiled, shrieking as they retreated from the force of my magic. But in that split second of hope, a realization struck me like a bolt of lightning: the shadow figure was not just a foe; he was a manifestation of everything we had fought against, every doubt that threatened to tear us apart.

"Together!" I shouted, my voice ringing with newfound clarity. "We are stronger than this!"

But as I focused on my companion, desperation clawing at my insides, I noticed the shadows creeping back, coiling around him with a sinister intent. Just as I gathered my strength for another strike, the ground beneath us trembled violently, a crack splitting the earth in a jagged line between us.

"NO!" I cried, reaching out, but the darkness surged forward, the shadows swallowing him whole as the ground erupted. I felt the pull of the abyss beneath me, a void threatening to consume everything in its path.

In that moment, time stood still, and all I could see was the look of sheer determination on his face as he vanished into the darkness. The light flickered, and with a heart-wrenching clarity, I realized that the battle was far from over.

The darkness roared around me, but I was not finished yet. Gripping the remnants of my magic tightly, I prepared to confront the shadow figure with renewed fury. I would not let fear dictate my fate; not when everything I loved hung in the balance.

With a fierce scream, I launched myself toward the swirling shadows, determined to reclaim what was lost, but as I leaped forward, the darkness engulfed me, and I felt the world slip away into the abyss.

Chapter 20: Bound by Fire

The air is thick with the acrid scent of burnt wood and scorched earth, remnants of a world caught in the grip of chaos. Shadows dance along the ruins, twisted remnants of what once was, their edges softened by the swirling smoke that clings to everything like a second skin. I can feel the weight of the night pressing down on me, a shroud that makes my heart race with both fear and determination. This isn't just a battlefield; it's a crucible, and we are forged in the flames of desperation.

I lean closer, cradling his head in my lap, feeling the roughness of the ground beneath me, gritty and unyielding. He's fading, and with every labored breath, the world shifts around us. The earth beneath is a silent witness to our pain, absorbing it like a sponge, and I can't help but think of the lives lost, the stories ended too soon. I brush my fingers across his brow, tracing the lines of his face, memorizing the angles that once held laughter and light. I can't let go. Not now. Not ever.

"Stay with me," I whisper, my voice cracking under the weight of desperation. "You can't leave. Not like this."

His eyelids flutter as if he's caught between two worlds, the one filled with the warmth of life and this bitter one, heavy with the scent of ash. "I'm... I'm trying," he rasps, and a spark ignites within me. It's faint but present, like the first rays of dawn pushing against the night.

I close my eyes, feeling the energy pulse between us, hot and electric. There's a history here, woven into the very fabric of our souls—a tapestry of shared glances, unspoken words, and moments that defy the passage of time. I can't fathom the depth of what we've experienced together, but I know it's not finished. Not yet.

A faint chuckle escapes his lips, laced with pain, and it pulls me back from the edge of despair. "You always did have a flair for the dramatic," he teases, his eyes flickering open to meet mine, their depths reflecting a kaleidoscope of emotions—fear, longing, love. It's enough to stoke the embers of my hope.

"Dramatic? You're the one bleeding out in the middle of a battlefield," I reply, forcing a grin through the tears threatening to spill. "I mean, really. Could you be any more cliché?"

The ghost of a smile flits across his face, illuminating the darkness momentarily. "And yet here you are, the heroine, saving the day... again."

"Someone has to," I quip, my heart swelling with a fierce pride. We've faced so much together, our lives intertwining like the branches of an ancient tree, each challenge only strengthening our bond. I draw in a breath, filling my lungs with the smoky air, tasting the bitter tang of fear and resolve. "I won't let you go. Not now. Not ever."

With every word, I channel my energy into him, willing him to fight, to draw upon the strength we've built together. The world around us fades into a blur, the distant sounds of the aftermath muffled as if we exist in a bubble, a moment suspended in time. I can feel the connection deepening, a swirling force that binds us, a magic I can't quite name but know in my bones. It's ancient and raw, and it pulls at the very core of who we are.

"Do you remember the fireflies?" he asks suddenly, his voice growing fainter, but the smile on his lips is bright, illuminating the shadowy recesses of our reality. "That summer by the lake? You danced like they were the stars, like you could catch them in your hands."

"Of course I remember," I reply, my voice steady despite the tremors of fear in my chest. "You were supposed to catch them for me, but you just stood there, mesmerized."

"I couldn't help it," he murmurs, his eyes drifting closed. "You were... you were magic. Just like this."

A swell of energy courses through me, igniting the air between us, and I clench his hand tighter. "Then let's create more magic. Remember the way they lit up the darkness? We can do that again."

His eyes flutter open again, the weight of reality crashing against the barrier I've created. "It's not... it's not that simple," he gasps, pain flickering across his features. "You can't save me. This—this is it."

But there's a stubbornness in my heart, a refusal to accept defeat. "You don't get to decide that. Not when I'm still here. Not when we have this connection."

As the darkness threatens to swallow him, I lean in, pressing my forehead against his. I can feel the warmth of his skin, the pulse of life still racing beneath the surface. "Fight for me," I plead, my voice barely a whisper, trembling with emotion. "Fight for us."

And in that moment, I realize that love is a fierce, unyielding force, a flame that can't be extinguished by fear or doubt. As he holds my gaze, I can see it—the flicker of hope reigniting in his eyes, a flicker that promises more than just survival. It promises a future, one we can seize together, and I won't let it slip away.

Together, we can rise from the ashes. Together, we are bound by fire, and nothing—nothing—can extinguish that flame.

His grip tightens around my fingers, sending a jolt of warmth surging through me, and for a fleeting moment, the battlefield dissolves into a hazy backdrop, replaced by memories that wash over us like waves. I can almost hear the laughter of our friends, echoing in the distance, where sunlight spills across the grass, and the air is filled with the sweet scent of wildflowers. It's strange how the heart can cling to such vivid snapshots, even amid the chaos and destruction.

"You remember that time at the fair?" he murmurs, his voice gaining strength. "The cotton candy incident?"

I can't help but chuckle, the sound bubbling up unexpectedly, a glimmer of normalcy piercing through the haze of despair. "Oh, how could I forget? You thought you could eat an entire bag without feeling sick. You were green for days."

His laughter mingles with mine, a melody stitched together with threads of memory, and it's enough to stoke the fire between us. "I still maintain it was worth it," he insists, a mischievous glint sparking in his eyes. "What's a little nausea in the name of sugar?"

"You're a true romantic, you know that?" I tease, relief flooding through me like a balm. "Nothing says love like a stomachache from a dubious food choice."

The laughter is a lifeline, tethering us to the world beyond the blood-stained earth. I can feel the pulse of magic between us, a shimmering thread weaving through the air, binding us together, even in this moment of peril. The energy is alive, thrumming with potential, and I can't shake the feeling that we're on the cusp of something extraordinary.

"I wish we could go back," he says, his expression softening as the laughter fades. "To before all this."

"Trust me, I'd love to. But we can't just sit here reminiscing forever," I reply, my voice a blend of determination and warmth. "We need to find a way out of this mess."

His brow furrows, a storm gathering in his gaze. "What if there isn't a way? What if this is it?"

A chill runs through me, and I force myself to meet his gaze, defiance coursing through my veins. "Not while I'm still breathing. We've faced worse, remember? We're a team. We don't give up."

A flicker of hope sparks in his eyes, but it's quickly eclipsed by uncertainty. "What if I'm too far gone? What if I can't fight anymore?"

"Don't you dare say that," I say, the words sharper than I intended. "You've survived everything thrown your way. You're not getting off that easily."

The tension in the air shifts, a palpable weight pressing against us, and for a moment, I wonder if I'm pushing too hard, testing the limits of his strength. But I can't back down. Not now. "You're stronger than you know. Remember the time you took on those bullies at school? You stood up for that kid even when you were outnumbered. You didn't hesitate."

"I had you cheering me on," he counters, his voice barely above a whisper. "I'm not sure I can do this alone."

"You're not alone," I insist, my heart racing as I squeeze his hand tighter. "I'm right here. You're not getting rid of me that easily."

As if to emphasize my point, the ground beneath us trembles, a low rumble resonating through the earth, and a plume of smoke rises into the night sky, swirling ominously. The distant sounds of battle echo, a reminder of the chaos still raging beyond our fragile bubble of connection.

"See? Just another obstacle," I say, forcing a grin, though my stomach knots with anxiety. "We've always thrived on chaos, haven't we?"

He exhales slowly, a mix of resignation and determination playing across his features. "What's the plan then, oh fearless leader?"

I pause, the weight of the moment crashing down as I sift through the chaotic mess of options in my mind. "First, we need to get you stabilized. We can't leave if you're still... like this."

He gestures weakly toward the remnants of our surroundings, his eyes narrowing with concentration. "What about the supplies? I saw a medic tent back there before the—"

I cut him off, urgency boiling in my blood. "We'll go to the medic tent, but I need you to focus on staying with me. No zoning out, no drifting away. Promise?"

"I promise," he replies, the corners of his mouth twitching in a half-smile. "But you know how stubborn I can be."

"Stubbornness is my favorite quality," I say, shooting him a wink. "Now let's get you on your feet."

With a careful heave, I pull him up, the effort leaving me breathless, and he leans against me, his weight both comforting and alarming. We move slowly, each step a dance with uncertainty, our surroundings cloaked in shadows, the scent of smoke still lingering, reminding us of the peril that lingers just outside our fragile sanctuary.

"Why do I get the feeling that this is one of those moments where we look back and laugh about how ridiculous we were?" he muses, his voice a low rumble against my shoulder.

"Because you're an optimist at heart," I reply, trying to mask the tremor of fear beneath my words. "And because I refuse to let this be the end of our story."

As we inch forward, I catch glimpses of the devastation around us—the charred remains of once-vibrant life, the flickering shadows of figures moving in the distance, a haunting reminder of what we're up against. The air crackles with tension, a promise of danger lurking just beyond the horizon, but there's also a thrill, a sense of purpose that fuels my every step.

Together, we push through the darkness, bound by a connection that defies all logic, fighting for a future that remains tantalizingly out of reach. But I refuse to let go, and I can feel the fire between us growing stronger with every heartbeat, igniting a determination that cannot be extinguished.

We stumble forward, our steps heavy with the weight of our shared resolve. The chaos around us is relentless—a symphony of distant shouts, the crackling of flames licking at the remnants of our world, and the low rumble of something ominous lurking just beyond our view. I can feel the adrenaline coursing through my veins, an electric pulse that ignites my every nerve ending, pushing me onward despite the dark tendrils of doubt creeping in at the edges of my mind.

"Are you sure you're up for this?" I ask, glancing sideways at him as we navigate the uneven ground. "I mean, I'm not exactly qualified to be a battlefield medic."

He smirks, though it's strained, a shadow of his usual brightness. "You've done enough saving for one night. I think we'll survive a few more minutes."

"Famous last words," I retort, trying to inject some levity into the dire situation. "You sound like my mom before a family road trip."

"Road trips? Is that your idea of a good time? Sounds like you're the one who needs to get out more."

"Hey! I'm just saying—if we survive this, we could hit the coast. It's got to be better than waiting for doom here."

He chuckles softly, and it warms my heart, driving away some of the encroaching darkness. We make our way through the debris, and I guide him with an arm around his waist, careful to keep him steady. The medic tent looms ahead, a stark white against the encroaching night, flickering lanterns illuminating the entrance like beacons of hope amidst the despair.

"Almost there," I assure him, my voice barely above a whisper, as if speaking too loudly might shatter the fragile moment we've created.

Just as we reach the entrance, a shadow looms nearby, a figure slipping through the smoke like a ghost. My heart races as I recognize the familiar outline. "Wait!" I call out, instinctively stepping forward, but the figure shifts back into the darkness.

"Who is it?" he asks, his brow furrowed, instinctively tensing beside me.

"I don't know," I reply, my pulse quickening as I strain to catch a glimpse. "But we should be careful."

Before I can decide our next move, the figure emerges from the shadows, revealing a face I thought I'd never see again. It's Leo, his expression a mix of relief and urgency that sends a jolt of energy through me.

"There you are!" he exclaims, his voice hoarse yet vibrant. "I've been looking everywhere! We need to get you both out of here!"

"Leo!" I gasp, half in disbelief, half in joy. "What happened? How did you find us?"

"I followed the smoke and the sound of chaos," he explains, glancing anxiously at the tent. "It's not safe here. The enemy is regrouping, and I don't think we have much time before they start sweeping through."

"Great, just what we need—more bad news," I mutter, but the resolve in Leo's eyes sharpens my focus.

"We have to move. You both look like you could use a miracle," he adds, glancing pointedly at the way my arm supports my companion. "Especially you," he says, turning his attention to him. "Can you walk?"

"I can manage," he replies, though his voice is strained.

"Let's get you inside for a moment," Leo urges, waving us toward the tent, and I reluctantly comply, dragging my feet. The air inside is heavy with antiseptic and the low hum of chatter. A few injured soldiers lie on makeshift cots, their expressions ranging from grim determination to sheer pain.

"Help is on the way," Leo assures me, motioning toward a nurse hustling nearby. "But we need to move quickly. There's a path through the back that leads to the forest. If we can get there, we might stand a chance."

"Why the forest?" I question, a wave of unease washing over me. "Isn't that where we just came from?"

"Yes, but the enemy isn't likely to pursue into the trees," Leo explains, his voice steady and calm. "They're more focused on the chaos in the city. We can slip away unnoticed."

"Not if we don't hurry," I urge, trying to keep panic at bay. "What if they find us before we escape?"

"That's why we can't waste time," Leo insists, glancing over his shoulder as if the shadows themselves might be listening. "We have to move. Now."

We make our way through the tent, weaving between the cots, and I can't shake the feeling of dread pooling in my stomach. I want to trust Leo, but the stakes are impossibly high, and I can't help but feel that time is slipping through my fingers like sand.

"Stay close to me," I instruct my companion, feeling the heat of his body pressing against mine as we reach the rear exit. I can hear the chaos outside—shouts, the crack of gunfire, the rumble of distant explosions—but I also hear something else, a low thrumming that resonates deep within my bones.

"Can you hear that?" I whisper, glancing at Leo.

"What?" he asks, pausing mid-step, his eyes scanning the darkness.

"That noise. It's...different. Almost like..."

The sound crescendos, drowning out the chaos of the night, a deep rumble that feels like it's pulling at the very core of the earth. I exchange a worried glance with my companion just as the ground shakes violently beneath our feet, and the air grows thick with dust and fear.

"Run!" Leo shouts, the urgency in his voice slicing through the confusion.

We dart out into the night, adrenaline propelling us forward, the medic tent disappearing behind us as the ground quakes beneath our feet. My heart pounds as I glance back, half expecting to see the remnants of the battle swallowing us whole.

But then I freeze, an icy wave of terror washing over me as I spot a dark shape emerging from the smoke—a figure cloaked in shadows, the very embodiment of menace, its presence like a harbinger of doom.

"Go! Now!" Leo urges, shoving us forward, and as we sprint into the forest's embrace, I can feel the darkness trailing behind us, a relentless force that refuses to be shaken off.

Branches whip at my face as we crash through the underbrush, and I can't help but feel the weight of fate pressing down upon us. The figure lingers in my mind, a haunting specter of the unknown, and I'm left with one burning question: how far can we run before it catches up to us?

The answer, I fear, lies just ahead, veiled in shadows and secrets waiting to unfold.

Chapter 21: Secrets in the Ashes

The cathedral, with its towering spires and intricate stained glass, stood like a guardian against the encroaching twilight, cloaked in shadows and the lingering scent of incense. Each breath I took was laced with a hint of aged wood and the faintest whisper of history, as if the very stones were alive, holding the echoes of prayers and confessions long past. We had stumbled into this sanctuary, seeking refuge from the chaos that had become our lives, and it felt as though we had been cradled in the arms of a benevolent spirit.

The flickering candlelight danced around us, illuminating the rough edges of our souls. I sank into the warmth of his embrace, feeling the steady thrum of his heartbeat against my cheek. It was a comforting rhythm amidst the uncertainty that had become our constant companion. As he held me, I could sense the weight of his past pressing against us, a heavy blanket woven from grief and unspoken truths. His voice, low and gravelly, cut through the silence like a blade, each word layered with emotion.

"I never wanted this life," he began, his gaze fixed on the flickering flames. "I thought I could carve out a future, one that didn't involve running or hiding."

I tightened my grip on him, urging him to continue. "What happened?"

He drew in a shuddering breath, the kind that seemed to pull from the depths of his being. "It's not a pretty story. I grew up in a place where survival meant loyalty, and loyalty meant blood." His voice cracked slightly, and I felt a pang in my chest as if I were catching a glimpse of the boy he once was, before the world had hardened him into the man standing before me. "When you're raised in the shadows, you learn to wear a mask. I had my share of secrets—things I'd rather forget."

I felt my heart twist in sympathy. "You don't have to share if you don't want to. I'm here for you, no matter what."

"No, you deserve to know." He turned to face me, and in the soft light, his eyes glimmered with a mixture of vulnerability and determination. "When I was sixteen, my father got involved with people who didn't play by the rules. They thought they could use our family's name to further their own ambitions. I watched him lose everything—his respect, his integrity. And in the end, he lost his life. I was supposed to protect him, to stand by his side, but I was just a kid."

The confession hung heavy in the air, and I could feel the bitterness seeping through the cracks in his facade. I brushed my fingers along his jawline, my touch tender, inviting him to release the burden he carried. "I can't imagine what that was like."

"It was hell," he said, the fire in his voice rising, fueled by memories. "I found myself at a crossroads. Either I followed in my father's footsteps, into a world of darkness, or I fought back. I chose the latter, but it cost me—my childhood, my friends, everything."

I wanted to reach into his past, to erase the scars that marred his soul, but I knew I couldn't. Instead, I focused on the present, the warmth of our shared space enveloping us like a cocoon. "And now?" I asked softly, hoping to guide him back to the light. "What do you want now?"

He paused, his brow furrowing as he searched for the right words. "I want to be free. Free from the ghosts that haunt me. Free to live without fear." His gaze met mine, fierce and unwavering. "But I can't do that alone. I need you."

The admission startled me, a surge of warmth flooding my chest. I had always thought of him as the protector, the one who held the pieces together while I shattered. Yet here he was, baring his soul, revealing his vulnerabilities. "You have me," I replied, my voice firm. "No matter what happens next, we're in this together."

He smiled then, a bittersweet curve of his lips that lit up his face. In that moment, the darkness that had shrouded us seemed to lift, replaced by a glimmer of hope. "You're the light I never knew I needed."

Outside, the night thickened, and a chill crept through the cracks in the ancient stone walls. Yet inside, the warmth of our connection ignited a fire that pushed back the encroaching cold. As he leaned in, his forehead resting against mine, I could feel the electricity between us, a spark that ignited the very air. The world around us faded, leaving only the two of us, entwined in the tender moment that felt both fragile and unbreakable.

"I wish I could give you the world," he murmured, his breath brushing against my lips like a caress.

I chuckled softly, the sound echoing in the hollow space. "You don't need to give me anything. Just be here. That's enough."

But his expression shifted, a shadow passing over his features. "What if being here puts you in danger? What if I can't protect you the way I want to?"

I pulled back slightly, looking deep into his eyes, searching for the doubts that lurked beneath the surface. "You've already done so much for me. You've protected me more than anyone ever has. But you can't keep me safe from everything. I'm not asking you to be my shield. I just want you—who you are, scars and all."

For a heartbeat, silence enveloped us, a fragile truce woven from trust and unspoken promises. In that sacred space, I understood: love was not just the moments of joy and light; it was the willingness to face the darkness together. The shadows of his past didn't frighten me; instead, they made me more resolute in my desire to stand by his side, to be the anchor he needed as much as I needed him.

And as the flickering candles continued to sway, casting whimsical shadows upon the walls, I knew that whatever lay ahead, we would face it together, united in our resolve and the hope of a future born from the ashes of our intertwined histories.

As we lingered in that sacred space, the soft flicker of candlelight illuminated the contours of his face, each shadow and highlight weaving a tapestry of emotions that left me breathless. I leaned in closer, the warmth of his body radiating against the cool stone, my heart racing with the uncharted territory we were exploring together. The air crackled with unspoken words, a tension that felt both exhilarating and terrifying.

"I wish I could forget all of it," he murmured, his voice barely more than a breath. "But memories are relentless little bastards." He chuckled softly, the sound tinged with irony, and it made my heart ache anew. The strength he exuded was undeniable, yet here he was, peeling back the layers, revealing the boy behind the warrior.

"What if we tried?" I suggested playfully, a mischievous grin breaking through the weight of our conversation. "We could just declare today a national 'Forget Your Past' day. Surely there's a holiday for that somewhere."

He laughed, a rich sound that reverberated through the empty nave, momentarily dispelling the darkness that clung to us. "I'm pretty sure that would be a short-lived celebration. But I like the spirit of it. Maybe we could at least make a pact to focus on the future instead of the shadows."

The prospect of a shared future felt like a fragile promise, a light at the end of a tunnel we had both been navigating. "Let's make it a grand adventure," I declared, my voice buoyed by a sudden surge of optimism. "We can create new memories that drown out the old ones. A scavenger hunt across the city, perhaps? We could map out our own little quests, collect stories instead of regrets."

His eyes sparkled with a mixture of intrigue and amusement. "You're on. But fair warning: I'm terrible at following maps. I'm more of a 'let's get lost and see what happens' type."

"Lost, huh? I'll keep that in mind next time we need to find our way to safety," I teased, nudging him playfully. There was something intoxicating about the ease of our banter, a delicate thread weaving us together even tighter.

"Let's hope we don't have to worry about safety anytime soon," he replied, his tone growing serious again. "I don't want to drag you into my mess."

"Too late for that," I shot back, my voice laced with playful defiance. "I'm already knee-deep in the chaos of your life, remember? Besides, if I didn't want to be here, I would've left when I had the chance."

The weight of my words hung between us, a delicate truce in the face of uncertainty. He took a breath, the tension shifting into something softer, as if the very act of sharing had lightened his burden, if only slightly. "You're stronger than you realize," he said, and there was an earnestness in his eyes that made me melt. "It's more than I deserve, really."

I reached for his hand, intertwining our fingers, grounding ourselves in this moment of connection. "You deserve to let someone in. I can't pretend to know the pain you carry, but I do know what it feels like to have walls built so high they almost touch the sky. Sometimes you just need someone willing to climb them."

His gaze held mine, and I could see a flicker of hope sparking within him, an ember that hadn't been extinguished. "Maybe I'm not as good at this as I thought," he admitted, a wry smile playing on his lips. "The whole vulnerability thing is a little outside my comfort zone."

"Join the club," I quipped. "I'm the president of 'Avoiding Vulnerability' right now. But hey, if we're going to be partners in this chaotic escapade, we might as well embrace it together. No more hiding."

He squeezed my hand, the simple gesture igniting a fire in my chest. "Alright then, partner. I'll hold you to that."

The soft sound of footsteps echoed in the vast emptiness of the cathedral, pulling us from our moment of serenity. I glanced over my shoulder, the sudden intrusion of reality unsettling the fragile peace we had crafted. An old priest emerged from the shadows, his long, white beard flowing like a river of wisdom. He paused, his gaze piercing yet gentle as it swept over us.

"Finding solace in shared burdens, I see," he said, his voice gravelly yet warm, like the earth itself. "It's a rare gift to connect in such a profound way."

"Something like that," I replied, feeling an odd mix of embarrassment and gratitude. It was as if he had seen right through the layers we had so carefully constructed.

The priest smiled knowingly, his eyes twinkling with a spark of mischief. "Just remember, love can be a double-edged sword. It has the power to heal, but it can also expose wounds you thought long buried."

His words hung in the air like a warning, but rather than inciting fear, they only deepened my resolve. I was willing to brave whatever storms lay ahead if it meant standing by his side. "We'll be careful," I assured him, squeezing my partner's hand tightly. "We've come too far to turn back now."

With a nod, the priest took a step back, leaving us to our thoughts. The flickering candles illuminated the path before us, casting shadows that danced like specters, reminding me that the past would always be a part of us. Yet I felt a shift in the atmosphere, a sense of possibility blossoming like wildflowers after a rainstorm.

"Ready for that adventure?" I asked, turning my attention back to him, my heart racing with excitement.

"Always," he replied, his voice steady and resolute. "Let's leave the shadows behind, at least for today."

And with that, we stepped out of the sanctuary, leaving the cathedral's embrace, and into the crisp air of the night, where the moon hung high and bright, illuminating a world waiting for us to explore. Each step we took was a declaration—a promise that we would navigate this labyrinth of life together, ready to face whatever came our way, armed with laughter, love, and the courage to embrace both the light and the dark.

The air outside was crisp and alive, imbued with the scent of damp earth and the distant promise of rain. The moon hung low in the sky, a luminescent orb casting silvery tendrils of light that flickered over the cobblestone streets like a fleeting whisper. As we stepped into the night, the world felt different—less daunting, more like a canvas awaiting our brushstrokes. I glanced up at him, the shadows of the cathedral still clinging to us, but they were fading, retreating before the warmth of our shared laughter.

"Okay, so what's our first quest?" I asked, adopting a mock-heroic tone. "Shall we rescue the damsel in distress or hunt down a mythical beast?"

He chuckled, the sound rich and inviting. "As tempting as slaying a dragon sounds, I think a coffee run would be a more manageable start."

"Ah, the quest for caffeine," I said dramatically, clutching my heart in mock despair. "How noble of you!"

"Desperate times call for desperate measures," he replied with a playful smirk. "Besides, I have my priorities straight. We'll need energy if we're to save the world."

With our mission clear, we set off, the cobblestones crunching beneath our feet. Each step resonated with newfound purpose, the air electric with possibility. The streets were mostly empty, the occasional flicker of movement revealing late-night wanderers or insomniac lovers, all lost in their own adventures. We meandered through the labyrinth of alleys, each twist and turn revealing quaint cafes and dimly lit bistros, the kind of places that felt like secrets waiting to be discovered.

As we approached a small, charming café tucked away beneath a flowering trellis, my heart leapt at the sight. The golden light spilling through the windows beckoned us like an old friend. "This looks perfect," I said, the anticipation bubbling inside me. "I can already taste the pastries."

"Let's hope they serve coffee strong enough to fuel our heroics," he replied, and I laughed, the sound dancing in the cool night air.

Inside, the café was a cozy refuge, filled with the aroma of freshly baked goods and rich coffee. The walls were lined with bookshelves, and mismatched chairs created a homey feel that invited lingering. We chose a table by the window, allowing the glow of the streetlight to wrap around us like a warm embrace.

"Okay, serious talk," I said, leaning forward, my voice dropping to a conspiratorial whisper. "What's the first thing we're going to do with our newfound freedom? After coffee, of course."

He leaned back, a thoughtful expression crossing his face. "We could drive to the coast. Watch the waves crash against the rocks. Maybe even throw some stones in for good measure. It sounds... freeing."

"Just us against the ocean," I mused, the imagery filling me with longing. "No ghosts, no pasts. Just the two of us."

"Exactly," he said, his gaze locking onto mine, the weight of his words wrapping around us like a comforting blanket. "We could leave it all behind, even if just for a day."

The waiter approached, interrupting our reverie, and we ordered a selection of pastries and the strongest coffee they had. As he walked away, I felt the anticipation buzzing in my veins, fueled by the excitement of our conversation. We could carve out a space that was just ours, untainted by the shadows of our pasts.

But as our coffee arrived, the atmosphere shifted subtly. The clinking of cups and the quiet chatter of patrons faded into a distant hum. I noticed a figure standing by the door, watching us. My heart raced as I recognized the familiar silhouette, a mixture of disbelief and unease pooling in my stomach. It was a man I had never wanted to see again, the embodiment of my own fears.

"Do you feel that?" I whispered, my voice barely audible as I leaned in closer to him, my pulse quickening.

He glanced up, following my gaze, and the smile vanished from his face. "What's wrong?"

I nodded toward the doorway. "It's him. The one from before."

His expression hardened, a protective instinct flickering to life as he turned fully in his seat. "Stay here," he said firmly, his tone leaving no room for argument.

"No, wait!" I hissed, panic rising within me. "You don't know what he wants!"

But he was already on his feet, moving toward the man who loomed like a specter from my past. I could feel my heart thudding in my chest as I watched them, my body coiled with anxiety. The man at the door, once a shadowy figure of menace, now seemed to exude an air of arrogance, his confidence practically oozing from his pores.

I strained to hear their conversation, but the café's lively ambiance drowned out their voices. My fingers tightened around the edge of the table, a nervous habit I couldn't shake. Moments felt like hours as I watched the two men exchange tense words, their postures shifting, the air around them thickening.

And then I saw it—a flash of something metallic in the man's hand. My breath caught in my throat as a sense of dread washed over me. "No," I whispered, as if the word alone could halt the impending disaster.

In a heartbeat, the atmosphere changed from casual to charged. The man leaned closer to him, his expression shifting to something darker, more threatening. I couldn't hear what he was saying, but I saw the challenge in his posture, the defiance that resonated between them.

Suddenly, my partner stepped back, his hands raised in a gesture of caution. "I don't want any trouble," he said, but his voice was steady, strong against the rising tide of tension.

The man smirked, a chilling expression that made my skin crawl. "Trouble finds you, my friend. You can't escape your past so easily."

That's when everything erupted. A loud crash echoed through the café as the man lunged forward, and in an instant, chaos ensued. Tables rattled, coffee spilled, and screams pierced the air, drowning out the sound of my racing heart.

I was on my feet before I even realized it, adrenaline surging through me as I pushed through the crowd. "Stop!" I shouted, desperate to reach him. But the scene before me had devolved into a frenzy, the reality of the moment both surreal and terrifying.

I caught a glimpse of my partner's face, a mixture of anger and determination, before the man collided into him, sending them both crashing to the ground. The world spun around me, but all I could focus on was the struggle unfolding in front of me, the shadows of our pasts colliding in a cacophony of chaos and fear.

"Get away from him!" I screamed, my voice barely carrying over the din. I rushed forward, propelled by a mixture of fear and fierce loyalty, knowing that I couldn't let this moment define us, not when we had only just begun to carve out a life together.

But as I reached them, everything shifted. The lights flickered, and for a split second, the world narrowed down to the two of them, locked in a fierce struggle, shadows dancing wildly around us. And just as I was about to intervene, a loud bang echoed through the air, freezing me in place, and the scream that followed sent chills down my spine.

Time seemed to stand still, suspended in a moment that felt as fragile as glass. I watched, heart pounding in my chest, as everything unraveled before me, knowing that nothing would ever be the same again.

Chapter 22: The Gathering Storm

The city breathes around me, its pulse quickening like a drumbeat in the twilight. Shadows stretch and yawn, casting long fingers across cobblestones worn smooth by years of hurried feet. I can almost taste the tension in the air, sharp and metallic, like the thrill of a storm on the horizon. It hangs heavy, a promise of change that whispers through the alleys and clings to the walls of the ancient buildings. I step onto the narrow street, where flickering lanterns cast a warm glow, and the scent of roasting chestnuts mingles with the dampness of the evening. Each breath I take is tinged with uncertainty, but beneath the anxiety, there's a spark—a flicker of hope igniting within me.

It is during moments like these that I find myself wandering towards the heart of our gathering place, a small square nestled between the looming silhouettes of two crumbling towers. The stone walls seem to lean in, as if eavesdropping on our whispered secrets. We've carved out a sanctuary here, a place where the clamor of the outside world fades to a dull roar, and the flickering flames of our campfire create a sanctuary against the encroaching darkness. The air hums with conversation as my comrades share stories, their voices rising and falling like the tide, weaving a tapestry of camaraderie that binds us closer in our shared resolve.

As I join the circle, the laughter dies down, replaced by a heavy silence. They look to me for strength, and in that moment, I feel the weight of their expectations settle on my shoulders. I smile, forcing the tension in my chest to ease, reminding myself that this isn't just about me. "We stand at the brink of something extraordinary," I say, my voice steady, as though the very act of speaking will shore up our faltering courage. "We've fought through darkness before, and together we can face whatever lies ahead."

The faces around me flicker with determination, each one a canvas of hopes and fears. Lucas, with his tousled dark hair and an easy smile that belies his fierce loyalty, leans forward. "And if we fall?" His question hangs heavy, a cloud in a clear sky. The murmurs that follow sound like the rustle of leaves caught in a sudden gust, a reminder of the uncertainty swirling in our midst.

I meet his gaze, the intensity of his brown eyes sparking something deep within me, a connection that goes beyond mere friendship. "If we fall," I reply, "we will do so with our heads held high, knowing we fought for something greater than ourselves." My words are laced with bravado, a shield against the gnawing fear that threatens to claw its way out.

Beside Lucas, Mira, our sharp-tongued strategist with a penchant for dry humor, rolls her eyes. "Great, but let's not fall just yet. I've got plans that involve not dying, preferably." A ripple of laughter dances through the group, the tension easing as if her words were a balm on our frayed nerves.

"Plans, eh? Care to share?" I challenge, grinning at her.

Mira smirks, the corner of her mouth lifting in that way that reminds me of a cat who's just spotted a particularly enticing bird. "Well, I was thinking something along the lines of 'hit them before they hit us'—classic."

"Revolutionary," Lucas quips, his tone dripping with mock seriousness. "Mira, you're a tactical genius."

Our laughter mingles with the crackling of the fire, but beneath the light-heartedness lies a current of tension. I can feel it thrumming through the air, an electric charge that amplifies every glance and every touch. The unspoken words linger, heavy and palpable, as if they are about to break free from the confines of our thoughts.

But then the moment shifts, the laughter fading as a shadow falls across our circle. It's Amara, her silhouette framed against the firelight, her presence commanding attention. "They've been spotted," she states, her voice low and steady, slicing through the camaraderie like a knife through soft cheese. "Scouts report movement near the east gate. They're gathering forces."

An uneasy silence blankets us, the laughter dying like a candle snuffed out in a sudden wind. My heart races as the implications sink in, the urgency of her words settling over us like a shroud. The finality of it all is stark, the reality of our situation slamming into me like a fist. The gathering storm we've sensed in the air is no longer an abstract threat; it's here, breathing down our necks.

"Prepare the defenses," I command, my voice ringing with an authority I didn't know I possessed. "We need to send scouts of our own. Every moment counts."

Nods of agreement ripple through the group as they leap into action, adrenaline replacing the lingering tension of moments before. I watch as Lucas and Mira begin plotting our strategy, their fingers moving deftly over a worn map, lines of ink crisscrossing like a web. The firelight dances in their eyes, igniting a fierce determination that mirrors my own.

But amidst the chaos of preparation, I can't shake the feeling of a storm brewing inside me as well. Each heartbeat thrums with anticipation, a relentless rhythm that urges me forward, into the unknown. And in that moment, as I glance at Lucas, our eyes locking in a shared understanding, I realize that this battle is more than just a fight for survival; it's a fight for the future we dream of, for the bonds we've forged amidst the darkness. The stakes have never been higher, and the storm may rage around us, but we will not go quietly into the night. Together, we will face whatever challenges lie ahead, united in our resolve, our hearts beating in synchrony against the howling winds of fate.

The night draped itself over us like a thick velvet curtain, rich and impenetrable, as the flickering flames from our fire cast long, wavering shadows against the surrounding buildings. I felt the crackle of anticipation in the air, sharp as the first snap of thunder heralding a storm. As I helped arrange the makeshift defenses—barrels, crates, and anything else we could scavenge—I was acutely aware of the adrenaline coursing through my veins. Each object was a shield, a silent promise that we wouldn't go down without a fight.

Mira moved beside me, her brow furrowed in concentration. "You know," she began, her voice laced with a mix of sarcasm and genuine curiosity, "if we survive this, I'm going to hold a seminar on how to properly barricade a square with an assortment of household items. I mean, have you ever seen such innovation? We could make a killing on the lecture circuit."

I chuckled despite the gravity of our situation, grateful for her ability to inject a sense of levity into the chaos. "Only if you promise to wear a PowerPoint presentation on your back. The audience would love it."

"Only if you promise to take me out for a celebratory drink afterward," she shot back, a glint of mischief in her eyes.

The sound of her laughter danced around us, briefly dispelling the shadows of doubt creeping in. But as I glanced towards the eastern horizon, the laughter faded like smoke in the wind. The clouds hung low and dark, their menace palpable, mirroring the anxiety building in my chest. Each moment felt like a countdown, a ticking clock echoing through the stillness, reminding us that our enemy was not far away.

Lucas was deep in conversation with Amara, their heads bent close together, exchanging hushed words laden with urgency. I drifted closer, hoping to catch snippets of their strategy. "The scouts are reporting increased activity," Lucas said, his voice a low rumble, a tone that demanded attention. "If they breach the gates, we'll need to be ready."

"Ready for what?" I interjected, crossing my arms. "They'll be ready for us. We're not the only ones preparing for a fight."

"Which is why we need to strike first," Amara replied, her voice as sharp as the blade she often carried. "A surprise attack could catch them off guard. We might stand a chance if we disrupt their formation."

"Disrupting their formation sounds a lot like getting ourselves killed," I countered, frustration bubbling to the surface. "Have you thought about what happens after we disrupt them? We might need to retreat, and I'm not keen on being the first one to turn tail."

"Good point," Lucas conceded, his eyes narrowing as he pondered my words. "But we can't let fear dictate our actions. We need a plan that keeps us mobile. If we're going to fight, we have to fight smart."

"Which I think we can agree is a rarity among this group," Mira chimed in, gesturing dramatically at our assembly of misfits. "Smart isn't exactly our strong suit, is it?"

"Speak for yourself," I shot back, suppressing a grin. "I'm known for my brilliant tactical maneuvers, such as that time I managed to trip over my own feet while attempting to sneak away from a party."

"Ah yes, the legendary 'stumble and tumble' tactic," Lucas said, feigning admiration. "Truly, you're a marvel."

Laughter erupted again, ringing like a bell, and for a fleeting moment, it felt as though the weight of our impending doom had lessened. But then the laughter faded as quickly as it came, reality crashing back in. The gravity of our circumstances hung heavy in the air, reminding us of the stakes involved.

Suddenly, a figure darted into the square, breathless and wild-eyed. It was Jonah, one of our scouts, his chest heaving as he leaned against the rough stone wall, gathering himself. "They're close," he gasped, the urgency in his voice snatching our attention. "I saw their encampment just a mile beyond the eastern ridge. They're preparing for an assault."

My stomach twisted into knots, the weight of his words sinking in. "How many?" I demanded, feeling the pulse of panic quicken.

"More than I could count. But they're not just soldiers. They've brought something else." His eyes darted around, ensuring he had our full attention. "Something darker."

"What do you mean, darker?" Mira's voice was sharp, laced with unease.

"Their mages," Jonah replied, each word dripping with foreboding. "I saw their banners fluttering in the wind. They're calling on powers we've only heard about in stories. I... I don't think we can face them."

The weight of despair crashed down on us like a wave. My heart raced, thoughts spiraling as the implications washed over me. Mages? Dark magic? This was a different kind of battle, one that demanded more than just swords and shields.

"Then we can't face them head-on," I said, forcing the resolve into my voice, though I felt the uncertainty clawing at my insides. "We need to prepare the people. The civilians can't be caught in the crossfire."

Amara nodded, her expression grim but determined. "Agreed. If they're targeting the city, we have to protect the ones we love. We can't let them become collateral damage."

"Right," Lucas said, pacing like a caged animal, the intensity of his gaze reflecting the firelight. "If we have any chance at all, we'll need to rally everyone. The more bodies we have, the better."

"Then let's not waste time," I urged, the call to action igniting something fierce within me. "We need to split up—some of us can secure the perimeter, while others gather the citizens and prepare them for what's to come."

"Make sure to avoid telling them about the mages," Mira cautioned, her tone serious. "Fear spreads faster than any magic they could conjure."

"Fear is already in the air," I replied, my voice a whisper. "Let's give them hope instead."

With that, we scattered like leaves caught in a tempest, urgency propelling us into the night. I felt the adrenaline flooding my veins, every heartbeat a reminder that we were on the cusp of something monumental. As I darted through the shadows, the city felt alive beneath my feet, the echoes of our plans intertwining with the deepening night. The storm was indeed gathering, but we would stand against it, side by side, ready to face whatever darkness came our way.

The flickering glow of lanterns created a dance of light and shadow in the narrow streets, casting an ethereal glow that belied the tension crackling in the air. I moved through the crowd, heart pounding, feeling the weight of every anxious face that turned towards me. There was a fierce energy rippling through the city, an undercurrent of both dread and defiance. It was infectious, a reminder that we were not alone in this fight.

I found Lucas near the town square, his brows knitted together in concentration as he spoke to a small group of volunteers. "We need to organize," he insisted, his voice cutting through the din. "If we spread ourselves too thin, we risk losing everything."

"Like my patience," I interjected, earning a knowing smile from him. "Let's prioritize the most vulnerable—families, the elderly. We can't afford to let them face this alone."

"Good idea," Mira added, appearing at my side, her arms crossed in that way that screamed she was ready to take on the world. "And maybe throw in some firecrackers or something loud to scare the enemy off. Because nothing says 'stay away' like an impromptu fireworks show."

"Right, because I'm sure that's just what they'll be worried about," Lucas replied dryly, but his eyes glinted with amusement. "Though I'm in favor of anything that might distract them from storming the gates."

We moved as a unit, a whirlwind of determination and purpose. People rallied around us, their faces a blend of anxiety and resolve, ready to take up arms or create barricades from whatever they could find. The streets buzzed with frantic energy as we divided into smaller groups, ready to fan out across the city, a plan unfolding as organically as the budding flowers in spring.

As I walked alongside Lucas, I felt a surge of gratitude for his steady presence. "You're the calm in my chaos," I said, glancing sideways at him. "How do you do that?"

"Years of practice," he replied with a grin, "and a healthy dose of denial. Besides, someone has to keep you from getting too dramatic."

"Dramatic?" I feigned shock, placing a hand over my heart. "Me? Never. I prefer to think of myself as passionately expressive."

"Is that what we're calling it now?" Lucas shot back, laughter lingering in his voice.

The laughter faded as we approached the edge of the town square, where makeshift barricades began to take shape. It felt like a scene from a dream, the chaotic beauty of solidarity weaving through fear and uncertainty. Just then, a familiar figure emerged from the shadows—Jonah, looking more frantic than ever.

"Guys, you need to see this," he panted, urgency written all over his features. "I just spotted something—"

But before he could finish, a low rumble echoed in the distance, sending a shiver down my spine. The ground seemed to vibrate beneath us, an ominous warning that pulled every eye to the horizon.

"What is that?" Mira asked, her voice barely above a whisper, tension tightening the air around us.

"It can't be..." I began, but the sight before us confirmed my fears. A massive dark cloud loomed, swirling ominously, casting an unnatural shadow over the landscape. The air grew thick, charged with an energy that felt alive, almost sentient.

"They're coming," Jonah hissed, his voice trembling. "I saw them preparing something—something big. We need to warn everyone!"

"Form the lines!" Lucas commanded, his voice breaking through the shock that had seized us all. "Get everyone into position! We need to be ready!"

I found myself at the front, adrenaline coursing through my veins as the panic in my chest transformed into a fierce determination. The laughter that had buoyed my spirits now felt distant, swallowed by the seriousness of our situation. The enemy was not just approaching; they were bringing their full force, and I could almost hear the distant echo of their battle cries on the wind.

"Stay together!" I shouted, my voice ringing with authority as I directed the volunteers. "We can't let fear divide us. We fight as one!"

The crowd surged forward, hearts pounding in unison, forming lines and defenses that felt too fragile against the approaching storm. As we prepared, I caught sight of Lucas, his expression a mixture of resolve and concern. He nodded at me, a silent promise that we would stand together.

But as the first sparks of lightning illuminated the sky, revealing shadowy figures marching closer, my breath hitched in my throat. They were not just soldiers; they were surrounded by tendrils of dark magic, swirling like smoke around them, a harbinger of the destruction they could unleash.

"What are we waiting for?" Mira shouted, brandishing her weapon, her voice fierce and defiant. "Let's show them what we're made of!"

And just as I opened my mouth to rally our forces, a sound ripped through the air—a piercing, otherworldly howl that made my skin prickle. It seemed to come from the heart of the dark cloud, an echo that resonated deep within me. The noise intensified, reverberating in the very bones of the earth.

"Get ready!" I yelled, my heart racing, as the enemy surged forward, the ground trembling under their weight. We were mere moments away from the clash that could change everything, the storm breaking around us with a force that threatened to swallow us whole.

But just as the first wave of soldiers broke from the shadows, a figure emerged at the front of their ranks, cloaked in darkness, eyes glowing with an unholy light. A shiver of recognition ran through me, chilling my blood. It couldn't be...

"Stay back!" I shouted, instinctively moving to shield those around me. But the reality was crashing down like the very storm threatening to engulf us.

"Prepare for battle!" Lucas yelled, stepping forward, determination etched on his face.

The first clash echoed through the night as we braced ourselves for the fight of our lives. And in that fleeting moment, with the darkness bearing down on us, I realized we were teetering on the edge of a precipice, where everything could change in the blink of an eye. With that thought spiraling in my mind, the storm broke, and the chaos began.

Chapter 23: Descent into Darkness

The walls of the fortress seem to close in around us, a living entity breathing in the darkness, whispering secrets that no one should hear. I can almost feel the cold stone beneath my fingertips as we tread softly through the shadowy passageways, our footsteps muffled by the dust of forgotten ages. Flickering torches cast an eerie glow, their flames dancing as if they too are afraid of what lies ahead. A gust of stale air rushes past, carrying with it a hint of damp earth and something more sinister—betrayal, perhaps.

Beside me, he remains a silent sentinel, his presence an anchor in this sea of uncertainty. I glance at him, catching the sharp line of his jaw and the determined set of his shoulders. There's a warmth in his gaze that melts away the chill of the air, and for a moment, I allow myself to believe we can emerge from this nightmare unscathed. But I know better. In a place like this, hope can be a fragile thing, easily crushed beneath the weight of despair.

Each corridor twists like a serpent, leading us deeper into the heart of the fortress. My pulse quickens as we approach a heavy wooden door, its surface marked by years of neglect and violence. I can feel the tension crackling in the air like static electricity, an omen of the confrontation waiting on the other side. He shifts slightly, his breath steady despite the rising dread. I can tell he's trying to project confidence, but I see the flicker of uncertainty in his eyes—a mirror to my own thoughts.

"Ready?" he asks, his voice low and rough, laced with an urgency that betrays the calm facade he attempts to maintain.

I nod, swallowing the lump in my throat. "As ready as I'll ever be."

Pushing the door open, we step into the chamber beyond, and the world shifts. The room is vast, illuminated by an otherworldly glow that seeps from the cracks in the stone walls. A raised dais sits at its center, draped in shadows that seem to pulse with a life of their own. And there, at the apex, stands our enemy—a figure draped in dark robes, their face obscured by a hood that casts a veil of secrecy.

"Welcome, intruders," the figure intones, their voice smooth as silk yet edged with malice. "I've been expecting you."

A shiver runs down my spine, but I refuse to show fear. "You've made a mistake if you think we'll be intimidated by your theatrics," I shoot back, surprising myself with the defiance that bubbles to the surface.

The figure chuckles, a low sound that echoes eerily in the chamber. "Intimidation? Oh, my dear, this is not intimidation. It is merely the beginning of your reckoning."

Before I can respond, the room erupts into chaos. Shadows detach from the walls, coalescing into forms that are almost human, but not quite. My heart races as I realize we've walked straight into a trap, the very darkness we feared manifesting before our eyes. He positions himself beside me, our backs pressed against one another, ready to fight as a horde of shadowy figures advances.

"Stay close!" he shouts, and I can hear the resolve in his voice, a promise wrapped in urgency.

I draw a deep breath, summoning every ounce of courage I possess. "We can't let them surround us!" I cry, moving in tandem with him, our movements choreographed by desperation and instinct.

The first of the shadows lunges at me, its form indistinct, a mere silhouette against the eerie light. I swing my arm, catching it off guard, and it dissipates like mist in the morning sun. A rush of adrenaline surges through me, momentarily blinding me to the danger as I realize I can fight back.

We dance together, two warriors moving in a deadly rhythm, every strike and parry a testament to our shared determination. He grunts with exertion as he takes on another shadow, his strength evident as he pushes back against its weight. I can hear the clash of our blows echoing, a symphony of defiance against the encroaching darkness.

But for every shadow we defeat, two more emerge, their numbers overwhelming. The realization sends a spike of panic through me, threatening to unravel the confidence I've built. "There are too many!" I shout, my voice rising above the din.

"Just keep fighting! We can't give up!" he replies, his tone unwavering.

In that moment, something shifts within me. The fear that once constricted my chest loosens, replaced by a fierce resolve. We are not alone in this fight; we have each other. I can feel the heat radiating from him, a steady flame against the cold, relentless dark.

"Right!" I say, determination igniting in my core. "Let's turn the tide!"

Together, we launch into a counterattack, a flurry of movement that feels almost choreographed. I aim low, sweeping the leg of a shadowy figure that lunges at him, while he thrusts his arm forward, driving a fist into the chest of another. We become a whirlwind of strength and agility, the shadows faltering in the face of our unity.

But then, just as victory seems within reach, the dark figure on the dais raises a hand, and the room falls silent. The shadows hesitate, retreating slightly, their forms flickering like candles in the wind. My heart sinks as a dreadful realization settles in—the enemy is not just a puppeteer of shadows but a master of their will.

"What are you doing?" I demand, my voice a defiant tremor in the silence.

"Witness the power of true darkness," the figure replies, their voice slicing through the air with an icy calm. "You are outmatched, and soon, you will learn that light cannot survive in my domain."

With a wave of their hand, the shadows surge forward again, their movements frenzied and chaotic, and I know this is our moment of reckoning. We cannot falter now. With a shared glance, we steel ourselves for the fight of our lives, ready to face whatever horrors the darkness may unleash. The weight of the fortress looms above us, but within my chest, I feel the flicker of hope, a promise that together, we might just carve a path through this abyss.

A surge of shadows crashes toward us, a roiling mass that seems intent on swallowing us whole. My heart pounds in my chest, each beat a reminder that we're not just fighting for our lives but for something far greater. The oppressive weight of despair hangs in the air, thick and suffocating, but somehow, against the tide of terror, a spark of defiance ignites within me.

"Do you always have to make things so dramatic?" I quip, attempting to lighten the grim atmosphere even as a shadow lunges at my face. My hands find purchase on the smooth hilt of my dagger, and I twist to the side, feeling the rush of air where the creature's grasp nearly caught me. "I mean, can't you just stick to the typical villain monologue? At least give us a chance to catch our breath."

He smirks, a flicker of amusement sparking in his eyes, even as he sidesteps another shadow and delivers a precise kick that sends it sprawling. "If only they knew how hard it is to come up with something original these days," he replies, panting slightly. "And here I thought we'd get a creative villain, not just a glorified ghost."

The shadows hesitate, as if thrown off by our banter, and for a heartbeat, I almost believe we can turn this tide. But the moment is fleeting. The dark figure on the dais raises an imperious hand again, and the shadows resume their relentless advance.

"Enough of this!" the figure snarls, their voice a tempest of rage that echoes ominously through the chamber. "You think you can disrupt my plans with your petty quips? You will pay dearly for your insolence!"

The air crackles with energy as the shadows begin to swirl, gathering strength, and I can feel a weight pressing down on me, like the very air is thickening with dread. "Just a thought," I say, my voice steady despite the rising chaos. "But what if we team up? You and your shadows versus... well, us?" I pause, giving him a sidelong glance. "I'm sure we could negotiate a better arrangement than this. Maybe throw in a coffee break?"

He chuckles, even as he dodges a particularly aggressive shadow. "And I thought I was the funny one," he shoots back, but his eyes are focused, scanning for weaknesses in our dark adversaries.

As if to taunt us further, the dark figure steps down from the dais, the shadows flowing around them like an angry tide. "You underestimate the power of true darkness," they hiss, advancing. "But you'll soon understand what it means to be swallowed by it."

With a flick of their wrist, the shadows snap forward like a pack of wild animals, and I feel a primal urge to run. But I won't—can't—abandon him. I brace myself, plunging forward with a newfound resolve. "You might want to rethink your strategy!" I call out, lunging toward the nearest shadow, blade aimed for the heart of its swirling form.

Our movements become a blur of energy and instinct, each blow an assertion of our will against the encroaching darkness. He fights like a storm, fierce and unyielding, while I weave around him, my heart racing in tandem with the intensity of our struggle. With every foe I take down, the shadows seem to thin, if only slightly.

But then I catch a glimpse of the figure watching us, their expression inscrutable behind the veil of their hood. There's a glimmer of something—satisfaction? Perhaps even curiosity?—and my stomach twists. It's as if they're testing us, gauging our strength against the tide of their power.

"Are we supposed to be impressed?" I shout defiantly, attempting to mask my growing unease. "Because honestly, I've seen better performances at the local theater. You really need to work on your delivery."

The figure's lips curl into a smile that chills my bones. "You have spirit, I'll give you that. But spirit alone cannot fend off the darkness. It is only a flicker in a storm."

With that, they gesture, and suddenly the shadows surge again, this time more focused, as if they've been given a singular command. I throw a glance at him, and we share a moment of understanding, a silent vow that we'll face whatever comes next together.

"Let's turn that flicker into a flame," he replies, and I can see the fire igniting in his eyes.

We push back against the tide, our blades carving arcs of defiance in the air. Each strike feels like a declaration, each shout a battle cry that shatters the oppressive silence. I swing wide, my dagger catching the glow of the torches as it slices through the air, connecting with a shadow that dissolves in a puff of darkness.

"Nice shot!" he calls out, his voice laced with exhilaration. "I knew you had it in you!"

But just as I begin to feel a semblance of control, a heavy weight settles on my chest. The shadows regroup, swirling like a tempest, their movement more organized now. They come at us in waves, and I feel the fatigue creeping into my limbs, every strike becoming a monumental effort.

"Remember that coffee break?" I manage to gasp between breaths. "I think I need one right now!"

"Just a little longer!" he encourages, but I can see the strain etched across his face. "We can't give in! Focus!"

Just then, a particularly strong shadow lunges at me from the side, a dark tendril reaching out with an intent to ensnare. I pivot just in time, but the movement sends me stumbling, and I feel myself teeter on the edge of panic. I'm losing ground, and for the first time, a deep-seated fear gnaws at me.

But then, in a flash of instinct, I remember the tiny charm hanging from my neck—a gift from my grandmother, a talisman of protection she insisted I keep close. I grip it tightly, feeling the familiar warmth radiate from it. "You think you can take me?" I shout defiantly, clutching the charm like a lifeline. "You'll have to do better than that!"

The shadows hesitate, their movements faltering for just a moment, as if my declaration has caught them off guard. It's a fleeting moment, but enough for me to regain my footing. I turn to him, a surge of determination igniting our bond. "Let's show them what we're made of!"

With renewed vigor, we launch ourselves back into the fray, a blur of motion and resolve. This time, as we fight, the shadows begin to break apart, their forms scattering like leaves caught in a tempest. I catch his eye, and we smile—genuine, unrestrained. In that moment, we are not just fighting to survive; we are pushing back against the darkness, carving our own path through the chaos.

But the figure watching from the dais is not finished yet. With a roar that reverberates through the chamber, they raise both hands, and I can feel the weight of their fury pressing down on us. The shadows swirl tighter, and I know that we're on the precipice of something even darker.

"Hold on!" I shout, reaching for him, our fingers brushing as we stand back to back once more, ready to face whatever storm is about to break. The darkness is closing in, but with him at my side, I'm determined to fight, to resist, to defy the very essence of despair. Whatever may come, we will face it together.

The shadows coalesce around us like a dark storm, swirling and thrumming with an energy that feels alive. I can almost hear their whispers, hissing secrets meant only for the darkness, and I can't shake the feeling that they're not merely pawns but a manifestation of our deepest fears. The figure on the dais observes us with a predatory intensity, their presence an anchor that keeps the shadows coiling in closer, seeking to ensnare us in their cold embrace.

"Okay, I really hope you have a brilliant plan brewing in that handsome head of yours," I shout to him, trying to keep the panic at bay. "Because I'm fresh out of ideas here!"

He shoots me a quick grin, a fleeting spark in the maelstrom. "Just keep swinging, and don't forget to look fabulous while doing it!"

With a deep breath, I dive into the fray, feeling the familiar weight of my dagger in my hand. I weave between the shadows, dodging and slicing, the air thick with a mixture of sweat and adrenaline. Each strike is fueled by a fierce determination, but I know we can't keep this up forever. The shadows are relentless, their numbers growing, and fatigue gnaws at my limbs, a hungry beast that won't be ignored.

"Are you sure they don't have a shadow union or something?" I pant as I pivot to evade a clawing tendril. "Because I'm starting to feel outnumbered here!"

His laughter bursts through the tension, a buoyant note amidst the chaos. "If they do, we're definitely not on their good side! Just think of this as an extremely misguided dance party!"

I can't help but laugh, even as I block a shadow that lunges for my throat. His humor cuts through the despair like sunlight piercing through dark clouds. "If this is a party, I want to be the first to leave!" I retort, my voice strained but laced with determination.

As we continue our desperate fight, I catch sight of the figure watching from the dais. They seem unfazed by our struggle, a smirk playing at the corners of their hidden mouth. My heart races with the realization that we are nothing more than entertainment for them—a spectacle of chaos and confusion. Anger flares within me, igniting a spark of resilience. "You think this is amusing?" I yell, brandishing my dagger at them. "You have no idea what you're up against!"

With a flick of their wrist, the shadows surge forward again, but this time I'm ready. I channel my anger into every movement, every slash of my dagger, my heart syncing with the rhythm of battle. "We're not just flickering lights, you know!" I shout. "We're a freaking wildfire!"

He glances over his shoulder, eyes gleaming with mirth despite the chaos. "Now you're talking! Let's turn this flicker into a blaze!"

Together, we push forward, moving as one. My heart pounds in my chest, the rhythm syncing with the power surging through us. With each foe we dismantle, the shadows begin to thin, revealing a glimpse of the dais once more. The figure's expression shifts from amusement to annoyance, and that shift fuels my resolve.

But just as it seems we might turn the tide, the ground beneath us trembles, sending vibrations through the stone. "What now?" I shout, glancing around in confusion.

"Brace yourself!" he yells, and before I can react, the shadows erupt, their forms morphing into grotesque figures, twisting and writhing like living nightmares.

"Okay, definitely not the type of party I envisioned!" I yell, adrenaline spiking as I back away from the onslaught. But the darkness shifts again, and I feel something pulse in the air, a current of energy that wraps around me like a shroud.

"Hold on!" he calls out, reaching for me, but just as our fingers brush, a shadow lunges between us, separating us with a deafening crash.

"NO!" I scream, a primal surge of fear and rage propelling me forward, but it's too late. The shadows close in around him, their forms melding into an impenetrable mass. "Get away from him!" I shout, my voice rising above the cacophony, desperation clawing at my throat.

The dark figure steps forward, their presence commanding and terrifying. "You cannot save him, child. You are out of your depth. Embrace the darkness; it is your only path to power."

"Power?" I spit back, fury fueling my every word. "What kind of power comes from stealing lives and shrouding everything in fear? That's not strength; it's cowardice!"

The figure's eyes narrow, and I see a flicker of something—anger or perhaps respect?—before the shadows begin to thrash violently, threatening to consume him whole. I can't let this happen. I refuse to let the darkness win, to take him away from me.

"Don't you dare touch him!" I scream, the power within me awakening as I draw upon the warmth of my charm, the flicker of hope that refuses to be extinguished. I grip it tightly, letting the energy surge through my veins like fire, pushing against the suffocating darkness. "You will not take him!"

In a burst of determination, I leap forward, throwing myself against the swirling mass of shadows. I feel the energy crackle around me, a force so potent that the very air seems to shimmer with potential. The shadows recoil, momentarily stunned, and I can hear the crackling of electricity as the light from my charm flares brightly.

"Together!" he yells, his voice cutting through the noise, a lifeline amidst the chaos. "We can break this!"

The shadows surge again, but I won't let them take him. "Together!" I shout, matching his resolve. "We are stronger than this darkness!"

I thrust my charm forward, the glow intensifying, and the shadows waver. In that moment, I realize the truth: we are not merely fighting against the dark; we are wielding our own light, and together, we can illuminate even the deepest shadows.

But just as I feel the tide shifting, a tremor ripples through the fortress. The ground shakes violently beneath us, and I stumble, momentarily losing my footing. Panic surges as I realize the entire structure is coming down around us, the darkness threatening to consume everything in its path.

"Hold on!" he cries, his voice slicing through the chaos, but I can barely hear him over the din. I reach for him again, my heart racing with fear as I feel the shadows closing in once more.

"Stay with me!" I shout, but the shadows surge like a living tide, and I'm left clinging to the edge of the chaos, watching as the darkness wraps around him, pulling him deeper into its cold embrace.

With one last burst of energy, I scream, "I won't let you take him!" The words are a declaration, a promise, and as I stand there, heart racing and breathless, the shadows recoil slightly, as if my defiance has struck a chord.

But in that brief moment of hope, the fortress trembles again, and a new, darker presence emerges from the depths. It's a figure cloaked in shadows so deep they seem to absorb the very light around them, their eyes gleaming with malevolence. "You think you can defy me?" they hiss, their voice like gravel, full of ancient power.

My heart sinks as the realization washes over me. This is no mere shadow—it is the embodiment of the darkness itself, a force far greater than anything we've faced. And as I feel the pull of despair threatening to consume me, I know that this is just the beginning.

"Together!" I yell, grasping my charm tightly, feeling its warmth against the encroaching cold. But as I look to him, my heart drops. The shadows tighten their grip, and the dark figure's laughter echoes ominously around the chamber, drowning out the last shreds of hope.

"Embrace your fate!" they roar, and in that moment, everything goes black.

Chapter 24: The Betrayer's Kiss

The cold, damp air clung to my skin like a shroud, a constant reminder of our captivity. The dim light flickered erratically, casting jagged shadows across the rough stone walls of the chamber. My heart raced, thrumming in my chest like a caged bird desperate for freedom, each beat echoing my fear. Bound to the chair, my wrists stung from the coarse ropes, but it was the helplessness that clawed at my insides, churning my stomach with anxiety. All around me, darkness loomed—thick, oppressive, and heavy with the scent of damp earth and something metallic, a tang that hinted at the violence that had taken place here before.

Before I could gather my thoughts, the heavy door creaked open, and he stepped into the light, silhouetted against the flickering torches. The enemy, with his cruel smile and eyes that glinted like shards of glass, advanced towards us, his every movement laced with confidence and malice. I fought to mask my fear, straightening in my seat, but it was like trying to hide a flame under a pile of ashes. The flicker of dread in my gut betrayed me, a warning that something terrible was about to unfold.

"Welcome, my dear guests," he drawled, his voice smooth as honey but dripping with disdain. "You've made quite a mess of my plans, haven't you?"

Beside me, the one who had stood by my side through every trial, every battle, shifted slightly. His presence was a balm against my rising panic, a reminder that I wasn't alone, even in this hellish moment. I caught his eye, searching for reassurance, for a plan. Instead, I found a tempest of emotions—determination, fear, and an unfathomable depth of love that set my heart racing anew.

"Is that what you call it?" he replied, his voice steady, imbued with a quiet strength. "You should learn to take rejection more gracefully."

A ripple of laughter ran through the enemy, a sound that chilled me to my bones. "Rejection? Oh, how charming! But this isn't about you or your fragile egos. It's about what you've taken from me. The power you wield—your very lives—are mere tools to achieve my true ambition."

"What is it you want?" I managed to say, forcing the words past the tightness in my throat. My mind raced through the possibilities, each more sinister than the last.

He stepped closer, the light catching his features—sharp cheekbones, a jawline that could slice through stone, and those eyes, devoid of warmth. "I want what's mine. I want revenge," he sneered, his breath a whisper of malice that brushed against my skin. "And I want to watch as you two crumble into dust."

The air grew heavy, each word punctuated by the weight of impending doom. I could feel the walls closing in, the darkness threatening to swallow me whole. Yet, amid that suffocating despair, I sensed a flicker of defiance rising within me. We had faced worse than this; we had fought tooth and nail to be where we were. We wouldn't fall without a fight.

"Then come at us," I said, surprised by the firmness of my voice. "You think you can scare us into submission? You're wrong."

"Ah, the fire in your heart is delightful!" he mocked, but his eyes narrowed, the flicker of irritation a crack in his otherwise composed facade. "You're just as stubborn as I was told."

In that moment, I glanced at my companion again, and our gazes locked, a silent conversation passing between us—an understanding forged in the heat of battle and tempered by the bond we had nurtured through every trial.

"Let me show you what stubborn really means," he said, a flicker of something like mischief in his voice. With that, he leaned closer to me, and I felt the world around us fade, the dark stone walls receding as he reached out in a way that made my breath hitch.

His lips brushed against mine, feather-light yet electrifying, igniting something deep within me. It was a brief moment, stolen amidst the chaos, but it sent shockwaves through my veins. The kiss tasted of defiance, of a promise unspoken—a reminder that we were not just pawns in his game but players with the power to turn the tide.

The enemy's laughter faltered, replaced by a look of surprise that quickly morphed into rage. "What is this? A distraction? How quaint."

But we were already moving, a surge of energy propelling us forward. With a sudden twist, my companion broke free from his bonds, the ropes falling away as if they had never existed. The tension in the air shifted; we were no longer the hunted but the hunters, emboldened by the very act of defiance that had sparked our rebellion.

"Now!" he shouted, and I lunged, feeling the adrenaline spike as I followed his lead. We dashed toward the door, the enemy momentarily stunned, confusion etched across his face.

Our hearts raced in unison, a rhythm of rebellion echoing through our bones. We were alive, fueled by the fire of our connection and the realization that even in the darkest corners, we could carve out our own light.

With every step, I felt the weight of our past pushing against us, yet it was a weight I could bear, a reminder of everything we had fought for. We were more than just individuals facing a common foe; we were a force intertwined, two souls igniting in the darkness. And together, we would rise, no matter the cost.

The moment we burst through the door, adrenaline surged through my veins like wildfire. The corridor stretched ahead, dark and foreboding, lit only by flickering sconces that threw long shadows across the rough stone floor. My heart pounded in my chest, a rapid drumbeat that drowned out the world around me. I could hear the distant sound of footsteps echoing behind us, the enemy's henchmen quickly realizing their mistake in underestimating us.

"Where do we go?" I gasped, my breath coming in sharp bursts. The layout of this place was a tangled labyrinth, one I had never had the chance to study.

"Follow me," my companion said, his voice steady and resolute. He took the lead, his presence a sturdy anchor in the storm of uncertainty. I hurried after him, stealing glances over my shoulder, the creeping dread of capture slithering back into my mind.

We turned sharply down another corridor, its walls closing in like the jaws of a beast ready to snap shut. A sense of urgency propelled us, each footfall echoing off the stone like a countdown clock to our freedom—or our demise. As we rounded a corner, the flicker of torchlight illuminated a pair of heavy wooden doors at the end of the hallway.

"There!" I pointed, my voice breaking slightly with excitement. We sprinted toward the doors, but just as we reached them, a figure emerged from the shadows, blocking our path.

It was one of his lieutenants, a tall man with a cruel smile and eyes that seemed to drink in the fear around him. He stepped forward, brandishing a sword that glinted menacingly in the torchlight. "You're not going anywhere," he sneered. "You think you can just escape? The master will not be pleased."

"We're not here for a chat," my companion shot back, his voice a low growl that sent a thrill of courage through me. In a swift movement, he positioned himself between me and the lieutenant, a human shield ready to defend what was precious.

"Step aside, or I will make you regret it," the lieutenant hissed, his grip tightening around the hilt of his sword.

I felt the air around us shift, thick with tension. In that moment, I was struck by a wild idea, a desperate gambit that surged up from the depths of my mind. "What if I told you that we have something the master would want?" I blurted, my voice shaking slightly but laced with a confidence I didn't quite feel.

The lieutenant's interest piqued, his brow furrowing in suspicion. "What do you mean?"

I glanced at my companion, who gave me a quick nod of encouragement. "We have knowledge—information about the defenses of the castle, secrets that could benefit the master. Let us pass, and we can discuss this in private."

For a heartbeat, uncertainty flickered in the lieutenant's eyes. It was enough. Seizing the moment, my companion lunged forward, catching the man off guard. They collided with a force that echoed through the corridor, and in the chaos, I dashed past them, my heart pounding a wild rhythm as I raced toward the doors.

With a fierce determination, I pushed against the heavy wood, adrenaline lending me strength as I threw the door open. Sunlight flooded the entrance, blinding me for a moment, but it was freedom—an intoxicating rush of possibility. I stepped outside, the cool breeze brushing against my face, invigorating and liberating.

"Come on!" I shouted, my voice ringing with urgency. I turned to see my companion grappling with the lieutenant, a struggle that seemed to stretch out forever. Just as I thought all hope was lost, he twisted away, throwing the lieutenant against the wall with a force that left the man gasping.

He rushed toward me, his eyes wide with determination, and we sprinted into the open expanse beyond the castle walls. The world outside was a tapestry of greens and blues, vibrant against the bleak backdrop of our recent captivity. I breathed deeply, inhaling the scent of grass and freedom, each breath igniting a fierce hope in my heart.

"We have to keep moving!" he urged, grasping my hand tightly as we sprinted across the courtyard. My heart soared at the contact, a reassuring reminder that we were still fighting together.

But the sound of alarm bells rang out, their clangor echoing across the landscape like a death knell. Shouts filled the air, the enemy mobilizing, and I felt a rush of dread as I realized we were not yet safe.

"Over there!" I pointed toward a dense thicket of trees at the edge of the courtyard. "If we can reach the woods, we might lose them."

We dashed toward the trees, limbs reaching out like welcoming arms. Just as we crossed the threshold, I turned to glance back, a spark of hope battling against the fear gripping my chest.

But the sight that met my eyes froze me in place. The lieutenant had recovered, and he was already barking orders to a group of armed men, their faces twisted with fury. "They're escaping!" he shouted, pointing directly at us.

"Go!" my companion shouted, yanking me forward as he pulled me deeper into the foliage. The underbrush crunched beneath our feet, the sound swallowed by the chaos of the world around us. Each step felt like a leap of faith into the unknown, and I couldn't shake the feeling that every heartbeat echoed like a countdown to our inevitable capture.

"Do you trust me?" he asked suddenly, his voice low and urgent, a fierce intensity in his gaze that sent a shiver of anticipation down my spine.

"More than anything," I replied without hesitation, the truth spilling forth like a confession. In that moment, nothing else mattered but us, and the strength of our connection felt like a shield against the darkness closing in.

"Then hold on tight."

With that, he took my hand, weaving through the trees, pulling me deeper into the embrace of nature's sanctuary. Each stride was filled with determination, and I could feel the warmth of his grip fortifying me against the chill of fear. As the sounds of pursuit faded,

I let myself believe in the possibility of escape, that together we could forge our own path, away from the shadows of the past and into the light of a new dawn.

The trees closed around us like the embrace of a long-lost friend, branches intertwining overhead, weaving a natural tapestry that cloaked us in shadow. We dashed through the underbrush, our footsteps muffled by the thick carpet of leaves and fallen pine needles. I could hear the distant shouts of our pursuers, but the sound seemed to fade, as if the forest itself was conspiring to hide us from view. Each breath felt like a gift, the crisp air filling my lungs with invigorating resolve.

"Are we safe?" I panted, glancing back, half-expecting to see the lieutenant burst through the foliage, sword drawn and fury blazing in his eyes.

"Not yet," my companion replied, his voice steady despite the urgency of our situation. He pulled me along, our hands still entwined, an anchor in this tempest of fear. "But we need to put as much distance between us and them as possible."

I followed him deeper into the woods, my heart racing not just from the exertion, but from the thrill of our escape. The sunlight filtered through the leaves above, dappling the ground with patches of gold, and for a moment, I let myself believe we might just make it. My mind drifted to thoughts of what lay ahead—a future free from the shadows of our captors, a world where we could breathe without looking over our shoulders.

The path narrowed, forcing us into an intimate proximity that felt both exhilarating and terrifying. I could feel his warmth beside me, the steady rhythm of his breath reassuring, yet my mind buzzed with uncertainty. "What if they find us? What if this is just a temporary reprieve?"

"We'll deal with that when it happens," he said, his tone light, but the underlying tension betrayed his resolve. "Right now, let's focus on putting one foot in front of the other."

Just then, a loud crash echoed behind us, branches snapping underfoot like thunderclaps in the otherwise serene forest. Panic surged through me, a visceral reaction that threatened to pull me under. "They're coming!" I cried, instinctively quickening my pace.

"Stay close!" he urged, pulling me along as we wove through the trees, my heart racing in sync with the pounding of my feet. The undergrowth grabbed at my clothes, as if trying to pull me back into the fray, but I resisted, determination propelling me forward.

Suddenly, we stumbled into a clearing, the vastness of the sky opening above us like a great blue eye. My breath caught at the sight—a shimmering lake lay ahead, its surface glassy and inviting, reflecting the sky like a mirror. "If we can reach the water," I suggested, glancing at him with hope, "we can hide beneath the surface."

He hesitated for a fraction of a second, then nodded, urgency etching his features. "Let's go." We dashed toward the edge of the lake, the cool breeze rustling through the trees behind us, and the gentle lap of the water against the shore beckoned us like a siren's call.

As we approached the water, I could hear the splashes of feet behind us, shouts echoing through the trees. We reached the lake's edge, and I turned to face him, uncertainty flaring in my chest. "What do we do now?"

"Dive," he said simply, his eyes fixed on mine, a mixture of determination and fear swirling within their depths. "We have to take a chance."

"Right," I said, the reality of our situation crashing down on me like the waves against the shore. "One, two..." I couldn't finish the count. Instead, I lunged forward, breaking through the surface of the water with a gasp, the shock of the cold enveloping me entirely.

I surfaced, shaking droplets from my hair, and turned to see him beside me, the water glistening on his skin, the sun casting silver highlights across his shoulders. There was a moment of pure connection, a brief stillness in the chaos, and I smiled despite the terror that still loomed just beyond the trees.

Then the sound of heavy footsteps thudded on the ground, muffled by the rush of water, and my stomach dropped. We ducked beneath the surface, our bodies entwined in an instinctive attempt to hide. I felt the water close over my head, a cool sanctuary against the chaos above.

Time seemed to stretch as we held our breath, the world above muted and distant. I could feel my heart pounding in my chest, each beat echoing in my ears. In that submerged silence, the weight of everything pressed down on us—the betrayal, the danger, the uncertainty of our future.

Suddenly, the surface erupted, the lieutenant's voice slicing through the tranquility like a knife. "They can't be far! They went this way!"

My heart raced as I glanced at my companion, his eyes wide with panic. The realization hit me like a jolt—if they were determined to find us, we had to act fast. As the bubbles around us danced in the light, I grabbed his hand, squeezing tightly. "We need to swim away from the shore," I whispered, feeling the urgency push me forward.

Together, we kicked hard, moving deeper into the lake, the cool water enveloping us like a protective blanket. I fought to keep my thoughts clear, focusing on the rhythm of our movements, the shared goal of escape. Each stroke took us further from the chaos, the sounds of pursuit fading as we moved into the depths.

Finally, we broke the surface several yards from the edge, gasping for air, and I turned back to see the frantic searchers. Their silhouettes were stark against the sunlight, moving along the shore like shadows looking for something that had already slipped through their fingers.

"Do you think they saw us?" I whispered, my voice trembling with the weight of my fear.

"I don't know," he said, scanning the shoreline. "But we can't stay here. We need to get to the other side before they realize we're not where they think."

With renewed determination, we started swimming, each stroke powered by desperation. The water, though cold, invigorated me, and I found strength in the rhythm we created together.

As we neared the opposite shore, the forest looming ahead was a promise of refuge, but a sudden splash echoed behind us. I turned just in time to see a dark figure break through the surface of the water—one of the enemy's men had followed us!

"Go!" I shouted, panic lacing my voice as the man began to swim toward us, the determination in his eyes unmistakable. "I'll hold him off!"

"No!" he exclaimed, his grip tightening on my arm. "We fight together!"

Before I could argue, I felt a surge of adrenaline as he propelled us forward. The shore was within reach, and I could see the trees waiting to engulf us. The man behind us was gaining, his strokes powerful and driven by purpose.

We reached the shallows, the water barely up to our waists, but as I turned to make one last stand, I caught sight of something glinting on the ground. A rock, jagged and sharp, gleamed like a beacon. My heart raced.

"Grab that!" I shouted, pointing it out to him. "It might buy us enough time!"

He nodded, a fierce look of resolve crossing his face. I turned to face our pursuer, adrenaline coursing through me as I prepared to defend our escape. Just as the man lunged for us, a shrill scream pierced the air—a cry of surprise mingled with rage.

The last thing I saw before the chaos engulfed us was my companion, determination etched into his features as he raised the rock high above his head. The world fell silent for a heartbeat, and then everything exploded into motion.

In that moment, I felt the weight of our choices crashing around us, the knowledge that nothing would ever be the same. We had made our stand, but at what cost? As I braced for the collision, everything around me blurred, the forest a swirl of colors and sounds, and I couldn't help but wonder if this was truly the beginning of our freedom or the end of everything we had fought for.

Chapter 25: Heart of the Flame

The air crackled with a tension that hummed in my veins, an electric charge that thrummed against the backdrop of chaos. Shadows danced in the flickering light, a chaotic ballet of fury and fear. I stood shoulder to shoulder with Rhys, the weight of our shared history settling like armor around us. The battlefield was a canvas painted in hues of desperation and determination, where every heartbeat felt like a drum, calling us to the center of the storm.

The enemy—a towering figure cloaked in darkness—loomed before us, his laughter a jagged echo that sliced through the din of clashing steel and cries of valor. He moved with a predatory grace, each step deliberate, a reminder that he thrived on fear. I could see it in his eyes, the twisted ambition that warped his soul into something unrecognizable. But we were more than the sum of our fears, more than the darkness he wielded like a weapon. Our bond pulsed between us, a vivid flame that illuminated even the deepest shadows.

"Are you ready?" Rhys's voice was a low rumble, a comforting thunder amidst the storm. His hand found mine, warm and reassuring, igniting a spark that chased away the chill of doubt.

"Ready as I'll ever be," I replied, my heart racing with a mix of anticipation and trepidation. I couldn't afford to falter—not now. Not when everything we held dear teetered on the edge of oblivion.

With a shared nod, we stepped forward, the world around us blurring into a tapestry of chaos and light. The enemy surged toward us, a living storm of fury, and in that moment, time slowed. I could see the glint of malice in his eyes, the promise of destruction that danced on his lips. But alongside that darkness, there was a flicker of something else—fear, perhaps, or recognition. Had he sensed the strength of our connection? The bond that transcended the tumult surrounding us?

Rhys launched himself forward, a bolt of energy and determination. I followed, the rhythm of our movements instinctual and fluid. It was as if we had become one, our hearts beating in tandem, our minds entwined in a shared purpose. Each strike was a testament to our resolve, each dodge a dance of defiance against the fate that sought to consume us.

The clash of our weapons rang out, a symphony of defiance that resonated deep within me. I could feel the heat radiating from Rhys, a beacon of strength that fueled my own. Together, we fought as if the world depended on our every move—because, in truth, it did. I blocked a devastating blow aimed at my side, the force reverberating through my bones. A shiver of pain sparked along my ribs, but I shrugged it off, pushing forward with renewed vigor.

"Watch your flank!" Rhys shouted, his eyes locked on mine, a grounding presence amidst the chaos. He wasn't just fighting for himself; he was fighting for us, for the world we dreamed of rebuilding together.

"I've got it!" I called back, executing a spin that brought me face to face with our adversary. The darkness roiled around him, tendrils of shadow reaching out as if trying to ensnare me in their cold embrace. I felt a flicker of fear, a reminder of the vulnerability that lay beneath my bravado. But then I remembered Rhys's steady presence, his unwavering belief in me.

Summoning every ounce of strength, I pushed back against the encroaching shadows. "This ends now!" I screamed, my voice ringing out with a defiance that pierced the darkness. The very air trembled in response, and I could feel the tide beginning to shift.

The enemy faltered, a flicker of uncertainty crossing his face. In that moment, I seized the opportunity. I lunged forward, my weapon slicing through the darkness like a comet streaking across the sky. The impact sent shockwaves through the ground, and for a heartbeat, I thought we might have finally gained the upper hand.

But the enemy was cunning. With a roar that echoed across the battlefield, he unleashed a surge of energy, dark and chaotic, like a storm unleashed. It crashed against us, a wall of malevolence that threatened to sweep us away. I braced myself, feeling the force slam into me, threatening to tear apart the bond that had become our strength.

"Stay with me!" Rhys's voice cut through the chaos, a lifeline anchoring me amidst the storm. Our hands tightened around our weapons, and I could feel the warmth of his skin against mine, a reminder that I was not alone.

"Always!" I shouted back, drawing on the strength of our shared purpose. With every ounce of willpower, I pushed against the tide, feeling Rhys's energy weaving through me, binding us together against the storm.

In that moment, the darkness surged again, but it was different this time. I could feel the weight of my fear lifting, replaced by a blazing inferno of courage that surged through my veins. It was as if every moment we had shared, every challenge we had faced together, had culminated in this singular, powerful moment.

With one final push, we unleashed our combined energy, a radiant wave of light that pierced through the darkness, consuming it in a blaze of brilliance. The enemy's roar turned to a scream of fury and despair as the shadows dissolved, unraveling like a tapestry pulled apart at the seams.

And just like that, the battlefield fell silent. The air hung heavy with the remnants of our battle, a stillness that felt almost reverent. As I stood there, hand in hand with Rhys, the reality of what we had accomplished began to settle in. We had not just faced the darkness; we had defeated it together.

The silence that followed our victory was almost disorienting. As the last remnants of darkness faded into nothingness, the battlefield transformed into a canvas of vibrant colors, a stark contrast to the chaos that had just engulfed us. I could hardly catch my breath, my heart still racing as the adrenaline coursed through my veins. Rhys's grip on my hand was firm, grounding me in this surreal moment where everything felt both achingly familiar and profoundly new.

Around us, the air shimmered with a golden light, a promise of hope and renewal. I could see the faces of our comrades emerging from the shadows, their expressions a blend of disbelief and triumph. We had done it. Together. The weight of that realization settled heavily on my chest, and I turned to Rhys, my heart swelling with unspoken words.

"Did we really just do that?" I breathed, still trying to wrap my mind around the victory we had forged from the ashes of despair. The warmth of his presence next to me was both comforting and electrifying, as if the very essence of our connection was now woven into the fabric of the universe.

"Believe it," he replied, a crooked smile dancing on his lips that made my heart flutter. "You were magnificent out there. I'm pretty sure I heard the enemy scream like a banshee when you landed that last blow."

I laughed, the sound ringing out like music in the quiet aftermath. "You should have seen your face. You looked like you were about to tackle a mountain instead of just fighting a rather irritable sorcerer."

Rhys chuckled, a low, rich sound that sent a pleasant shiver down my spine. "Well, I'll admit, the whole scenario did feel a bit like a bad horror flick. But we're here, and that's what matters."

As we stood in the golden light, a subtle change began to ripple through the air. The very earth seemed to sigh with relief, the tension that had crackled like a live wire now dissipating into a gentle warmth. Yet, beneath the surface of this peace, a question nagged at the back of my mind. What now? The victory felt monumental, but it was only the beginning of a new reality.

Suddenly, the ground beneath our feet trembled, a subtle reminder that the battle may have been won, but the war was far from over. I exchanged a worried glance with Rhys, the laughter fading as we sensed the shift in the atmosphere. The energy around us changed, becoming thick with uncertainty, and the vibrant colors began to dim as shadows flickered at the edges of our vision.

"What's happening?" I asked, my voice barely a whisper as the ground continued to vibrate ominously.

"I don't know, but I don't like it," Rhys said, his expression tightening. He took a step closer, our bodies instinctively aligning, ready to face whatever new threat loomed ahead.

Just then, a figure emerged from the shadows—a woman cloaked in a mantle of shimmering silver, her features obscured by the cascade of her dark hair. She moved with an ethereal grace, each step deliberate, as if she floated above the ground rather than walked upon it. The moment she stepped into the light, I felt a chill race down my spine, a warning bell ringing in the depths of my intuition.

"Do you think she's here to congratulate us on our little victory?" I quipped, though my voice trembled with unease.

"Or perhaps to deliver bad news," Rhys replied, his eyes narrowing in caution.

As the woman drew nearer, I could see her face clearly—striking, with sharp cheekbones and eyes that glinted like steel. There was a fierce intelligence in her gaze, but it was shadowed by something deeper, a profound sadness that resonated in the air around her.

"Your victory was not without cost," she spoke, her voice like silk draped over a blade. "The darkness you vanquished was merely a pawn in a greater game. There are forces at work that you cannot begin to comprehend."

"Great," I muttered under my breath, shooting a glance at Rhys. "Just when we thought we'd earned a moment of peace."

"Who are you?" Rhys asked, his voice steady, but I could sense the tension rippling through him. "And what do you mean by 'greater game'?"

"I am Elara," she said, her gaze unwavering. "And what you face now is not just an enemy. It is a reckoning that will shake the very foundations of your world."

I felt my heart drop. The weight of her words hung in the air like a storm cloud, heavy and foreboding. "What are we supposed to do?" I asked, desperation creeping into my voice.

Elara studied us for a moment, her expression inscrutable. "You must seek the Heart of the Flame," she said, and the name sent a shiver down my spine. "It is the source of your strength, the catalyst for the light that vanquishes darkness. But it is hidden, protected by trials that will test the very essence of who you are."

Rhys and I exchanged glances, the weight of this new challenge settling heavily between us. "How do we find it?" he asked, his determination clear.

"You will know when the time is right," Elara replied cryptically. "But be wary. There are those who will stop at nothing to keep you from it. Trust in your bond, for it is your greatest weapon."

With that, she turned and melted back into the shadows, leaving us standing in the growing twilight, a mix of uncertainty and resolve swirling in the air around us.

"What do you think?" I asked, my voice shaky. "Did she just drop a cryptic warning and vanish, or do we have to worry about a world-ending catastrophe now?"

Rhys squeezed my hand, his touch grounding me. "Let's take a moment to catch our breath before we dive into the abyss. We've just won a battle; it's okay to celebrate for a second."

A smile broke through the tension, and I couldn't help but feel a glimmer of hope. "Okay, but if the next time we face a mysterious figure, they try to hand us riddles, I'm definitely going to need a bigger sword."

Rhys chuckled, and for a fleeting moment, the weight of the world felt a little lighter. But as the shadows began to creep back, I knew we couldn't ignore the reality of what lay ahead. Our path was uncertain, but together, we would face whatever darkness awaited us.

The shadows receded, but a lingering tension hung in the air, thick and oppressive, like a storm cloud waiting to unleash its fury. I glanced around, still trying to process the monumental shift we had just experienced. Victory tasted sweet, yet I couldn't shake the feeling that we were standing on the precipice of something far more complex.

"Are you ready for a new adventure?" Rhys asked, breaking the silence, his tone teasing yet edged with sincerity. The light flickered, casting playful shadows that danced across his features, highlighting the determination in his eyes.

"An adventure? I feel like I've just survived a cataclysmic event, and you want to dive headfirst into another one?" I raised an eyebrow, fighting back a grin. "Let's at least take a moment to appreciate our survival before we start looking for the next dragon to slay."

"Survival isn't enough for you?" He leaned closer, his breath warm against my ear. "I thought we were in this for the thrill."

"Thrill?" I laughed, shaking my head. "That's a word for it. I was thinking more along the lines of 'terrifyingly chaotic nightmare.'" But as I said it, I felt the tension in my shoulders ease slightly. There was something exhilarating about our current predicament, the uncertainty of it all igniting a fire deep within me.

"Ah, but you know what they say about nightmares," Rhys replied, his tone conspiratorial. "They often lead to the best stories. And we've only just begun to write ours."

His optimism was contagious, and I found myself relaxing into the moment. "Alright, you win. But if we end up chased by a horde of angry specters, I'm blaming you."

With a playful roll of his eyes, he took a step back, surveying our surroundings. "Okay, let's find out what Elara meant by the Heart of the Flame. Any ideas on where we should start?"

"Maybe we could ask the nearest tree for directions?" I suggested, gesturing toward a gnarled old oak that had survived the chaos. "They've been around long enough to have seen a thing or two."

Rhys laughed, his eyes twinkling with mischief. "You know, I think that's a solid plan. Trees are great listeners. But we might need to sweeten the deal with some well-placed compliments about its bark."

Before I could respond, a strange rustling in the underbrush drew our attention. The forest, once alive with the sounds of life, now felt eerily quiet. My heart raced as I turned toward the noise, adrenaline surging through my veins. "What was that?" I whispered, instinctively inching closer to Rhys.

"I don't know, but it sounds like something is moving," he said, his voice low. "Stay close."

As if on cue, a creature burst from the foliage—a small fox with fur as bright as embers and eyes that glimmered like polished amber. It paused, its delicate ears twitching as it regarded us with an almost curious intelligence. I couldn't help but smile at its antics, the tension momentarily forgotten.

"Look at that little guy," I said, crouching down to get a better look. "He's adorable!"

"Cute, yes," Rhys replied, keeping his eyes on the creature. "But remember, it's often the cutest ones that hide the darkest secrets."

"Are you saying this fox is secretly plotting world domination?" I shot back, unable to hide my amusement.

"More like leading us into a trap," he countered, amusement dancing in his gaze. "But I suppose we can't let fear dictate our every move. Besides, if it turns out to be an ally, we'll want to befriend it."

With a cautious yet playful smile, I held out my hand. "Hey there, little friend! Are you going to lead us to the Heart of the Flame?" The fox sniffed my fingers, then turned abruptly, glancing back as if inviting us to follow.

"Is it just me, or does that seem a bit too convenient?" Rhys asked, but there was a hint of intrigue in his tone.

"Convenient or not, it's our best lead," I replied, glancing at him with renewed determination. "Let's see where it goes."

We moved carefully, the forest around us shifting from a place of despair to one filled with potential. The fox led us through tangled roots and under branches, its movements quick and purposeful. It darted ahead, pausing occasionally to ensure we were still following, a mischievous flick of its tail encouraging us onward.

"Do you think it actually knows where it's going, or are we just following a cute furball into a wild goose chase?" I asked, my voice barely above a whisper as we navigated the dense underbrush.

"Given our luck so far, I wouldn't rule out the wild goose chase," Rhys replied dryly, but the corner of his mouth twitched with a suppressed smile.

As we ventured deeper, the trees began to thin, revealing a clearing bathed in soft, dappled sunlight. In the center stood a stone pedestal, weathered yet dignified, and atop it rested a small, flickering flame, vibrant and alive. My breath caught in my throat, a sense of reverence washing over me. The Heart of the Flame.

"Is that...?" I began, stepping closer, awe taking hold of my voice.

"It has to be," Rhys confirmed, his eyes wide. "This must be it."

As we approached the pedestal, the fox settled at our feet, watching us with an expectant gaze. I reached out tentatively, feeling the warmth radiating from the flame, a pulse of energy that seemed to resonate with my very core. It flickered and danced, casting playful shadows across the ground, inviting and enticing.

"Do you feel that?" I asked, glancing at Rhys. "It's like it's alive."

"Yeah," he replied, a hint of reverence in his voice. "It's powerful."

Before I could reach for it, the ground trembled once more, more violently this time, as if the earth itself was protesting our approach. A rumbling sound echoed through the clearing, and I stumbled back, instinctively grabbing Rhys's arm for support.

"What now?" I gasped, my heart racing as I scanned the trees surrounding us, which began to sway ominously.

Just then, a figure stepped into the clearing from the shadows, tall and imposing, cloaked in darkness, his presence eclipsing the light of the flame. The air thickened with tension as he raised a hand, and I felt a chill grip my heart.

"Foolish mortals," he hissed, a cruel smile playing on his lips. "Did you think you could claim the Heart without consequence?"

Rhys and I exchanged glances, fear and determination intertwining within us. "We didn't come this far to back down now," I said, my voice steadier than I felt.

"Then you shall face the consequences," he sneered, advancing toward us, the shadows swirling around him like a living cloak. The flame flickered in response, and I realized with dawning horror that it was reacting to his presence.

"Get ready," Rhys murmured, his grip tightening around my hand. "This isn't over yet."

As the ground beneath us trembled once more, I felt the reality of our situation crashing down upon me like a wave. The path ahead was fraught with danger, and with the flickering flame caught in the crossfire, everything we had fought for hung precariously in the balance.

Chapter 26: Beyond the Ashes

The soft murmur of the city awakening wraps around us like a comforting shawl, the light creeping over rooftops and spilling into the narrow alleys, where shadows once danced in the aftermath of chaos. We meander through cobbled streets, our fingers intertwined, each step an affirmation of our new reality. Gone are the haunting echoes of betrayal and fear that once reverberated in my mind. In their place is the soothing melody of possibility, punctuated by the laughter of children playing in the distance and the gentle rustle of leaves stirring in the crisp morning air.

I glance sideways at him, my heart swelling with an affection that feels as though it could lift me from the ground. He catches my gaze and smiles, a lopsided grin that crinkles the corners of his blue eyes, igniting a warmth in my chest that rivals the dawn. His hair, tousled and slightly damp from the early morning dew, reflects the sun like a halo, and I can't help but chuckle at how effortless he makes everything seem. In this moment, he is my anchor, a solid presence that steadies me amid the whirlpool of emotions threatening to overwhelm.

"Do you think we'll ever get used to this?" I ask, my voice low, almost conspiratorial. It feels like we're the only two souls awake in a world filled with lingering echoes of the past.

He raises an eyebrow, feigning deep thought, then shrugs. "I think that would be boring. Besides, what's the fun in predictability?" There's a twinkle in his eye that makes my heart leap, a reminder of all the moments that led us here—each challenge we faced, each secret we unraveled, has only woven our lives closer together.

We pass a quaint café, the aroma of freshly brewed coffee wafting through the open door, teasing our senses. I can almost taste the rich blend on my tongue, the warm, dark liquid promising to kickstart my day. "How about a pit stop?" I suggest, my stomach grumbling in agreement, the sound comically loud in the stillness of the morning.

He nods, leading the way inside, and I can't help but admire the eclectic decor—vintage posters peeling at the corners, mismatched furniture that somehow fits together like a puzzle. The barista greets us with a friendly smile, her hands deftly maneuvering the espresso machine, steam curling around her like the tendrils of a spell.

"What can I get for you?" she asks, her voice warm like the golden light flooding in from the windows.

"Two coffees, please. One with a splash of cream and a sprinkle of hope," he quips, his charm effortless. I roll my eyes but can't suppress the smile that creeps across my face.

"And the other?" the barista asks, her brow arched playfully.

"Black. Like my soul before I met her," he replies, nodding at me. The barista giggles, and I can't help but lean into him, relishing the warmth radiating from his body.

As we wait for our drinks, I take in the small details—the sound of laughter from a couple at a corner table, the soft clinking of dishes, the sunlight dancing on the hardwood floor. This is what life is supposed to be—a series of ordinary moments strung together, each one a bead on the necklace of existence. And yet, it feels extraordinary because we've emerged from something that threatened to extinguish our light.

With steaming cups in hand, we step back outside, the chill of the morning air brushing against my skin. I wrap my fingers around the warmth of the cup, letting it seep into my being. "What's next for us?" I ask, the question lingering in the air like the scent of coffee, rich and intoxicating.

He takes a sip, contemplating my question, his brow furrowing adorably. "Well, I was thinking we could spend the day exploring the city. We've fought for our freedom; we should enjoy it."

I bite my lip, suppressing a grin. "Are you suggesting we become tourists in our own city? Because I can already envision us getting lost in the labyrinth of streets and ending up somewhere ridiculous."

"Exactly!" He laughs, a sound so genuine it sends a thrill through me. "We'll make it an adventure. We'll get lost, and I'll have to heroically rescue you from a wayward pigeon or something."

The image of him valiantly warding off a feathery foe makes me giggle, and for a moment, I forget the weight of our past. The promise of exploration beckons, and I can't help but feel the excitement bubbling within me. "Okay, then! Let's go on this grand adventure. Just promise me that if we run into a pigeon, you won't scream like a little girl."

His laughter is infectious, and I find myself swept away in the moment, ready to embrace whatever absurdities lie ahead. As we stroll further into the heart of the city, our conversations flitting from trivial to profound, I realize that this is the life I've always craved—the one that thrives in the wake of chaos, where love reigns supreme and the future glimmers with untold potential.

Around us, the city is slowly coming alive, storefronts waking from their slumber, each one a potential treasure trove waiting to be uncovered. It feels like a blank canvas, a stage set for our story to unfold, and I can't wait to see where this path will lead us. With every step, I feel the tendrils of hope wrap around my heart, entwining themselves with the reality of our newfound freedom. The world is vast, and we are ready to embrace it, hand in hand, heart to heart.

The streets begin to hum with life as we weave through the vibrant tapestry of our city, the air crackling with the energy of a new day. Sunlight pours through the trees lining the sidewalk, dappling the ground with patches of gold, and I can't help but feel a sense of wonder at the beauty surrounding us. Each moment feels like a celebration, as if the city itself has shed its old skin and is reveling in its rebirth.

"I bet you five bucks we get lost before we reach the old market," he challenges, a playful smirk dancing on his lips. I raise an eyebrow, my competitive spirit igniting.

"Five bucks? That's chump change. Let's make it ten, and if we get lost, you'll also have to buy me lunch," I retort, crossing my arms defiantly.

"Deal! But if we don't get lost, I get to choose the restaurant." His eyes glimmer with mischief, and I can't help but laugh.

"Fine, but only if it's not some hole-in-the-wall that serves questionable meat."

He feigns shock, a hand on his heart. "You wound me! I happen to love hole-in-the-wall restaurants. They have character!"

"Character or health violations?" I shoot back, my voice playful, and we both dissolve into laughter, our lighthearted banter filling the spaces where shadows once lingered.

As we stroll, I can't help but marvel at the way the world seems to embrace us. Vendors are setting up stalls, displaying their colorful wares—bright fruits and vegetables, handmade crafts, and sweet pastries that practically beg to be tasted. The tantalizing aroma of cinnamon wafts through the air, and my stomach growls again, this time with more urgency.

"Let's make a quick stop for those pastries," I suggest, pointing at a stall adorned with baskets overflowing with golden-brown treats.

He nods, and we approach the vendor, a jovial woman with twinkling eyes and flour-dusted hands. "Good morning, you two! What can I tempt you with today?"

"Everything looks amazing, but I think I need to start with one of those cinnamon rolls," I reply, trying to suppress my excitement.

"Make it two," he adds, shooting me a conspiratorial glance. "After all, we might need the energy for our grand adventure."

With a wink, the vendor hands us two warm rolls, the icing glistening in the sunlight. I take a big bite, the sweetness exploding in my mouth, a perfect counterpoint to the cinnamon's warm spice.

"This is what heaven must taste like," I murmur around a mouthful, and he chuckles, shaking his head.

"Careful there. You might start drooling, and then I'll really have to rescue you."

"Rescue me? From a pastry?" I laugh, feigning horror. "That sounds like a plot twist worthy of a bad romance novel."

"Hey, don't knock the classics!" He teases, finishing his roll and licking the icing from his fingers with exaggerated delight.

We devour the pastries, savoring each bite, our laughter weaving a spell of normalcy around us, a fragile bubble of joy that I'm determined to protect. As we finish, I glance at him, a question forming in my mind. "So, what's the first stop on our adventure?"

"Let's visit the park—there's a beautiful garden there I think you'll love. And I hear the ducks are particularly charming this time of year."

"Oh, the majestic ducks of the city park. How could I resist?" I tease, and he grins, clearly pleased with my enthusiasm.

The park is a sanctuary amidst the city's hustle, the sounds of chirping birds mingling with the soft rustle of leaves. As we enter, I feel the weight of the world lift off my shoulders. The flowers are in full bloom, a riot of colors that make my heart sing. I wander down the path, letting my fingers brush against the vibrant petals, feeling the delicate textures under my skin.

"You really do love flowers, don't you?" he observes, watching me with an amused expression.

"They remind me that beauty can flourish, even in the most unexpected places," I reply, my voice soft. "Especially after everything we've been through."

He nods, the gravity of my words hanging between us. "You know, I think that's what makes you so special. You always find the light, even when things get dark."

I meet his gaze, feeling a warmth spread through me, a sense of belonging. "And you help me see it. I wouldn't have made it through without you."

Just then, a gaggle of ducks waddles past, quacking and flapping their wings, and I burst into laughter. "Look at them! They're like tiny, feathery royalty, strutting around like they own the place!"

He watches the spectacle, his face breaking into a wide smile. "And just like royalty, they demand attention."

As we follow the ducks toward the pond, I notice a small group of children feeding them bread. Their giggles ring out, innocent and pure, and I can't help but feel a pang of longing. It's a reminder of simpler times, moments untainted by the weight of the world.

"Do you ever think about having kids?" I ask suddenly, my curiosity getting the better of me.

He glances at me, surprise flashing across his face. "Wow, diving straight into the heavy stuff, aren't we?"

"Only because you make me feel safe enough to explore it," I say, my voice steady. "Besides, I'm just curious about what you envision for the future."

He takes a moment, considering my question. "Honestly? I think about it. I imagine having a family, maybe a couple of kids who laugh like those kids over there." He gestures toward the children, his eyes softening. "But it's a big responsibility, and I want to make sure we're ready for that."

I nod, a flutter of hope mixing with uncertainty in my chest. "It's a big step, for sure. But I can see it, you know? Us, with a little one running around, exploring the world."

His gaze sharpens, and he leans closer. "And what about you? What do you want?"

"Me?" I laugh lightly, feeling the weight of the question. "I want to create a home filled with laughter, where adventure is just outside the door. I want to be the kind of parent who encourages curiosity and exploration."

We share a moment of understanding, our dreams swirling around us like the blossoms in the breeze. But just as the air feels charged with possibility, a figure appears at the edge of the park, shattering the serenity we've built.

A woman stands there, her dark hair whipping in the wind, eyes scanning the crowd as if searching for something—or someone. My heart sinks as recognition dawns. It's the woman from our past, the one whose presence always felt like a storm on the horizon, lurking just out of reach. She strides forward, her expression a mix of determination and desperation, and I can feel the atmosphere shift around us, charged with an unspoken tension.

"Maybe our adventure just took an unexpected turn," I whisper, my heart racing as I try to gauge his reaction.

Her approach feels like a thunderclap in a serene sky, a sudden disruption that sends a chill racing down my spine. The warmth of the moment we'd been sharing evaporates, replaced by an uneasy tension that wraps around us like a thick fog. I can see the recognition dawning in his eyes, and a flicker of something—fear, perhaps—crosses his face.

"Is that who I think it is?" he asks, his voice low, almost a whisper, as if saying her name aloud would summon the worst of our memories.

I nod slowly, unable to tear my gaze from her. She seems to carry the weight of the world on her shoulders, and yet there's an urgency in her stride that suggests she's not just here for a casual chat. The way she scans the park, her eyes darting from face to face, sends my heart racing.

"Why is she here?" I murmur, a question tinged with a mixture of dread and curiosity.

"I don't know, but it can't be good," he replies, his grip on my hand tightening. The atmosphere crackles with unspoken fears and unresolved conflicts, reminding me of the stormy seas we've navigated to reach this point.

Just then, she stops a few feet away, her gaze locking onto us, and I can see the conflict warring in her expression. There's desperation, yes, but also something softer—regret? Hope? It's enough to make my heart ache.

"Can we talk?" she asks, her voice shaky but resolute. "Please?"

I steal a glance at him, and the indecision etched on his face mirrors my own. "Talk about what?" he counters, his tone laced with suspicion.

"About everything," she replies, her eyes welling with unshed tears. "About what happened. About you... both of you."

"You think we want to relive that nightmare?" I snap, my voice sharper than intended, the anger bubbling up at the mere thought of our past.

"Please," she begs, her hands clasped together, the raw emotion evident. "I just need a chance to explain. I made mistakes, terrible mistakes. But I didn't realize how deep it ran until it was too late."

"Spare us the theatrics," he says, his voice hardening. "You're the reason we're here, the reason we had to fight for our lives."

"I know," she says, her voice barely above a whisper. "But I've come to warn you. It's not over. Not yet."

The air grows thick with tension, and my heart races at her words. "What do you mean, 'not over'?" I demand, stepping closer, driven by a mix of fear and adrenaline.

"There are people who won't let it end like this," she continues, glancing around as if expecting someone to leap out from behind a tree. "They're looking for you. For both of you."

His grip on my hand tightens further, and I can feel the pulse of his heart matching my own, a frantic rhythm that speaks of urgency. "Why should we believe you? After everything?"

She takes a step forward, her expression earnest. "Because I care. Because I thought I was helping, and I was wrong. I need you to understand the danger isn't gone. It's lurking, waiting for the right moment to strike."

"What are you talking about?" I press, my voice tinged with disbelief. "Who's after us?"

"People who want power, who want to control what you've fought to protect," she explains, desperation clawing at her tone. "They think they can erase you both, and you need to be ready."

"Ready for what?" he asks, his voice hardening.

Her eyes dart around again, her posture tense. "For anything. They won't stop until they get what they want."

The weight of her words settles in the pit of my stomach like a stone, the laughter and light of moments ago feeling like a distant memory. My mind races through the possibilities, the implications of her warning spiraling outwards. "What do we do?" I manage to say, my voice steady despite the tremor of fear coursing through me.

"You need to stay hidden for a while, figure out your next move," she urges, urgency dripping from every syllable. "Trust no one. Not even me."

"Great advice," he retorts, skepticism dripping from his tone. "How do we know you're not just leading us into a trap?"

She opens her mouth to protest, but a sudden noise—a rustling in the nearby bushes—interrupts us. We all turn instinctively, eyes narrowing as we try to discern the source. The moment stretches taut, the quiet of the park amplifying every sound, every heartbeat.

"What was that?" I whisper, a chill creeping up my spine as a shadow flits past the trees.

"I don't know," she replies, her eyes wide with fear, glancing back towards the bushes. "But we should go. Now."

Before I can respond, a figure emerges from the foliage—a tall man, his face obscured by the shadow of a wide-brimmed hat. He moves with an unsettling confidence, the type that sends a shiver down my spine.

"Not so fast," he calls out, his voice smooth, almost mocking. "I wouldn't want you to leave without a proper goodbye."

Panic spikes in my chest as the reality of our situation settles in. "We need to run," I say urgently, pulling at his hand, but he stands rooted to the spot, his eyes locked on the newcomer.

"Who are you?" the man asks, his gaze shifting between us and the woman who stands, trembling beside me.

"I—I don't know," she stammers, and I can see the fear in her eyes.

"Time to stop playing games," he replies, stepping closer, his expression darkening. "You've caused enough trouble already."

"Leave her alone!" he shouts, stepping in front of me, instinctively shielding me from the threat.

The man's lips curl into a smirk, his confidence radiating like a shield. "Oh, I'm just getting started."

And then, before I can react, he lunges forward, and the world seems to shatter around us—chaos erupting in a flurry of movement as I grapple with the reality that our fight is far from over. The park, once a refuge, transforms into a battleground, and as I glance at him, the fear reflected in his eyes mirrors my own.

"Run!" he yells, but the words seem to hang in the air, caught in the whirlwind of uncertainty, as I realize the stakes have never been higher.